THE SACRED WOOD

JOANNA LEYLAND

Copyright © 2013 Joanna Leyland

All rights reserved.

ISBN:148279-083-1
ISBN-13: 978-1482790832

For Charles and Giuseppe

CONTENTS

1	Thursday 30th July	1
2	Friday 31st July	12
3	Saturday 1st August	25
4	Sunday 2nd August – morning	41
5	Sunday 2nd August - afternoon	57
6	Sunday 2nd August - evening	67
7	Monday 3rd August	80
8	Tuesday 4th August	94
9	Wednesday 5th August	117
10	Thursday 6th August	134
11	Friday 7th August	156
12	Saturday 8th August	174
13	Sunday 9th August	200
14	Monday 10th August	222
15	Tuesday 11th August	236
16	Wednesday 12th August	250
17	Thursday 13th August	269
18	Friday 14th August	294
19	Saturday 15th August - Ferragosto	308

1 THURSDAY 30ᵀᴴ JULY

The dead man staggered from the shadows of the alleyway, mouth stretched in – what seemed at the time – a loose-lipped drunken leer, and it was there that the strangeness first started, since drunks were rarely seen in Rome, not in the Saturday-night English sense anyway.

The middle-aged British couple passing the alley instinctively took a step backwards to avoid the stumbling figure, only to find themselves bumping into three young Italian couples, who exclaimed and laughed and waved aside the flustered mutters of, "Oh, sorry", "I beg your pardon," even though an ice-cream cone had fallen to the ground in the jostling dance and was starting to melt stickily between the cobblestones.

Ahead of them – she had spotted an empty table outside the bar in the piazza, just the place to end the evening with a last Sambuca – their daughter had turned back, taken in the scene and was about to go to their aid when her gaze locked with that of the bulky swaying figure. She took in the blackness of dilated pupils, the greasy sheen of sweat on the swarthy face, and recognised the agonised appeal, but even as she stretched out her hand, he took an uncertain step backwards, then another, pawed at a building wall, then slid slowly to the ground, shards and wafers of greyish cement showering around him. What should she do? Help the man? Help her parents? She glanced at them – No, it was all right, the young couples had already gone – and with sudden decision crossed to the wall.

"Be careful, darling – he might lash out," called her mother, still embarrassed by the first fuss and now fearful of a second; though her voice was hushed a sudden lull in the general background noise made it ring out, loud and clearly concerned.

People sitting outside the café where the family had had after-dinner coffee craned their necks to see what was happening, while late-night strollers stopped to look. A babble of voices, and then shouts of *"Qua! C'è qualcuno che sta male!"* started to lap outwards towards the police van in the main piazza, as Jane knelt beside the man, her woven shoulder bag folding to the ground beside her. The sourness of sweat and the mustiness of a suit past its best and worn too often came from the man. He was half-sitting, half-lying, one hand pressed to his side, the other groping for hers, and it was then she smelt the metallic odour of blood, and saw the wetness soaking the dust-smudged dark jacket.

"*Deve essere protetto,*" he whispered. "*E' arrivata – e questa volta sarà …*"

Someone else had seen the blood – more confused shouts – and now the police were coming, forcing their way through the excited crowd, as Jane held the man's hand, telling him that help was coming, to hold on; his fingers, blunt and leathery, clung to hers, and she tightened her grip, trying to keep him with her, willing him not to die.

For a moment time slowed, the scene caught and held in the soft summer air. A camera set above would have captured the symmetry of the three streets that came together just outside the café, one street lined with pizzerias, bars and small shops that led to Viale di Trastevere, a second, less frequented, bounded by the ochre walls of a Vatican-owned *palazzo* and the third, a stubby tract that gave onto the main piazza of Santa Maria in Trastevere. At that hour, diners were still sitting over crumb-strewn tables littered with wine glasses, while foreign tourists enjoyed the magic of medieval Rome, with its ivy-clad walls and small balconies glowing in the reflected light.

The grasping hand loosed its grip, a gentle leaving like that of two lovers in an old painting, outstretched fingers reluctantly touching for the last time. For a second she still clung to him, and then, equally gently, laid his hand beside him, mechanically brushing away the pieces of cement so that their roughness would not press into his skin. Two young police officers had arrived, one helping her to her feet and drawing her away, the other checking the man's pulse and speaking urgently into his mobile phone; her parents stood silent and worried but uninvolved.

South-east of Rome, in a private nursing home set in wooded grounds in the Alban Hills, an old woman stirred and woke. She had been dreaming of her friend Barbara. Barbara was young in the dream and had been her old self, affectionate in her brusque, matter-of-fact way and, as always, extremely pragmatic. "You'll know them when they come." she said. "Then just tell them and let them get on with it – I mean, it's not as though you can go haring off with them. You're old now, you know."

Lena opened her eyes, turning her head to gaze at the night sky through the gap in the shutters, and smiled. "Even so ...," she murmured in gentle protest. "But you're right, of course. I am old. I just don't feel it." In her imagination Barbara laughed and gave that abrupt little nod she had when she agreed but had nothing to add.

There was the call of a night bird from the trees and the far-off sound of a car winding down the hill. Lena smiled again at the thought of her friend, then sighed as she considered what lay ahead.

The time spent at the *comando di polizia* was as long

as Jane had expected. At the scene there had been noise and confusion, with the arrival and manoeuvrings of the ambulance at the car-cluttered intersection, while Jane stood to one side, fingers twined in the woven strap of her shoulder bag, a habit acquired in her years in Rome with its ever-present threat of bag-snatchers. Her parents had been allowed to go back to their hotel, but she had had to go to the local police station to make a statement, though no one seemed in a hurry to take one. She sat dutifully in the small waiting room, mind empty, regarding the dirty walls, where an out-of date police calendar and a set of fire regulations were the only decoration. Finally the policeman who had been at the scene talking into a mobile phone escorted her to a small office, where he cleared a space between teetering heaps of files. He was tall with the reddish hair and pale skin of the Venetians; his face was serious and his uniform immaculate.

"He just came out of the alleyway next to Mario's café," she explained in answer to his first question.

"Ah, you know Trastevere, *signorina*?"

"Yes, I live here. In Via del Moro – number 34, "she added, fishing her identity card from her bag as he found a report form. A slip of paper was caught in the plastic cover of her ID card, probably a receipt, and she put it in the back of her diary. "My parents are staying in a hotel – my flat is too small for them to stay with me. And it's not really that comfortable – not for older people anyway." That's what people do in films, she thought distractedly, always over-explaining, adding details the police aren't interested in, and then they get aggressive and say, "Are we done here?" and the police say, "For now," and pull a face and let them go though they are obviously guilty as sin. She could not imagine saying to this policeman, "Are we done here?"

He took the identity card and copied out the details.

"Teacher?" he said.

"Yes. I teach English language. For a private school, but I do contract work, in companies, you know?" There I go again, she thought. Not that he seemed impressed. I should just have said, "I am a professor of English."

"Jane! What are you doing here? Is everything all right?" Both Jane and the policeman looked over at the door, where another policeman, dark-haired with a thin face, had appeared.

"Tommaso – hello," said Jane feebly.

"She is just a witness, sir," said the Venetian quickly, getting up and coming round the desk; his arm brushed one of the heaps of files that shifted, wobbled, but then settled back, even more awry. "A stabbing near Santa Maria. Probably drugs but the man is unknown to us."

"He seemed ... worried about someone," offered Jane tentatively.

"What made you think that?" asked Tommaso,

coming further into the room. The Venetian officer went back to the desk and sat down, now leaving procedure to his superior.

"He caught hold of my hand and said, 'He must be protected. She has arrived and this time ...' then he di... stopped." She felt tears well as reaction finally set in. Tommaso patted her arm.

"Yes, it is most upsetting. And you saw no one else? No one who could have been responsible for the attack?"

"No, I was only looking at him. And it all happened so quickly."

She repeated what little she knew – the man's agitation, the actual Italian words he had said, but really she had noticed nothing else. Those few minutes, when the tranquillity of a summer night was invaded by distress and death, were transformed into the strange language of police reports the world over. "I was proceeding" rather than "I was going," "The victim was unknown to me" rather than "I didn't know the man", so that any humanity or reality was lost. And – as Tommaso explained when she questioned it – police reports used exclamation marks instead of full stops, so that every sentence had a dramatic declamatory tone: 'The victim was unknown to me!' seemed a cry of innocence, and not a simple statement of fact, and "I cannot add anything further!" the anguished answer to persistent questioning.

She thanked her stars that Tommaso had been

on duty, a former student who had graduated in language and literature, then followed family tradition when an uncle found him a post in the police. She had known he was stationed in Trastevere, and they had had coffee a couple of times. His presence lightened the lengthy procedure but it was after midnight when she stepped out into the street again, Tommaso, who insisted on accompanying her home, beside her.

There were still tourists and locals in the streets enjoying the relative cool of the late evening. July had been hot, no, searing, that year, with travelling on public transport a misery and even the hardiest of foreign sightseers huddled in patches of shade rather than basking in sunshine at bus-stops. The city was already emptying – it would be almost deserted in the month of August – with many shops closed and an almost complete disappearance of cars and traffic.

"Come. Let us drink something," said Tommaso, guiding her into a small bar near where she lived. They collected two beers and sat outside at one of the small metal tables perched precariously on the cobbles. Jane took a long swallow and lit a cigarette.

"You are still smoking."

"Yes. Would you like one?" And she held out the packet.

"I am reformed," he said smiling, shaking his head. "I need my breath to catch criminals."

She laughed, put the packet on the table, and

then drank again, feeling the coils of tension start to fall away. She looked much younger than her thirty four years, her usual expression being one of alert interest, rather like a baby bird; a pleasant face, not beautiful except for the eyes, which were a golden hazel.

"That man ...," she started, wiping her mouth with the back of her hand.

"Yes?"

She shook her head. "No, I don't know. He ... he wasn't thinking about himself at all. I mean, he didn't ask for help, just wanted to ... well, I told you what he said.

"He – or it – must be protected," repeated Tommaso musingly. "She – or it - has arrived. He might not have been talking about people."

"Oh, yes, of course," Jane agreed. "I hadn't thought, just assumed ..." But deep down she was convinced of what she had understood. He must be protected, she has arrived – that was what the man had meant. She pressed one hand to her forehead, the other hovering indecisively between her glass and her cigarettes; she chose the glass; the last cigarette had seared her throat.

"And you had never seen him here in Trastevere before?" asked Tommaso, his voice deliberately casual. When people were in shock a matter-of-fact tone often minimised the horror and smoothed things back to normality, so that a witness might remember additional details.

"No. But then – I have the city habit – I don't

really look at people." She paused, then, "Tommaso, what do you think he meant? " She knew there was no way he could know, but she wanted to hear something, anything, that might begin to explain the mystery.

Predictably he shrugged, then picked up his own drink. "We see many strange people in Trastevere – the area is always full of tourists and their presence attracts petty thieves. Then there are the drug pushers, and the rich who come to eat in the expensive restaurants, the young who come to eat a pizza. Everyone. It is a moving population. We keep a presence – the van in the piazza – and we know the regulars, but there are always the new ones arriving, those passing through or looking for a new angle." He paused, then, "Did you notice if he had an accent?" he went on.

Jane tried to replay the man's words in her mind. Accent? She could identify the main ones – Roman, Neapolitan, Florentine too if it was exaggerated enough, the c pronounced as an h so that Coca Cola became Hoca Hola. She pulled herself up; she must stop wool-gathering. Accent?

"I didn't recognise it," she said slowly, tracing a squiggle in the condensation on the half-empty beer glass. "It seemed to have a definite cadence. He wasn't from Rome, I don't think, or Naples."

"We shall see," said Tommaso. "We will have a better idea once he has been identified. And now, I will accompany you home, and you must try to forget this. You did all you could, Jane – more than

The Sacred Wood

most people would have done – and at the very least he did not die alone."

2 FRIDAY 31ST JULY

Mrs Pleiades was a very lacquered lady. All was varnished and sealed, from the burnished backsweep of unnaturally chestnut hair to the hard crimson nails to the shiny black high-heels with their knife-shaped toes. Whatever early morning rites were conducted in her private rooms, rites presided over by the trained maid who accompanied her on her travels, at their completion she emerged in a polished carapace of fashionable perfection.

It was whispered that her late husband had soon given up the effort of trying to penetrate that unyielding gloss, that he had taken his pleasure with barmaids and secretaries and undemanding 'normal' girls who would be thrilled by the present of a single red rose or dinner in an expensive restaurant. Mrs Pleiades led her own life. She spent autumn in London (opera), winter in New York (art and culture), spring in Paris (fashion), and summer in her native Greece, where – as well as an apartment in Athens and a villa on Rhodes – she had an estate near Troezen. She came to Rome and Italy but rarely, calling it the charnel house of western civilisation, a landfill heaped with the remnants of those twin relics, the Roman Church and the Roman Empire. She made her friends laugh when she said it had been better in the 19th century, when the city was half-empty and the malaria-ridden night air of the Colosseum kept tourists away. Or even – this with a droll twist of the lips – when the early barbarians swept from the north, appalling the anally-retentive Romans who were too busy fussing with their lumpy aqueducts and finicky street plans. Such bores, she said, making them laugh still more, with a few exceptions like Caligula and Nero, and they had not been truly appreciated at all.

That she was Greek was an accepted fact but where she actually came from remained a mystery. In passing she might refer to Crete or Rhodes or Athens in a way that suggested she had known them intimately in her youth but to the question (dared by some few) "And where do you actually come from, Mrs Pleiades?" she would smile and make some reference to being a citizen of the world. The spiteful might hint at an imagined meeting with her husband at some gathering of shady business associates, a gathering thoughtfully supplied with high-class whores, and even add that his death was an all-too-convenient coincidence, given that he was about to be reconciled with his estranged son. The generous, on the other hand, might wonder aloud if perhaps she had had a poverty-stricken childhood and re-invented herself as a consequence.

Whatever the truth of the matter, she was now an accepted figure in the fashionable world. Her presence met with glad cries from charity organisers and head-waiters, and if some found themselves repelled by the shining shell and the veiled eyes, such people tended to be peripheral to the mainstream of polite society.

She had arrived in Rome, that charnel house of western civilisation, on 1st July, but had almost immediately left again for a rented villa near Genzano in the Alban Hills. It was a large two-storey building, set in the midst of open lawns studded with massed oleanders and intersected by winding white-gravel paths, the whole beautifully maintained by the gardener who had come with the villa, and who had proved useful in other ways. Hidden from the road outside by thick shrubbery and high stone walls, the villa also possessed a squat one-storey annex containing a gymnasium, which a former owner, a fitness fanatic, had had installed. That Friday morning found her in the brocaded salon, seated by the ornate marble fireplace, a cup of coffee on the small antique table beside her; behind her, her private secretary David Levant was in attendance, and before them, standing awkwardly side by side on the lush carpet, two of the "local help" he had engaged in Rome.

"And have you cleared up that rubbish in a satisfactory way?" Mrs Pleiades asked carelessly, as if asking the time of day. Her metallic voice held a slight accent, the "r's" rolled a little and the "i's" gently elongated.

One of the two men before her, a skinny sunburnt man with darting eyes and coarse black hair, shuffled his feet nervously, undeceived by the calmness of her tone.

"He's dead, yes …," he blurted out, "but he … he managed to get away. We had no time to search him – there was an English woman … a tourist … and many people … then the police. It was … many people …," he repeated mechanically.

"I see." She took a sip of coffee. Levant bent to murmur in her ear, and, after some seconds, she nodded.

"You will make sure," she said slowly. The static of menace faded from the air and the local help visibly relaxed, though their foreheads gleamed with sweat. "Lay a false trail so that their investigations go no further – and monitor the situation. But *discreetly*. Do you understand?"

They fell over themselves to reassure Mrs Pleiades that all would be done as she desired, a false trail would be laid, information would be obtained – but with the maximum discretion, suspicion would not be aroused. She dismissed them with a flick of the hand, then turned her attention to Levant, a pale Englishman with light thinning hair and the sharp profile of a bird of prey.

"Keep me informed, David." She paused, scarlet nails curling about the emeralds of her heavy necklace, so that the sparkling green appeared encased in thin blood-red shells, and then, "Go now and continue your preparation of Varian. He is still untutored. Oh, and ensure that his physical training is still being maintained."

Levant nodded and went out. Mrs Pleiades finished her coffee, studied the delicate china cup as if seeing it for the first time, then softly snapped off the fragile handle.

"But why did you tell them I worked in television?" she asked with exasperation watching the young couple walk off down the street. The trattoria was almost empty now after the lunch-time flurry.

"Oh, come on, Jane," drawled Gabriel, flicking a balled paper napkin to the ground with one finger and lounging back. "No one listens or is interested anyway."

She gazed at him in baffled anger – not for the first time in their uneasy friendship. The trouble with Gabriel, she thought, no, the troubles, plural, since there were many of them, but the trouble connected to this particular occasion, was that telling lies came as naturally to him as breathing. Nothing was fixed, nothing was obvious, it all had to be needlessly complicated. Now he was sitting quite unrepentant, gazing after the departing couple who had stopped at their table to say hello. They had been in their twenties and Gabriel had said the girl was a Greek scholar and the boy an archaeologist, which could be true but they could just as easily be American exchange students or backpackers or someone's nephew and niece. And perhaps all three of us were trapped in Gabriel's story, Jane thought, and not one of us had the courage to say, "No, that's not true, I'm a ...," whatever they really were.

Thank God her parents had left that morning; otherwise she could have ended up having to introduce them to Gabriel and who knows what he might have decided to be or say? Anyway, she had seen them off with a mixture of affection and relief, and they were safely away, reassured that the events of their last night were of no importance: she had told them she hadn't understood what the man was trying to say. And I have the face to criticise Gabriel about lying, she thought.

Then, after she had just got back from the station, Gabriel had phoned, popped up from nowhere, as was his habit, coming from somewhere unspecified to do something unspecified in Rome, then off (this was specified) to a Greek island for the summer. He had a house there, which seemed real enough since she had seen a photograph of it, and the "Greek scholar" and the "archaeologist" were going there to visit him in a couple of weeks. Or so Gabriel had said. Wants an audience for his world-weary pronouncements, she thought sourly, then repented. After all ... but she couldn't think of anything positive, was still annoyed at the pointless lie.

"You shouldn't take things so much to heart," he said as if he had heard the thought. She lit a cigarette to have something to do, feeling limp and washed-out; it would have been better to eat in the air-conditioned interior rather than outside, even though they were in the shade. And there were flies too ... Tears filled her eyes, as – surely not again – residual reaction to the previous evening kicked in.

"I saw a man die last night," she said abruptly.

"What?" Now he sat bolt upright and was looking at her with a satisfying mixture of concern and curiosity. Not a tall man, he gave an impression of solidity, with strong-looking shoulders, and had an attractive face when it was not marred by a knowing smile.

She took a sip of water, and recounted what had happened. She was thankful that he asked no questions nor did he exclaim and cluck. No, clucking definitely wasn't Gabriel. He just nodded, then asked a passing waiter for two *caffè corretti*. For a while they just sat there, Jane thinking, the nice thing about Gabriel ... then almost smiled as she realised that – as so often when she was with him – she had done a complete turn-about. The tiny espresso with a shot of brandy was put in front of her while she was rummaging in her shoulder-bag for a paper tissue. The woven material slipped to one side, treacherously creating a funnel for the contents of the bag to spill onto the ground, and with an exclamation of annoyance, she bent down to gather them up; Gabriel too leaned down too to help.

"A Greek lover?" he asked smirking.

She had been packing the rest of her things away, thinking, not for the first time, that she must get another bag, but she had found the packet of paper tissues and was fumbling one free. Gabriel's question completely confused her, and she looked across at him. He was holding up her diary and a slip of paper.

"What?"

"Lover. Greek. Assignation," he enunciated, as if she were a deaf person who had to read his lips. "And a professor too."

"Gabriel, just what are you talking about?"

He grinned, obviously enjoying her confusion, and waved the paper at her. "I didn't know you could speak Greek."

"I don't ... what is that? What do you mean by 'professor' anyway?" The trouble with Gabriel, she thought …

"It fell out of your diary." He was still grinning, perhaps sure that he had caught her out in some way.

Irritated and ruffled, she took the paper from him. It was crumpled and dirty, with a small brown smear on one corner. Written in black ink there were five lines in Greek and an English name. The last few lines were illegible. She looked at it uncomprehendingly.

"What does it say?" she asked, for, among other things, Gabriel spoke several languages, including Greek. The trouble … or the good thing about Gabriel …

"Let me see it again."

"No, wait a minute. There's a name – Professor H.E. Caseman." She held it up to look at it more closely. "The last bit is all smeared – but it could be an address." She handed it back to him. "What does the Greek part say?"

He looked at it again. "'The artefact is ready. Where is the original?' then a date – the 13th August – something by or perhaps it's until the 13th August. Then this Professor Caseman."

"It's not mine," began Jane, and then stopped. She had had the bag with her the night before, it had folded down onto the cobblestones when she knelt beside the dying man, and he had clutched at her.

"I think it's from last night," she went on slowly, "the man who was killed, he must have put it in my bag. Perhaps it's connected with what he said."

"What was it?"

Again she repeated the words *"Deve essere protetto. E' arrivata e questa volta.* Then he said *sarà* so it could be 'he will be', or 'she will be'."

"Or it will be," Gabriel reminded her; he also spoke Italian. "And the two others could be 'it' as well."

"That's what Tommaso said." And then, hurriedly, because Gabriel was grinning again, she added, "A *policeman,* and an old student of mine. He was on duty last night. I must take it to him – it's evidence, isn't it?"

"I wouldn't get involved if I were you," said Gabriel. "Unless you want to spend most of the summer hanging around police stations."

"Don't be silly," she said tartly. "I just have to deliver it."

"Old student or not, he – or if not him, his colleagues – might think you're more involved than you are. Why should the man give you the paper anyway?"

"There was no one else. If it was important, I was his only chance to ... I don't know ... deliver the message?"

Gabriel laughed. "Then the police are the last people to ask."

"Well, what would you do, then?" she challenged.

"Nothing," he said flatly, lounging back again. "A man is dead, you have no idea what this is about, and in my – not inconsiderable – experience …"

Oh, God, not the secret service routine, Jane thought.

"… it's a mistake to get involved without any background information."

She could feel the stubbornness setting in. Gabriel always had that effect on her, and she wondered why she went on seeing him. He made her feel … young and inexperienced. And there was only six years between them, her thirty-four to his forty, but it felt more like twenty years sometimes.

"I still think I should … I don't know … carry out his last wishes?" And he makes me end every statement with a question, she thought. Oh, do brace up, you idiot.

Gabriel sighed as if he had expected nothing else, and got up, pushing his chair back.

"Where are you going?"

"Photocopy," he said tersely, jerking his head down the road towards a small tobacconist; it was owned by an old man who appeared to live there since it was always open. "Might as well do the thing properly. Then, if you're set on going to the police, I'll come with you. But I still think it's a mistake."

She watched as he walked down the street, crossed a narrow intersection, and disappeared inside the tiny shop. He really looks like the archetypal ex-pat with that linen jacket, she thought idly, but it's probably ideal for someone who refuses to be seen in public in his shirt-sleeves. She leant back, pushed her hair away from her forehead, eyes still on the tobacconist's. The heat! And why was there always a slight smell of rubbish? After all, they emptied the bins every morning, and hosed down the cobblestones, but then ... Gabriel was coming out of the tobacconist's, head bent as he checked the copy. From where she was sitting Jane suddenly noticed that his path would intersect with a horse-drawn tourist carriage coming slowly from the side road. Still, he would hear it ...

Apparently he didn't, being intent on the copy, and Jane giggled as Gabriel and the horse came face to face at the corner. Gabriel meet Horse, Horse meet Gabriel, she thought inanely, then was amazed when he leapt back, a swift limber leap at odds with his stocky frame, and suddenly crouched as though expecting an attack. The carriage, empty of passengers, trundled across the crossroads and away, the driver laughing raucously – gave that foreigner a shock all right, and raised his whip in a derisory salute.

"I didn't know you were frightened of horses," Jane said mockingly as Gabriel came back and sat down; it felt good to be the one teasing him for a change.

"Filthy brutes," he commented, handing her one of the two copies. "All bulk and shit. Now, do you want to walk round to the police station now?

Joanna Leyland

Might as well get it out of the way."

3 SATURDAY 1ST AUGUST

George's holiday was the fulfilment of a long-held dream – to travel round the area south of Rome and visit some of the roads and aqueducts that had converged on the ancient city. He had studied Roman construction techniques as a student many years before, and now, as a moderately successful freelance engineer, he could more or less choose the projects he worked on. The most recent – a particularly trying assignment but with a particularly large salary – was in Syria, and on his return to torrential rain in England – this at the beginning of July – he had looked at the sodden trees and glum faces and decided to make the trip before he was "too gaga to enjoy it".

He had already spent two weeks following the

course of the Claudian Aqueduct from its source in the River Aniene, some 69 kilometres north-east of Rome, to – for him – its symbolic end in the city, where a water distribution tower was disguised as a huge monumental fountain in Piazza Vittorio, near the main station.

That done, he decided to "do a few roads", but was now more inclined to take it easy, "potter about", as he put it, and he rented a car and left the city for the Alban Hills; it would not only be more relaxing but cooler as well. In the area there was a long tract of the Sacred Way still be seen on Monte Cavo, and also some few remains of an off-shoot of the Appian Way, the little-known Via Virbia. This last led to a small lake in the deep valley below Genzano di Roma, and it was here in the valley that the road had reached its destination, the ancient Sanctuary of Diana.

Little could now be seen of what had once been one of the largest and most important sacred complexes in ancient times. Set in a small steeply-sided crater of the huge extinct volcano that made up the Alban Hills, it bordered the north-eastern shores of the lake, filling the small area of land that was not covered by water. Most of the area was now under cultivation, small untidy fields with the occasional shack giving the impression of a patchwork of English-style allotments.

George was staying at an *agriturismo* in the valley, about mid-way between the local museum and the ruins of the sanctuary, which he decided to visit first; he wanted to take it easy, leave the Sacred Way for later. He had to apply for the visit at the museum, having found out that there was no unaccompanied access, and on Saturday morning a man from the museum (he couldn't be called a guide since he knew very little about the actual history) duly accompanied him.

The initial formality turned out to be just that: a formality and unnecessary in practice, for although the entrance had a high padlocked gate, the equally high link fence stretching from either side of it was sagging and had a large oval hole cut next to the gate pole. The man from the museum jerked his head at the hole (while stepping through it) and said, "Big problem ... *neo-pagani*. They still come, you know – at night – for do ... *things* ..." Pagan things presumably, thought George, stepping through the hole himself.

That was not the only evidence of the neo-pagans. In one of the excavated areas, a sunken room or courtyard roofed over with rigid Perspex sheeting, in the corner formed by two of the original walls, there was a plinth, where a collection of offerings had been arranged: three apples and some glossy sprays of bay leaves, a misshapen biscuit rather like a child's attempt to make a gingerbread man, and a small wooden bowl containing a few of the tiny wild strawberries characteristic of the area, apparently still fresh.

"*Fragole*," said his guide, pointing at the strawberries, his small stock of English deserting him. "*Dicevano ... lacrime di Diana.*"

George recognised "Dee-ana" as Diana, then thumbed through his pocket dictionary for *lacrime*. Tears, he discovered. The tears of Diana.

"Ah," he said nodding encouragingly. "Good ... uh ... yes."

"*Neo-pagani,*" repeated the man from the museum, shaking his head. "What people ...!" He turned to go, shrugging his shoulders, but he surreptitiously touched his crotch in the ancient gesture to ward off the evil eye, and did not approach the plinth or disturb the offerings.

And that would have been all George would have seen – or wanted to see – of the sanctuary had he not discovered after lunch that he no longer had his guidebook. He had been planning to put his feet up on the bed and plan his visit up to Monte Cavo and the Sacred Way, but now he stood indecisively in the middle of his chalet, a tall, lanky man with a slight stoop from courteously bending down to listen to shorter people, clad in knee-length khaki shorts, a worn but well-washed shirt and large walking boots. He rubbed his right ear in a characteristic gesture as he thought, his pleasant sun-reddened face creased with perplexity. Then, an image of himself sitting on a fallen pillar in a shady corner and putting the book down beside him came into his mind. That was it. On their way back to the gate the man from the museum had gone to check the lock on a corrugated storage shed, and as George sat and waited, looking down towards the lake, the shriek and flap of some large bird flashing close by made him duck nervously, and he had got up leaving the book behind.

For a moment he considered alternatives. The heat would be oppressive, the inside of the car an oven, and he could just as easily go later, about sixish when it would be cooler, but the thought of the book lying there, and – though unlikely – being found by some stray visitor (and he had left some notes in it) made him turn round and leave the chalet.

The *agriturismo* where he was staying had a central two-storey building, where the reception area, dining-room and kitchens were situated, with a large vine-shaded patio area bordered by high hedges of bay. In one corner a path through a gap in the hedge led to an olive grove and eight chalets, each with a tiny roofed veranda, set among olive trees. The car park was at the back, behind the kitchen. Everywhere was deserted, the staff and guests probably dozing after lunch. Even in the shade of the veranda the afternoon heat was intense. As he skirted the main building to reach the car park, the smell of lavender hung in the air, tainted with a slight mouldy smell, probably from the old covered well at the back, and the car park, a dusty expanse of sun-baked earth, shimmered in the heat. George wiped the sweat from his eyes and sighed; the car was sitting in full sun. When he opened the door a furnace blast of hot plastic-smelling air rushed out and he almost yelped when he touched the burning seat. Get a towel to put on it? Leave the door open and wait? With sudden decision he closed the door again, locked the car, and set off on foot. Getting nesh if I can't walk a bit, he thought. Not far. Can get there in the time I'm messing about waiting for it to cool.

As he plodded forward, the flick of a frightened lizard scuttling for safety sent a small puff of dust into the still air, while from somewhere across the valley came the muted sound of a horse's neigh. Then, there was only the droning and whirring of cicadas, fiddling away in their assiduous monotonous way.

It was actually further than he remembered and the sun beat down relentlessly on the tarmacked road; it was a relief to turn off the road into the tunnel formed by the sunken track and the dappled shade of holm oaks and olives. A climb up the track, a small olive grove with *proprietà privata* prominently displayed on hand-written signs nailed to the trees, then a short grassy track to the sanctuary, and through the hole in the sagging fence.

He found the book where he had left it, the cover warm and sticky to the touch from the sunlight that now flooded the shady corner. Taking a swallow of water from the small plastic bottle he always carried in his battered rucksack, he stowed the bottle and the book away and started back down the hill.

The way down was cool but the sunken track

seemed more treacherous, the hard-baked earth rutted and grooved and stippled with sharp stones. He was now very near the main road, and stopped briefly to switch his rucksack to the other shoulder and wipe his forehead, savouring the last of the shade before facing the hot tarmac. Suddenly, the boughs above him rustled, there was a flap and a piercing shriek, as if the large bird of the morning had returned, and George's head jerked back. He could see nothing above him, though the boughs were still swaying. Had the bird taken off? What kind of bird was it anyway? It had been large, large but fast and with that (threatening? warning?) shriek.

All at once he felt uneasy, some atavistic sense of danger making his skin cool and his breath short. He looked round warily, feeling foolish, the rucksack held defensively in front of him. One hand tried to wander up to rub his ear but the fingers were caught in the rucksack strap. A fly buzzed in some brambles by the track and he realised that – after the shriek of the bird – the cicadas had fallen silent. Now, apart from the sound of the fly, the whole of the sheltered bowl of the valley was silent.

He strained his ears, glanced to the left at the olive grove above the track, narrowing his eyes against the sunlight spearing through the leaves, then right towards the untidy fields. For a couple of seconds the fly buzzed on, then stopped. There was no sound at all now.

"*Poû autós esti?*" whispered a voice.

George whipped round, rucksack still clutched before him, the reality of its canvas hard under his fingertips. Before him, on the stony track, stood a woman, her features indistinct against the bright backdrop of sky and road at the end of the tunnel. She could have been anything from thirty to sixty, with unkempt shoulder-length hair and large (black?) eyes. He had an impression of some long garment and some sort of shawl. He had heard no sound of her approach yet there she was, not two yards from him. The small hairs on the back of his neck prickled and stood up.

"*Poû autós esti?*" she whispered once more, and like a ghostly echo "*Where is he?*" seemed to sound in his mind. "*Poû autós esti?*"

"… uh … g … good … uh … afternoon," said George, striving for politeness and a sense of the normality that his body had already rejected.

She took a step closer, and George instinctively took a step back. The valley remained hushed and waiting.

"*Oida oti autòs entháde estí,*" she hissed. "*Chrésimón esti autòn krúptein – chrésimón.*" Again he heard the faint eerie echo: "*I know he is here. It is useless to hide him – useless.*"

Her (black?) eyes glinted in the shade, mouth slipping to the side as she attempted to smile (reassuringly? invitingly?) at him. "*Just tell me … where.*" And the "*where*" seemed to whisper on and on.

Speechless with surprise and – yes – fear, George tried to smile back into the grimacing travesty of a smile.

"S...sorry, madam ... uh ... *signora*," he stuttered. "I don't ..."

She started to circle around him with the gliding motion of a snake, her fingers twisting and twining in the shawl. George, his thoughts a chaos of unreality, fear and a kind of frantic embarrassment, started to back away, turning to follow her movements so that he could still see her. If she got behind him ...

Suddenly she began to shriek though – horribly – she still seemed to be trying to smile at him. George understood nothing of the words; whatever connection had existed between them was now severed.

A neighing whinny sounded from the road below. She whirled to look, face fearful, fingers still twisting and twining. Then she grimaced, that strange slipping of the face occurring once more.

"*It cannot enter,*" came the confiding and somehow regretful whisper. "*Not even now – no, it cannot.*"

Horse hoofs clopped nearer, then the horse and rider appeared, blocking out the light at the tunnel end. George was infinitely relieved by the interruption of 'the unpleasantness'. He was no longer alone and things would be sorted out. The woman was probably some villager's feeble-minded relative who had escaped supervision, they were probably looking for her and he could get the rider to recognise her and say where she belonged. It would all be sorted out. He glanced back at the woman.

But she had gone. The path was empty. The fly took up its interrupted buzzing, and then the cicadas too resumed their fiddling and clacking.

That morning, while George was at the sanctuary viewing the strawberries left by the neo-pagans, Jane and Gabriel were again at the *comando di polizia* in Trastevere. Their first visit had been fruitless since Tommaso – Jane did not want to speak to anyone else – was away from Rome but would be returning on Saturday. Gabriel of course was late, and it was after 11.00 when they were shown to Tommaso's office. He was on the phone but gestured at them to sit down. Jane sat, guiltily aware of the photocopy in her bag, not the woven shoulder-bag, which she had started to hate, but a brown leather one with rigid sides and a proper flap.

"Actually, it *was* drug-related," said Tommaso, when he came off the phone, and Jane had introduced Gabriel, said her piece and given him the paper. He read the few words, then the translation of the Greek part that Gabriel had jotted down.

"This probably refers to some shipment," commented Tommaso.

"What about Professor H.E. Caseman?" asked Jane, ignoring a look from Gabriel that said, "You've given him the paper – against my advice – just *leave* it."

"Probably a nickname for one of them." Tommaso didn't seem that interested. "Look, Jane. You did the right thing bringing this to me but the case seems quite clear. We identified the man, and found half a kilo of heroin in his apartment. It was obvious what was going on – some dispute between suppliers and pushers, some vendetta, it goes on all the time."

This time Jane heeded Gabriel's warning look and did not pursue it. She had done what she considered her duty, and that was that. The phone rang and Tommaso answered it. For a moment he listened, then said wearily, "Yes, I will see her but there is no point – I told her all that was known yesterday. Ask her to wait." He hung up, but the phone started ringing again almost at once. Raising his voice to be heard, Tommaso thanked them for coming, obviously a dismissal. He was already speaking rapidly into the phone when they got up and made farewell gestures.

"Coffee," said Gabriel, as they went out into the sunshine. Jane groped for her sunglasses, half-blinded by the light. "No, an *aperitivo*, then perhaps something to eat."

"Is that all you can say?"

"What do you want me to say? You insisted on going, and you went. Ah, here, I think."

It was the intersection outside Mario's café, Jane realised as she sat down. Gabriel went off to order. It looked so different by daylight. She looked over to the spot where the dead man had slumped against the wall. It was just a wall now, the only sign of what had occurred the small heaps of the shards and dust of cement. But she felt dissatisfied. The man may have been a pusher, but she was sure there was more. If only the last part of the paper hadn't been smeared. But there was the name, H.E. Caseman. Presumably a real person. Perhaps she could do a search on the computer. The whole thing felt … unfinished … no, not just unfinished … important. She looked up as Gabriel put the drinks down.

"No," he said.

"What do you mean?" she asked, raising her eyebrows, glad her eyes were hidden behind dark glasses.

"Leave it, Jane."

"All right." She sipped at the drink, dipped into her bag for her cigarettes and lit one.

"Bloody women," he muttered, slumping back and reaching for his own drink. "And those things are no good for you, you know."

She ignored the potential red herring of nicotine addiction. "You despise us, don't you?" she said in a tone of discovery, still safe behind the sunglasses.

"No, I don't."

"I've seen you in a group." she retorted. "You only have proper conversations with the men while you're all charming and flirty with the women – as if we don't understand anything else," she finished, suddenly thinking: Oh, God, truth is the last thing we should be getting into.

Apparently the shaft had struck home, and seeing him look so crest-fallen, Jane repented. After all, though maddening, he was completely consistent. They had first met when she had only been in Rome about six months. On the phone, as it happened: she was phoning around looking for a job in a private school, ready with her prepared sentence *'Vorrei parlare con il direttore'*, since the secretary or whoever answered the phone didn't necessarily speak English. That was fine if the *direttore*, who *could* be counted on to speak English, was there and she was put through. But it all became much more difficult if the person said something complicated like "He's at lunch" or "She's not here but will be back at four."

It had been Gabriel who answered the phone at that particular school, and, being Gabriel, had let her stumble on in Italian before saying: "Would you prefer to speak in English?" The autumn classes hadn't been organised yet but he asked her if she would like to see the school. That had been the beginning of their friendship, if such a conflict of wills and characters could be called a friendship. And that first meeting – a tour around a set of dingy rooms with grubby chairs and lop-sided blackboards (a school?) – was somehow typical of Gabriel as Jane would later discover. After the tour they went to a pleasant trattoria with large tables covered with snowy-white tablecloths, had a good meal served by a middle-aged waiter complete with black suit and large apron, and the first example of Gabriel's (malicious?) sense of humour – or was it something else again?

At the next table there was an older man eating on his own who had struck up conversation. He asked the stock question, 'Where do you come from?', and Gabriel said he was Russian and Jane was Lithuanian. (Was it because I had my hair scraped back and was wearing purple lipstick, Jane wondered afterwards). She was struck dumb by the sheer ease and effrontery of the lie, not the last one by any means (what about the 'Greek scholar' and the 'archaeologist' and saying I worked in television?), and – of course – had said nothing, had even tried to look more Lithuanian (and just how did I think I was doing *that*, she wondered).

But after the meal Gabriel had put her in a taxi, which he paid for in advance, showing no sign of trying to go home with her, and said he would phone if any jobs came up.

And he did phone. He was at Moscow airport – he said – but had wanted to hear how she was, or – a little tipsy – at some boring drinks party and was looking for a 'cuddly lady', which she made clear wasn't her since she was very wary of Gabriel.

But there were also the nice times when they perfectly understood each other: he came to Sunday lunch, bringing three books as a present

(*The Varieties of Religious Experience* by William James, Georgina Masson's *Rome*, and *The Quiet American* by Graham Greene – and what does *that* combination say? she thought), or they met up at a bar for beer and filled rolls and sat in the sun peacefully reading.

He was a strange mixture of infinite generosity as far as meals and practical things went (he had also unblocked a drain for her), and infinite parsimony in revealing anything emotional or recounting anything personal. She knew nothing of his family, nothing of other friends he might have, nothing to ... put him into context (Pigeon-hole, you mean, said a voice in her head that sounded remarkably like Gabriel's). It was all quite confusing. She sighed, went back to the first thought: after all, though maddening, he was completely consistent. And now he was looking crest-fallen and uncomprehending. She took off the sunglasses, looked at him squarely.

"Sorry," she said. "I'm still ... hyper about the other night."

Gabriel relaxed, picked up his drink. "But you *are* going to leave it now, aren't you?"

"Yes," she lied, picking up her drink as a diversion, and then, "You're right."

"Yes, I am." He was his usual arrogant self. "Now, how about something to eat? Pietro's perhaps."

Jane giggled. "Pietro the Poisoner?" she asked, and then, at his interrogative look, "No, not really, it's just what one of the students called him. I said how handy and cheap Pietro's was, and this student said darkly, 'Pietro the Poisoner'."

"Darkly," Gabriel repeated with enjoyment. "Maybe – but all you've got to remember at Pietro's is to have something simple and recognisable – no sauces, and absolutely nothing fancy."

"And avoid the house wine," Jane added, still smiling. "Don't forget that."

4 SUNDAY 2ND AUGUST – MORNING

Rome, ever more empty now that August had begun, sweltered in the unabated heat, with temperatures already in the high twenties by nine in the morning. There were very few people around and the backstreets of the old city had a lazy somnolent atmosphere.

On that hot quiet day two very different women were pursuing very different activities. In the Alban Hills Lena was following what she thought of as her summer routine: awake about five to have coffee on the balcony, then perhaps a walk in the garden followed by breakfast in the communal dining-room, reading perhaps until noon – though her eyes had started to give her problems recently – then a light lunch and a nap in the afternoon. She liked the heat – her bones pained her less – and the sight of the first sunlight coming through the slats of the shutters always heartened and cheered her. Still here, she thought. If I can just last a little longer. Afterwards it will be up to others, but this time it is my responsibility.

It was not that she was worried, though she better than anyone knew how crucial the next few weeks would be. She waited serenely – that was her part, and then, when the time came, she must be ready to help in any way she could. There was Barbara to be considered as well. She would be arriving later that day for her annual visit, which Lena had first planned to put off and then decided that now of all times she needed her old friend with her. Am I being selfish, she wondered.

While Lena was thinking about others, Mrs Pleiades was watching Varian torture a kitten. They were in the annex of the rented villa; he had wanted to bring the tiny animal into the house but she said. "No, the gymnasium – that's where we train, Varian."

He really is perfect, she thought. Young – only twenty-three – tall and strong, with a beautifully sculptured body. Physically he was perfect, mentally perhaps a little ... slow. He didn't seem to realise that the kitten had died. Not surprising, she thought idly, looking at the pathetic remains.

"And how are your lessons progressing, Varian?"

He looked up, a sudden smile showing white

teeth in the sun-tanned beautiful face. With one hand he brushed a lock of dark blonde hair out of his eyes, while the other closed into a fist round the kitten's small head; there was a brief crunching sound.

"I am strong, fast and born to fight," he recited proudly, now licking at his blood-dappled fingers.

She smiled down at him, "I am extremely pleased with you. Go now and wash, you have blood on your face."

"And I will have more," he said with another beautiful smile. She patted his head, watched as he got up from the tiled floor, and smiled again. "Oh, yes, dear one, much more."

But as she watched him go, still sucking at his fingers, her expression darkened and became calculating. He was her instrument, she had created him, given him – as she believed – those qualities that would achieve victory, but ... With an impatient movement of the head, she glanced around, dismissed the matter, smiled again as she viewed the bloody and now-shapeless results of Varian's training. Her beautifully-manicured hand hovered over the bell push and she was about to ring when the air seemed to shift a little, a tiny displacement, and her eyes flicked to the doorway. "Good," she murmured in her soft metallic tones, withdrawing her hand from the bell push. "Clear this mess up." As she went out, she glanced down at the so-useful gardener, thinking, Funny little man. Sooner or later they would have to get rid of him but all in due course.

Near Piazza Farnese, in a flat borrowed from a friend who had gone away for the summer, Gabriel was looking for his passport and swearing quietly but forcefully. He was actually leaving the next day but, being habitually secretive, had not said as such to Jane. "In a few days' time," he had murmured vaguely. "Things to do. Be in touch." Since then he had turned his attention to his own arrangements, but – unusually – he felt uneasy for no good reason he could think of, and, though he would have scoffed had someone said the two were connected, he was worried about Jane.

He knew she had no intention of letting the matter drop, and had first mentally shrugged his shoulders – it was her business if she wanted to be stupidly stubborn – only to find it much more difficult than usual to dismiss the matter. Two unusuals – he was unable to dismiss the matter, and he was considering someone other than himself.

"Damn stupid woman!" he muttered, glancing round in annoyance. "And where's that bloody passport?"

His mobile phone rang just as he spotted the passport half-hidden by a book. He picked it up with one hand while answering the phone with the other.

"Yes?"

"Gabriel? It's Jane here."

"Are you all right?" he said sharply.

"Yes, I mean … look, I'm sorry to bother you – I know you're getting ready to leave – but I think my flat's been broken into."

"Are you in the flat?"

"No, I'm in a bar near the synagogue."

He was suddenly amused. She really was extraordinary. He couldn't think of another person who would be "in a bar near the synagogue" after their flat had been broken into. He thought quickly. No, no good on the phone.

"Go over to Campo de' Fiori. I'll meet you at the bar on the corner of Via dei Baullari, the opposite end from the cinema, OK?"

"Yes, thank you. I'm sorry I …"

"I'll see you there," he said shortly and hung up. He still held the passport in one hand, looked at it for a moment, tapped it gently against his chin, then replaced it where he had found it and went out.

The small oval of Campo de' Fiori was empty of the clutter of fruit and vegetable stalls that made it a bustling marketplace on weekdays though there were a few stalls, one selling football shirts, another bags of coloured pasta, and a third hung about with cheap jewellery sparkling and flashing in the morning sunlight. The austere figure of Giordano Bruno, cowled head bent, gazed thoughtfully down at the hot cobblestones while water from a Roman-style drinking fountain poured endlessly into a grill-covered drain. The sides of the piazza were lined with the huge white umbrellas of five or six bars doing leisurely Sunday business, serving breakfast cappuccinos and cornettos to the late-risers, pre-lunch cold drinks and beers to the early-risers. Gabriel ordered a beer, and sat sipping and gazing idly up at the greenery of the tiny terraces crammed between gabled rooftops, and then across, where a section of the elegant Palazzo Farnese was visible in an adjoining piazza; he had bought a paper at the news kiosk but after glancing at the front page (EMERGENZA CALDO read the headline) discarded it on the chair beside him.

He was about half way through his beer when Jane appeared from the direction of the cinema. She was walking slowly as if tired but quickened her pace when she spotted him where he sat, deep in the shade of one of the white umbrellas, back resting against the blackboard advertising *Dolci della Casa: tiramisu – cassata siciliana – cheesecake – mousse di ricotta*. He'll get chalk on his jacket, she thought mechanically. She sat down, ordered a beer as well, and took off her dark glasses, laying them on the table. Although she seemed calm, the flame of the lighter wavered as she lit a cigarette.

"Tell me," he ordered.

"Look, don't start getting at me, Gabriel, but ..." She groped for her sunglasses but did not put them on again, being momentarily distracted by the sight of a short jowly dog drinking with practised ease straight from the flow of water from the drinking fountain.

"I knew it!" he said with exasperation, then, "You think it's connected, don't you?"

She glared back at him, jaw set. "Yes – can you just *listen* for once!" It was not a question. Gabriel sat back scowling, drank some more beer; there were a few mellow notes from a wandering flute-player working the bars.

"I just wanted to see if I could find something about H.E. Caseman but the server was down and I couldn't use my computer – to do a search, you know?" She wasn't sure how much Gabriel knew about technology. He had a mobile phone, but hated computers and could not say the word without putting the adjective 'fucking' in front of it. He had nodded though so she went on:

"That was after I got home after lunch, so I went out about six to see if there was an internet point open." She checked his face again to make sure he knew what an internet point was. Apparently he did.

"When I got back, the door was open. I'm *sure* I didn't leave it open, and some papers had been moved on the table." Her hand went out to the sunglasses again, but she just moved them from one spot to another.

"Was anything taken?"

"No, that's why I think there's a connection with … that man." She stopped and relinquished her grip on the sunglasses, obscurely relieved that Gabriel was there. The good thing about Gabriel …

He was sitting, forehead creased, the beer forgotten for the moment. She took a sip of hers and glanced around: over towards the street leading to Piazza Farnese there was a *Unità Mobile di Soccorso*, a white van blazoned with florescent yellow and orange bands, ready for any emergencies. It reminded her of the police van in Piazza Santa Maria in Trastevere, and despite the warm air she shivered, again remembering the man slumped against the flaking wall, his jacket wet with blood. *Deve essere protetto. E' arrivata ...*

"What were you doing near the synagogue?" he asked suddenly, inexplicably smiling.

She pulled herself together. "I was spooked," she explained. "I went over to Silvia's place in the old ghetto – I'm looking after her plants while she's away. I slept there last night. I didn't want to stay in my flat in case they came back."

"They?"

"That was the other thing." Jane was being less than honest. It was not really 'the other thing', it was the main thing, but she was pushing the thought away. "I started to go out again – I had some idea of asking Tommaso or something – and I met Loretta, you know, my neighbour upstairs. She asked if my friends had found me. I ... asked her about them, and she said they were two young men. She got quite ... waggish about them. That's when I took off. I didn't even go back inside to pack some things."

Waggish, Gabriel was thinking, now there's a

word you don't hear every day. He did not like the sound of the two men. He sighed.

"What?" asked Jane, bracing herself for a lecture; she picked up her sunglasses again and this time did put them on.

"I presume you didn't find out anything about this Caseman?"

"No," she said in disgust, leaning back, relieved no lecture was forthcoming; the sunglasses came off again. "I only found two places in the whole of the centre – one had their server down and the other was mobbed with American students. I love Rome, but honestly – a capital city that more or less closes as midnight strikes on 31st July."

Again he sat, brow creased. "We'll go and check now. See if anything is open." he said finally. "Where are the two places?"

"Not far from here."

He sighed again, went in to pay for the beers, and they set off towards Piazza Navona, where the first, an Internet café, was not only open but now on line. The café had a few customers – all late-risers having breakfast or drinking coffee – but the back was empty. Jane sat at a work station, while Gabriel dragged a chair over. She found Google and entered "H.E. Caseman". Gabriel sat moody but resigned.

They leaned forward as the page flashed up, the screen blinding in the dim corner:

Tenenbaum of Vently said that **he, Caseman** and

other lawyers at the firm often serve as parliamentarians at meetings of associations because of their ...

followed by:

Oh Dogman, you obviously don't know Bob, does **he Caseman**. There aint noghting small about Bob including his trucks and tractors. He drives a 350 ford, ...

"And that's the fucking computer for you," muttered Gabriel.

"No, wait a minute." She scrolled down. "Here's something. H.E Caseman *Study of the Sanctuary of Diana Nemorensis*, Oxhall Monograph, 38, 1990." She saw that Gabriel had got out a small notebook and was writing the reference down. "What do you think?" she asked. "Could that be the person?"

"Nemorensis," he said slowly. "Nemi, in the Castelli."

"It's famous for the strawberries, isn't it?" said Jane. "Those tiny woodland ones. And they have a festival there."

George had spent the first part of Sunday morning "dithering", as he termed it. The fortuitous arrival of the rider had been of no further help. As George hurried down the last stretch of the stony path, torn between the urge to look behind him and the need to watch his footing – a conflict that resulted in an ungainly loping crouch – he saw that it was Massimo, the owners' son from the *agriturismo*.

"Engineer George!" Massimo hailed him. "What are you doing here in this heat? Not good – you will get – how do you say? – sunstroke?" he laughed. "Stroked by the sun! Ah, you English are not so cold if your sun strokes, eh?"

George, who was indeed red in face, gave a sheepish smile. "Left my book," he explained, and then, "Massimo, do you know …?"

But Massimo, still laughing and planning to tell his girlfriend of the English sun that stroked, was already riding off with, "See you later, Engineer!"

George was left standing there, mouth still open from his incomplete question, feeling unsettled and perturbed. His relief at finding the guidebook gave him no pleasure. If he had not returned to the sanctuary, if he had waited till later …

All of which had caused the dithering on Sunday. Some family's feeble-minded relative, he thought yet again, as he walked back to his chalet after breakfast, but the very words, "feeble-minded relative", were beginning to sound increasingly hollow, and could not begin to explain the feelings of repulsion and dread aroused by her slow circling and twisting fingers. "Where is he?" "I know he is here," she had said. "It is useless to hide him – useless!" And then that confiding and somehow regretful last whisper: "It cannot enter. Not even now – no, it cannot." It? The horse? Or maybe he had misunderstood; she had said 'he' not 'it'. His mind was already protecting him from the knowledge she had not actually spoken in English, that somehow he had understood whatever language she had used. Haven't got a clue, he concluded. Not much I can do about it anyway. Best to just leave it. For now at least.

More cheerful now he had made some kind of decision, he glanced around the chalet, then down at his watch. Although he had dawdled over breakfast it was still relatively early, about ten, but even so it was too late – and would be too hot – to go up to Monte Cavo and the Sacred Way. Daytrip to Rome, he thought with sudden inspiration. That ACEA place. With a feeling of relief he fished his rucksack out from under the bed, and briefly rummaged through its contents until he found the leaflet. This was it. The front showed two Roman statues against a dark background of machinery with the words SISTEMA MUSEI CAPITOLINI. CENTRALE MONTEMARTINI written at the top. The chalet contained a canvas director's chair and George now carried this out onto the small veranda, and made himself comfortable. First things first. Opening hours, which were at the back: Sunday 9.00-19.00. Good. He read the brief paragraphs of the English text:

The power plant named after Giovanni Montemartini is a splendid museum housing over 400 pieces of ancient sculpture from the Capitoline Museums.

Masterpieces of antique sculpture and precious artefacts discovered in the course of excavations carried out at the end of the previous century and in the Thirties, (Roman archaeology's two most fruitful periods) are on exhibit side by side with the original machinery of the first Roman power plant.

Power plant. That had been the part that had first caught George's attention, and he opened out the leaflet. The text on the left read:

Two colossal diesel motors made by the Franco Tosi di Legnano firm divide the Machine Room into a nave and two aisles. A statue gallery and some beautiful Roman copies of the most celebrated Greek masterpieces precede the extensive archaeological collections on display in the room.

He left the rest, which was about the collection, and studied the photograph, which took up nearly the whole spread of the fully-open leaflet. Three colours of warm beige (the ceiling), dark grey (the machinery) and light blue (the floor) cleverly formed three visual blocks, the dark bulk of one of the colossal diesel motors stretching away lengthways. Impressive, thought George. His eyes skipped over the pictured heads of marble statues, smaller blocks of white on light blue pedestals along the side of the diesel motor. He sat back, absent-mindedly fanned himself with the leaflet, and then looked at his watch again. Ten past ten.

Driving up to Rome would take an hour or less, and it would then be almost lunchtime. Maybe find an English newspaper – who knows what was happening back home? – and catch up a bit, something to eat – would that little place in Trastevere be open? – and off to the power plant. There was no hurry; his time was his own. His thoughts ran on happily as he got up, put the canvas chair back inside, and collected his rucksack; he was whistling as he strode to the dusty car park on the other side of the *agriturismo*, and was filled with quiet excitement as he drove off.

From the dusty track that led out of the *agriturismo*, he turned left, then right onto the only tarmacked road in the valley. This ran past the modern construction of the Museum of Roman Ships and followed the curve of the lakeshore, before beginning a gentle uphill climb to the town of Genzano di Roma on the lip of the crater. George began whistling again as he drove up the hill. The valley, the lake and the buried sanctuary dropped away.

The journey was uneventful, the traffic light, and once in Rome, he parked in one of the streets in the less-frequented part of Trastevere, then walked over to where the main piazza of Santa Maria in Trastevere formed the centre of the district. He could not quite remember where the trattoria was and took more than one wrong turn in the slightly smelly back alleys between the main piazza and the river, noticing in passing that there was a tiny English bookshop. He brightened – a browse would be nice – then saw it was closed. Well, it was Sunday and August, though the hand-written sign said that it would be open "as usual" until 10th August. Today was only the 2nd. There the information stopped however, for there was no explanation of what "as usual" meant. Not Sundays anyway.

The trattoria, *Da Pietro*, which he finally came upon almost by chance, was closed as well, but George wasn't surprised. He merely walked on towards the Tiber and Ponte Sisto, the stone footbridge that led to the large area within the bulge formed by the river's wide curve. George was in the mood to be a tourist, and many of the main tourist sights were inside the bulge, including the Pantheon, Campo de' Fiori, and Piazza Navona; it was just nice to be out and about in the city. Here, the streets held middle-aged holiday-makers in roomy shorts and aertex T-shirts, camera at the ready, young backpackers, suntanned and serious, Italian couples and families in stylish summer wear and dark glasses. There were no whirring cicadas, no abrupt silences in leafy tunnels, no deserted fields, and any birds were city birds, plump bustling pigeons and skinny darting sparrows, *normal* birds; they did not shriek from some invisible vantage point and then mysteriously disappear.

By this time George had emerged into Piazza

Farnese, an empty expanse under the midday sun; he paused briefly to look back at the imposing façade of Palazzo Farnese, whose blank shuttered windows rebuffed the world outside, then continued past one of the huge monumental fountains, the sound of splashing water reminding him he was now hungry and thirsty. He would pick up a piece of pizza, rather than have a sit-down lunch, and there was that ice cream place near the Pantheon; it wasn't that far away. He left the patrician piazza to enter Campo de' Fiori, busier and much more populated than its aristocratic neighbour, then stopped again to look at the statue of a brooding monk, and fill up his water bottle at the drinking fountain. There was another road leading off the piazza that promised to take him in the general direction of the Pantheon. Near anyway. Just past the bar here …

From one the tables came a woman's voice, raised in half-comical half-angry emphasis. "I love Rome, but honestly – a capital city that more or less closes as midnight strikes on 31st July."

I know what you mean, thought George as he continued on his way.

5 SUNDAY 2ND AUGUST - AFTERNOON

In the Internet café Jane and Gabriel had continued their computer search for more information about H.E. Caseman but it yielded thin results. They did find a site for Oxhall Monographs, which apparently was based in Oxford and specialised in the publishing of erudite papers with names like *Farm Decay in Medieval and Post-Medieval Iceland* and *Amber in Prehistoric France*. Another monograph by H.E. Caseman was listed, *Pre-Roman Cults – Origins of the Sacred Wood*, Oxhall Monograph, 46, 1995, which Gabriel had noted down as well, but when they tried to find the monographs themselves, only the names appeared with "withdrawn" after each one.

Jane tentatively brought up the subject of whether she could go home, but Gabriel cut her short and was quite adamant that she remain in Silvia's flat, vetoing even the suggestion that she should go and get more clothes.

"Look, Jane," he said, with the tone of weary "isn't-it-obvious-even-to-an-idiot-like-you", "perhaps there is no connection and it doesn't matter where you are, or ...," he paused for emphasis, "the two men *were* looking for you and not to give you flowers either, and may still be doing so for all you know. If there is even the slightest chance the latter is true, it's worth the inconvenience of staying away until we know what's going on."

Jane, subdued, agreed, though she was glad she had gone to the police with the piece of paper. Her conscience was clear. What to do next though ...?

"We could phone them," she suggested.

"The two men?"

"No, of course not. Oxhall Monographs. You wrote down the address and phone number, didn't you? There'll be someone there. They must have contact addresses for their authors."

"We don't even know that it's the right H.E. Caseman."

"It's the only one with anything to do with Italy."

In the end Gabriel agreed. Now that he had – indefinitely – put off his departure and become involved, he gave it his full attention. If Jane had been able to read his mind, she would have thought "The good thing about Gabriel …" but she did not, and was only relieved that – for whatever reason – he was still in Rome. As for Oxhall Monographs, no one would be there on Sunday so nothing could be done immediately.

They went their separate ways, Gabriel somewhere unspecified, Jane to MAS in Piazza Vittorio near the main station. MAS, short for Magazzini dello Statuto, blessedly open on Sundays even in August, was a Roman institution, being officially a big department store, but in reality, as one enthusiastic Italian blogger put it, "the atmosphere is between Porta Portese and an Arab bazaar. The clothes are vulgar and the prices astounding: ten euros for trousers, bras at two euros and knickers at 50 cents, and the quality is what you'd expect – terrible, but so terrible that you can't help getting excited and buying something."

She was extremely glad she had thought of it – the prices were indeed rock-bottom, and it also had a small section with shampoo, face cream and other toiletries, though here the prices were normal. She collected one of the huge clear-plastic bags that MAS provided as a shopping basket, and started to browse the ground floor, the part that resembled a second-hand clothes market. It occurred to her that she was doing what people on the run in American crime films did, though not as dramatically as they did. They rushed around shops grabbing shirts in cellophane, scooping up socks and sundries, not even getting a trolley in their haste, to emerge breathless with large brown-paper sacks. They never show them getting knickers, she thought with amusement as she picked through a mound of one-euro T-shirts, and then she gasped and recoiled, snatching her hand back out of the mound. It was nothing, a skimpy pink T-shirt with a vivid red splash of design on the front, but for a moment ... Taking a quavering breath, she applied herself anew to the task of hunting for clothes. Must remember knickers, she thought, but all amusement had gone.

A couple of hours later she was back in Silvia's flat, where she unpacked her new but hopefully temporary wardrobe. Definitely temporary, she thought, apart from these, and draped a pair of olive green combat trousers over the back of a chair. These I really like. She then sat down to eat the ham and tomato roll she had picked up on the way back, before having a look at Silvia's bookshelves. Would her friend have anything about Nemi?

In a well-thumbed Pirelli guide called *Viaggiare Bene in Italia* she found that it was 33 km. from Rome with a population of 1,420 (in 1994, the date of the book), an "agricultural centre on the lake of the same name", and was noted for its production of strawberries; the name derived from Nemus Dianae, the wood sacred to Diana, of which "traces" remained. I suppose I'm lucky to get that much, she reflected. After all, it's on the whole of Italy.

The second book, nearer home, was called *Roma e Lazio*, published in 1988. Why hasn't she got something more *recent*? thought Jane irritably, pushing her hair back from her damp forehead; the flat was cool in the morning but gradually heated up in the afternoon when the sun shone full on that side of the building. She glanced towards the window, realised she hadn't closed the shutters and got up. The room sank into a muted half-light, and she propped herself up on the couch by the window. *Roma e Lazio*, 1988. This too said that Nemi was famous for the strawberries, and added that it was "even more famous" for the remains of the luxurious ship belonging to the Emperor Caligula plus other Roman "imbarcations", which had been excavated from the bottom of the lake; a special museum, *Il Museo delle Navi Romane*, had been designed and built to hold the remains of the ships, which had been destroyed by fire in 1944.

Jane noted down the few facts on a scrap of paper, and then decided to do a search on Silvia's computer, only to find that she needed a password to get on-line (which I should have remembered, she told herself), and switched the computer off again. She thought longingly of her own computer at home but killed the thought before it could get a hold; her reaction to the pink T-shirt with the red splash had been enough. Why on earth didn't we do this at the Internet point? she thought, but she knew why. They had got into another squabble about computers and had not progressed with information about Nemi. For a moment she stood indecisively, before sitting down on the couch again and lighting a cigarette.

The dead man had said *"deve essere protetto"* – "he must be protected" (or perhaps "it must be protected", she corrected herself, dammit), then *"è arrivata"* – "she (or perhaps 'it' again, dammit) has arrived", and *"e questa volta sarà"* – "and this time "it (or he or she, damn Italian nouns with their genders and Italian verbs that didn't need a subject) will be ..." whatever.

She got out the photocopy of the paper the dead man had slipped into her bag: there was the part in Greek, which Gabriel had translated, "The artefact is ready. Where is the original?", the smeared part (an address?), then the date – the 13th August – *by* or *until* the 13th August, then the name, Professor H.E. Caseman.

There were the two monographs by H.E. Caseman, *Study of the Sanctuary of Diana Nemorensis*, and *Pre-Roman Cults – Origins of the Sacred Wood* (both "withdrawn"), then the few facts about Nemi and the lake (obviously the setting for the monographs): strawberries, the Nemus Dianae, the sacred wood ("traces remaining"), Caligula's luxurious ships and the Museum of Roman Ships.

She tried to clear her mind. The sacred wood – Caligula's ship – ancient history – that could all be linked with "artefact", but what about "Where is the original?" The artefact must be a fake – traffic in faked antiquities? But Tommaso said that they had found half a kilo of heroin – so perhaps it was all drug-related. Drugs hidden in faked artefacts? He (or it) must be protected. Well, the word for heroin was feminine in Italian so it couldn't be heroin that had to be protected. She or it has arrived, which could refer to the drug. But then there was H.E. Caseman. Why on earth would a professor with two monographs (withdrawn) be involved in drug trafficking?

She lay back and closed her eyes, her notes slipping to the floor. It was no good. They would have to wait until they could get in touch with someone at Oxhall Monographs.

The *Centrale Montemartini*, the power plant "housing over 400 pieces of ancient sculpture from the Capitoline Museums" was situated in the south of Rome, away from the main tourist sights in the centre. This was an area that George had never visited and had not included in his planning of the road-and-aqueduct-tour – there was not enough of interest. Most aqueducts had entered Rome from their sources in the eastern hills, and the Via Ostiense, here a wide tree-lined avenue, followed the course of the ancient road to the port of Ostia so closely that nothing remained of its Roman counterpart.

The former generating station was an attractive

19th-century building set between a sprawling industrial complex and what appeared to be an abandoned building site. Once through the main gate however, the green of a well-tended garden with tall palm trees contrasted pleasantly with the warm cream and ochre of the building's walls; water sprinklers played gently over lush green grass, and a faint perfume of flowers seemed to hang suspended in the misty cool of the spray.

The entrance with its ticket office and cloakroom was small and low-ceilinged and had no natural light; to George's trained eye it was obviously a prefabricated box constructed within a much larger space, its size and shape dictated by the constraints of the existing structure. Two restored turbines, black and shiny under their spotlights, stood against the far wall, and a faint smell of warm oil still seemed to cling about them. George paused and sniffed appreciatively before going down a short corridor lined with the tall tubes of compressed air canisters. Probably used to work the diesel engines in the Machine Room upstairs, he thought as he went up the metal steps, still happily breathing in the warm familiar scent of oil.

Immediately above the stairwell were the backs of the two huge diesels, looking for all the world like two colossal railway engines without wheels. Their massive presence threw the steps into shadow, while the rest of the Machine Room was flooded with natural light from windows set high above the work space. George sighed with pleasure, began to immerse himself in contemplation of the engines, then became aware of the marble heads, statues and carved fragments displayed on plinths along the engines' sides. He shook his head slightly, much as a horse would when bothered by a fly, and went back to his study of the engines; he was after all there for the power station.

But as he continued the sculptures intruded on his attention more and more: marble faces, stern or playful or dreaming, stone arms, smooth and rounded or taut with muscle, garlands of leaves and flowers meticulously traced, all thrown into high relief against the dark bulk of heavy industrial machinery, one past placed against another and seemingly content to be there. George too felt calm and contented, even began to saunter slightly as he walked into the Boiler Room, where artificial light predominated and the surviving boiler, a mammoth construction of tubes, bricks and metal struts, resembled a discarded prop from the set of *Modern Times*.

This should have been one of the highlights of his visit but, even as he walked towards it, George was distracted by the guardian-like presences of statues set around the assembled pieces of a large mosaic. He stopped to look. Slightly raised above floor level, the mosaic itself was roughly executed and parts were missing, but the scene was quite clear: a forest, where men and horses were frozen in a moment of their pursuit of deer and wild boar.

George paced down its length, following the hunt. And all at once the cool scents of the garden downstairs seemed to rise to the first floor and permeate the dim room, the stylized trees and plants took on colour and depth, the roughly-executed figures of men and animals wavered for a moment and became three-dimensional and real. George gazed and marvelled, feeling no trace of dismay, or fear or revulsion.

For a moment the scene held – was that birdsong? – then men and beasts were gone, the forest empty and quiet. Only the dense undergrowth swayed and dipped, the far-off notes of a horn sounding faintly as the hunt went on its way. Another moment, and the mosaic was as before, incomplete, roughly-executed and static.

George was smiling as he walked from the room, leaving the boiler unvisited and unadmired. He felt refreshed and invigorated, in a split second had decided to cancel the "impression". Nothing like the countryside, he thought as his one conscious concession to the occurrence. He glanced to one side, where a marble head nearly six-feet tall stood. It was of a woman with full lips and heavy eyelids. A card said it was thought to be the goddess Fortune in her aspect of 'Seize the Moment'; a slight enigmatic smile curved the full mouth. Yes, thought George, uncharacteristically philosophical, that's the trick, recognising the moment when it comes.

6 SUNDAY 2^(ND) AUGUST - EVENING

At six o'clock the daytime heat was reluctantly loosing its grip of the parched countryside, and there was even the slightest breath of a breeze gently ruffling the calm waters of the lake. Barbara and Lena were sitting in the shade of a cypress tree on the lawn outside the nursing home, and each of them tipped back her head to enjoy the coolness on her skin, then caught the other's eye and smiled. Barbara, who over the years had filled out where her friend had thinned down, was a robust-looking sixty-five-year-old with grey hair roughly chopped into a kind of helmet. She looked like the kind of woman who would own dogs and speak her mind, which she did now:

"Are you sure you're well enough?" She asked

brusquely. "You're looking frail."

"I have to be well enough," replied Lena with spirit. Barbara's response was a muted annoyed "hrummp". She knew there was no point in arguing. Once Lena had made up her mind …

"So, you're waiting for him?" she went on after a moment.

"Yes," said Lena. "As I said, it was quite clear, but now I wonder if I became too complacent, just took it for granted that everything would happen as it was supposed to happen. I will admit I'm beginning to feel a little worried." She glanced towards the lake, then towards the rough fields covering the sanctuary. Barbara followed her gaze. Nothing there that I can see, she was thinking, but if it's worrying Lena … "Is there anything I can do to help?" she asked gruffly.

Lena looked at her, suddenly penitent: "Barbara, it was selfish of me to ask you come now. September, now, perhaps would have been … better."

"Nonsense!" said Barbara forcefully to cover her amazement: she had never heard Lena regret a decision in her life. "I wouldn't *not* have come, however … loony I think you are." This was astonishingly tactful on the Barbara-scale. When Lena had confided in her some years back, Barbara had first said her friend was losing it (an expression she had picked up from her niece), then said Lena should never have got involved and there was probably some kind of con-trick going on and had

Lena been asked for money, or to rewrite her will? Since the answer was twice negative, she had finally settled for a "you're-being-fey" kind of attitude towards the affair, deciding that if Lena really believed in it, the best Barbara could do was to humour her friend and keep an eye on her.

Lena settled her legs a little more comfortably on the padded stool they had brought for her. They do look stick-like, she thought. "How's the *agriturismo*?" she asked. Perhaps if they stopped picking at the subject, something might come.

"Plain, simple. Much cosier than that hotel in the village – and much nearer here, of course. I walked up."

"Did you? After your journey? That's quite a long way."

"Good to stretch my legs after being cooped up in trains and planes. It's no further than I take the dogs at home. Bit hot, but going back will be nice with that bit of breeze."

"And how are the dogs?" This was kind of Lena since she was not an animal lover; but she always asked after Barbara's two spoilt setters, which ruled her life for the rest of the year. The conversation settled into anecdotes about the dogs, touched on local gossip in the village where Barbara lived, then took a detour into a university reminiscence involving a pair of tights and a smashed bottle of vodka that had them both laughing.

"Well," said Barbara finally, glancing at her chunky practical watch with the big numbers, "I'll be off now. Seven-thirty and they start serving dinner about 8.00. Tomorrow for our drive?"

"Lovely!" said Lena. "I'll phone Alfredo and ask him to come about eleven-thirty."

"Is that beat-up Mercedes of his still working?"

"Oh, don't let him hear you say that – it's his pride and joy. He's got the air-conditioning working, he told me."

"Air-conditioning!" snorted Barbara. "Probably means he's got the windows unstuck."

They began to giggle, the years dropping away, and Barbara set off, glad of the walk after sitting for so long. I'm lucky, she thought. Just a few aches and pains, normal for my age, but poor Lena, you can see she's suffering, whatever she says. What was it she had said years back when she was first diagnosed with arthritis? "I won't let it take over. I had a good run for my money anyway."

It was a lovely evening, still and golden, with shadows gathering gently on the slopes and beneath the trees. Barbara wished her dogs were there – they would so enjoy nosing along the roadside, tails in the air, discovering some tantalising trail that …

… a hissing muttering sound was coming from somewhere nearby. Barbara looked around but could not pinpoint the source. It was extremely unpleasant, rising and falling, as if whatever was making the sound was trying to croon or chant. Barbara kept peering around until a sudden cracking *smack*, like the sound of a rotten branch being broken, put an end to it. Barbara let out the breath she had not known she was holding.

George spent much more time in the museum than he had expected, but had actually seen little of the power plant equipment that had first appealed to him. He went back to the beginning, found rooms of further statues on the ground floor, and repeated the whole visit, including the mosaic. It was about eight when he began a leisurely walk back to Trastevere, now across the Tiber, a longish walk that took him up to Piramide, where he sat outside a kiosk and drank cold beer, contemplating the pyramid itself (Proportions are wrong, he thought. Sides too steep. Not enough room to build it maybe) before continuing on to the river. There he paused again and leant on the parapet, feeling hot and sticky. Though the sun was now beginning its downward journey, the buildings and pavements radiated heat, and exhaust fumes and air-conditioning systems added their own heat and waste to the heavy air. Arriving back in Trastevere, George added his own car to the traffic and even went so far as to turn on the air-conditioning. Just till I cool down a bit and get out of Rome, he promised himself.

The valley was already in shadow as he drove down the road from Genzano, the lake softly gleaming, the slopes dark but showing lights here and there from the few villas on the hills, the night sky now unveiling a gleam of stars. It was much cooler now, and as George locked the car he gratefully took in a deep breath of evening air, and went round to the vine-covered patio to see if he could get a last beer before showering and turning in.

As he sipped his beer – and they had thoughtfully brought a plate of *antipasti* as well – he felt ready to return to the encounter of the day before. The obvious course of action was to ask someone at the *agriturismo* about the strange woman but was at a loss as quite how to bring the subject up. "Is there a mad woman in the area?" seemed too abrupt, and "I had a strange experience when I went out yesterday" too attention-seeking. He was not a man who was at his ease when he first met people, not like his sister who was enviably adept at chatting to complete strangers, and soon had the stranger recounting the most intimate details of his or her life. What would she have said, he wondered. She would have probably launched into the story of the lost guidebook, recounted the strawberries and the neo-pagans, and then asked if there were any in the area, explaining that she had seen such a strange sad-looking woman. George could imagine her saying all that but lacked the facility himself, and besides he still did not know how to ... categorise the encounter.

He was rescued from his unhappy musings by Massimo, the son and a university student who was home for the holidays to help his parents at the *agriturismo*. He sometimes chatted with George in the evening to practise his English, and found immense enjoyment in translating Italian literally into English.

"Engineer George!" said Massimo, his dark attractive face alight with fun and laughter.

"Massimo, good evening," returned George, feeling old and stodgy by comparison.

"You are back – good!" went on the young student boisterously. "You should leave those old ruins alone – stay with your aqueducts and roads. That place is no good. Not healthy. We leave it alone."

"Why?" asked George, not correcting Massimo about where he had been that day, Rome and not the sanctuary, and was now alert with the possibility of finding out more.

"Unsafe," said Massimo, suddenly monosyllabic and bending down to brush a few crumbs from the tablecloth with quick jerky dabs. "Holes in the ground, falling walls. You could break your ankle, hurt yourself. And sometimes there are strange types."

"Neo-pagans?" suggested George, then wished he had asked "What kind of strange types?" which might have elicited more information.

"Exactly!" agreed Massimo quickly, looking up and smiling. "But enough of that – I want to present someone to you." He turned, and then waved to someone. "Tayo!" he called.

A young man, tall and dark-haired, with an open tranquil expression, came across the patio.

"This is Tayo," said Massimo, "one of our helpers. He is an American student and he studies Italian. Tayo, sit down, talk to George, we know you Anglo-Saxons like to meet yourselves." And with that he went cheerfully off, pausing at one or two of the tables to greet other guests having a drink or ice cream. Laughter came floating back.

George and Tayo, under instructions to talk to each other, found nothing to say.

"Theo, actually."

"Pardon?"

"Not Tayo – Theo, Theodore."

"Oh, right. Theo. Like a beer?" offered George, glancing to see if Massimo was still around so he could order one.

"No, it's OK – I'll go." And Theo went off, was back in a few minutes, sitting down again with his beer and drinking straight from the bottle student-style; George felt rather a fuddy-duddy with his glass, but picked it up and took a gulp; Theo, like Massimo, seemed so young to him.

But the business of drinks had only filled in a couple of minutes, and now it was time to meet themselves. George racked his brains for something to say. Theo seemed content to drink his beer, holding the bottle in one hand and regarding George with a friendly smile.

"So you're a … uh … student," said George, a little desperately. "Here … uh … to study Italian."

"I was." said Theo. "Here in Italy to study the language, I mean. But, actually – apart from that – I'm in Nemi on a kind of spiritual quest." He spoke naturally and matter-of-factly, gave another friendly smile.

George's heart sank. "Uh, yes ...," he said, clutching at his glass, and taking another swallow. Ten minutes should be enough, he thought, then, tired ... day in Rome ... heat ... early night ... nice to meet you ... hope all goes well for you and your ... uh ... quest here.

"I was working up in Tuscany before," Theo went on. Oh, Lord, thought George with despair. I'm going to get the whole bloomin' story. "And I was speaking to one of the guests there – a German guy. He had just been here, and was talking about it. He showed me a book he had, *Nemi and the Valley of the Sacred Wood*. I only had a quick look – the guy was leaving the next day – but it was really cool. The sanctuary to Diana, the moon goddess, and there was a link with a Greek legend. A queen was in love with her stepson, and when he rejected her, she accused him of rape. Can't remember the details now but he was reborn, hidden here, became another Roman god. Something like that."

The concepts 'love', 'rejected', 'rape' and 'hidden' suddenly came together in George's mind and the frantic whispers of the mad woman echoed in his memory. What had she said? *"Where is he? I know he is here. It is useless to hide him."* Hide – hidden, he thought disjointedly.

"Some places are places of the spirit," remarked Theo.

"Pardon?" asked George, pulling himself together; he picked up his glass, realised it was empty.

"Some places are places of the spirit," Theo repeated patiently. "This is one, a sacred place for hundreds – thousands – of years."

"But ... uh ... pagan," said George, drawn in despite himself.

"All religions are expressions of the spiritual," said Theo, looking up towards the dark slopes and the lights of the village above. His tone was still quiet and matter-of-fact. "The belief of the worshippers, their offerings and prayers – it all opens the way."

George thought of the neo-pagans and the strawberries. "So ... you think the valley here is ..." He broke off, unsure how to complete the thought.

"Spiritually charged – like a battery. Yes." agreed Theo. "And it was here that the old world, the world of nature, gave rise to organised religion. I had to come." He smiled, seemingly at the beer bottle in his hand but it was obvious his thoughts were elsewhere.

"And so ... you came?" said George, marvelling at the easy simplicity with which Theo had decided to come to Nemi, and even found a job when he got there. Like the drinking beer from the bottle, it seemed a young carefree thing to do. The ten minutes (tired ... day in Rome ... heat ... early night … nice to meet you … hope all goes well for you.) was forgotten.

"Yes," agreed Theo. "I just came. I've got Tuesday morning off so I'll take a walk over to the sanctuary then."

George glanced around. The other tables were empty now – he had not even noticed people leaving, though in retrospect he seemed to remember movement and scattered calls of "*Buona notte*". Massimo waved from the door of the kitchen, made a 'more beer?' gesture, and George waved back. Definitely another beer. During the time it took to arrive, and there was another bottle for Theo as well, George had considered –and rejected – recounting the strange meeting with the mad woman. Instead he told Theo about his own visit to the ruins with the man from the museum, how the neo-pagans left gifts, the strawberries, bay leaves and misshapen biscuit. He would wait and see what Theo said after visiting the sanctuary before broaching the subject of the mad woman.

"Massimo called you Engineer George," said Theo. "What kind of engineering?"

"Uh … civil. Mostly site, but some hydraulics as well. Freelance."

Theo fastened on this last. "Freelance? So you're your own boss. Cool."

"Yes, uh …" George was feeling old again; he would never be able to call something 'cool'. "Different projects, here and there, you know …," he ended lamely.

"Wow! Great! Bet you've travelled all over." And George found himself first an audience, then a participant in reminiscences and impressions of various countries. He himself had worked in Africa, Australia and South America, while Theo had back-packed all over Europe and South America as well. Massimo appeared briefly and grinned, pleased at the success of his introduction, and when Theo got to his feet rather guiltily, waved him back down.

"No, Enjoy, enjoy! Keep open the bar for Engineer George, Tayo, but write down the beers, eh? Engineer George will find them on his bill. We are not your Father Christmas here! Our *Babbo Natale* does not drink!" And with a last cheerful wave, he went inside. Shortly afterwards the patio lights dimmed, leaving a muted night-time glow, but George and Theo were talking about Guatemala; they had even been to the same area in the south-west of the country, Lake Atitlán.

"You know it's endor … endorheic," said George rather woozily. "Like this one …"

"What's *that* in plain language'" asked Theo laughing. "You're not talking to one of your own, you know."

"Oh, yes, sorry," said George, waking up a bit. "Fed by underground springs and rainfall, and doesn't flow into the sea."

"Right. Where were you on the lake?" Theo went on. "I stayed in Panajachel as a base. And then went round other places from there."

"Santiago Atitlán – I was there for work so I didn't really get anyway else."

"Right! That's one place I stopped a couple of days – it was their holy week with a procession moving their local god. Now, there's one that's really weird. Maximón, mix of Mayan and Catholic, and known for his drinking and cigar-smoking."

Theo had pronounced the name correctly but George's tired brain interpreted "mah-shee-mohn" as Theo being drunk too. In addition he had had enough of deities and spirituality and was now longing for bed. He drained his glass, and dredged up his original excuse. "Uh, sorry, Theo, but that's me for the night. Long day in Rome … uh … with the heat, you know." He did not add, "Hope all goes well for you and your … uh … quest here." It no longer seemed appropriate somehow.

7 MONDAY 3ᴿᴰ AUGUST

The local help had returned to report to Mrs Pleiades, but only because they were more afraid of not returning than returning. This was the first time they had worked for her, and initially they had congratulated themselves on their good fortune; she paid five times the going rate. It is true that they had heard things about her, things they simply did not believe at the time, and then, when they did meet her (already committed by even the acceptance to meet), believed utterly and with appalling certainty that what they had heard was true. Five times the going rate did not seem enough then.

She was her perfect varnished self that day, expertly made-up, beautifully coiffured and elegantly dressed in dark reddish-brown, oxblood as it is called, with nails enamelled to match, and the mirrored patent-leather shoes she favoured. When David Levant showed the two men into the ornate sitting-room, she was sitting on the couch with Varian, speaking to him quietly and slowly with one hand cupping his cheek. He was nodding seriously, his face smooth and blank. She did not look round when the door opened.

"So?" she asked. She smoothed back Varian's dark blonde hair, then patted his cheek. "It is successfully concluded, I trust?" Now she did look at them.

"The police suspect nothing. They are following the drug trail."

"And what about the English tourist?" Uneasily they realised that she had missed none of the blurted words at their previous meeting.

"Tell Mrs Pleiades what happened," said David Levant, then, shockingly, launched into a stream of invective in Italian, moisture appearing at the roots of his thin hair, plastering it to the pale bony forehead.

"Thank you, David," murmured Mrs Pleiades when the tirade had finished. "Now - the English tourist."

"Not a tourist," said the braver of the two. "She lives and works here. Jane Harrison. A teacher. We saw the police report. And we have a copy of her identity card. Here." He brought out a folded sheet of paper and half-offered it in the direction of Mrs

Pleiades, who ignored it.

"And?"

"He spoke to her." The man reported the words that Tommaso had scrupulously noted down – *'Deve essere protetto. E' arrivata - e questa volta sarà ...'*

Mrs Pleiades showed her teeth. "Ah, quite the chatterbox, wasn't he? And?"

"And nothing," said the man with a hint of spirit. He held up the photocopy of Jane's identity card as if it were an exhibit. "I know these English. They help the police, answer their questions, do what they see as their duty." This last uttered with enormous contempt. "But we checked anyway – went to her flat. There was nothing."

"Did you ... speak with her?"

This was the bad news, and neither man wanted to be the first.

"There was a neighbour, we could not get her alone, and then she went to the ghetto, we followed but ... we lost her. She did not see us, Mrs Pleiades. I assure you ... but ... those alleyways, so narrow, such sharp corners. She turned a corner and must have entered a building but how to know which one? Those thick walls. We heard nothing."

The ornate sitting-room was quiet. David Levant stood by the door, hands clasped before him. Varian, who was lounging in his corner of the couch, looked bored. Mrs Pleiades was thinking. A few enigmatic words from a dying man, words faithfully reported to the police. She was inclined to believe the help's assessment. Jane Harrison had done her duty, and the police were following the drug trail. However ...

"I cannot pay you for your work, of course," she said slowly. "It has been ... sloppy."

They broke into a chorus of agreement, of course no payment was required, Mrs Pleiades was completely justified, completely in the right, they were mortified, no, more than mortified, desolate, if there was anything they could do ... without charge, of course. Mrs Pleiades listened, nodded as though agreeing ...

"David ...," she said.

He had been standing behind them. At her words he took two quick steps forward and before they had time to hear him or react, had hooked a hand round each head and crashed them together with bone-shattering force. The two men crumpled untidily to the carpet. One of them gave a faint moan.

Mrs Pleiades leaned back, admired her ox-blood nails. "The gymnasium, I think, David, but make it the shower-room. Varian can have them to practise on. Oh, and give me that photocopy."

Hidden by the copious red blossoms of massed oleander bushes, the gardener peered through their spiky leaves to watch The Pallid One and The Thing drag two bodies from the house to the annex. Ah, they would have blood! And the prey were not dead yet, there had been some feeble resistance – fingers pawing weakly at the gravel – so, if he moved closer to the annex in a short while he would hear the screams and pleas for mercy, the crunch of bone and whimperings of despair. He licked his lips and smiled, baring tobacco-stained teeth, pushing his small cowboy hat to the back of his head. His fingers fondled the worn handle of his rake, and then he grasped it more securely, crossed silently to the path, and scrutinised the grooves and welts scored in the small white stones. Still silently, save for a whispering rattle, he smoothed the uneven surface, the rake moving in small concentric circles, and then withdrew to the grass and studied the gravel anew. And now …

The walls of the annex had been sound-proofed, but only for normal purposes. It was not designed to muffle completely those sounds beyond a certain pitch, and the sounds that the gardener heard were well beyond that certain pitch. For a short while he listened, obsidian eyes glinting in the shade of his hat, but then moved away and reflected, with a curl of the lip, that prey was always repetitive and these could offer no new sensations. As he walked, he looked up at the sun. Midday was drawing close, and it was time to repeat the call. All must return to their essence, be reborn, tread the cosmic circle in this fourth of worlds. As did his native lake: first water, then clouds, then rain, then water. Here, beneath the town, this puny body of water could not compare, a mere puddle, and yet … and yet.

He stopped suddenly in his tracks, nostrils flaring, head cocked as though he had heard a faint

The Sacred Wood

far-off call. For a moment he stood, eyes questing, and then with dawning awareness, gazed in the direction of Nemi. He could see nothing, but he nodded, smiled again, and this time it was a smile of recognition and salutation. So there was another Old One, another who waited as he was waiting, at this the crossroads of the world. Well, he would find the other, but first the call ...

He continued on his way, entered a door at the back of the house, and went down the short, unpainted corridor to his quarters, a small narrow room with an alcove set in the far end. The air inside was stiflingly hot, heavy with the mingled smells of sweat, stale tobacco smoke and candle wax, smells of home for the gardener. Doffing the small cowboy hat and throwing it onto the unmade bed, he went to the alcove, drew back the red bedspread that served as a curtain, and bent to relight the stubs of candles set in metal jar-tops. They flared hungrily towards the match, to show the small table on which they stood, together with a charm flask and a picture of a moustachioed man seated at a crossroads, wearing a black suit, red tie and wide-brimmed hat. The gardener nodded to the picture before drawing up a battered wicker chair and lighting a cigarette.

He fixed his gaze on the flask, narrowing his eyes to focus on first one and then another of the seven layers: mustard seed against all harm, red bean against the evil eye, rosemary to protect him. He drew heavily on the cigarette, then let it fall still burning into one of the jar-tops, and leant back, his eyes gradually closing as he whispered the words that would recall the wandering spirit and bind it to the cycle of the whole.

At this time in the morning, Barbara should have been on her way to the nursing-home in Alfredo's Mercedes to pick up Lena for their trip and lunch out, but a phone call had come the evening before to say Lena was scheduled for blood tests and X-rays that morning, but would be free in the afternoon. Barbara was not surprised since it had happened before. They never seemed to give any advance warning, or at least, not the kind of advance warning that Barbara was used to in England; Lena said that the night before was quite thoughtful really, usually they told her the same morning but they knew she had a visitor.

Barbara decided she would go up to Nemi and spend the morning there. She had forgotten to pack her flannel and wanted to buy a new one, and she might get a few postcards even though it was early in her stay. As for getting there, she would walk, with no hanging around waiting for a lift. There was a narrow road winding up the hillside that began quite close to the *agriturismo* and would take her straight to the imposing arch next to that castle and into the village. From the valley it looked a good stretch of the legs but the slope was fairly gentle, and Barbara liked both walking and not having to rely on others; besides, she'd used it to come down the hill to the nursing home in the past. She put on her walking shoes, picked up her handbag and set off.

George slept in on Monday – a rare occurrence. He was only just in time for breakfast, brought to him by Theo with a sympathetic grin but mercifully no talk, and then sat rather grumpily over his tea, feeling as if the day had got away from him. He still wanted to go to Monte Cavo and the stretch of the Sacred Way, but not just yet; he wished Theo's time-off and visit to the sanctuary was that day, rather than the next. He rightly attributed his grumpiness to his vague hangover, another rare occurrence, while Theo had looked annoyingly awake and bright-eyed. And what about the mad woman? If only that bookshop in Rome had been open …

Bookshop! Now, that was an idea. He would go up to Nemi itself, which he hadn't visited yet, and see if there was one there. He was not to know that the village that had had a population of 1,420 in 1994 had hardly changed at all since then, and that he was in fact being overly optimistic as regards the range of shops to be found there. He went to get his rucksack, took one look at his travel thermometer propped up by his bed (28°), another at the road up to the village as he left the chalet, and headed purposefully for the car park, keys in hand. Walking was definitely not on the cards, not in the heat with a headache; and he could buy some Aspirin as well.

At that hour the car was merely uncomfortably hot, and the thick khaki of his shorts would block the heat temporarily so he got in, started up the car, and moved it to the meagre patch of shade afforded by an olive tree, opening all the car doors once he had got out. That done, he leant against the tree thinking. If there *were* no bookshop in Nemi, tomorrow he could go back to the English one in Rome, which should then be "open as usual". Theo would be going to the sanctuary, and if George stayed here, he would just hang around the *agriturismo* waiting to hear what he had to say; at this point he had forgotten Monte Cavo yet again. Better to go to the city and get some gen. As for today – he had another inspiration. Perhaps Nemi had a tourist office – brochures, a bit of background to the place. Something, anyway, to be going on with. He got into the car and reversed carefully out of the shade.

As he drove up the slope to Nemi, he was very glad indeed he had taken the car; he had even switched the air-conditioning on; his head was still gently throbbing. He drove slowly and carefully for it was more a lane than a road but with two-way traffic, and George had seen the way locals drove. They were used to it no doubt but even so … the unexpected could occur at any time; it wasn't as though there were long stretches with unrestricted views.

By this time he was about two-thirds of the way up, still driving slowly, little more than a walking pace, and unconsciously hunching slightly over the wheel. He saw that there was someone up ahead sitting by the side of the road, a middle-aged woman – obviously English from her roomy blue skirt and white cotton blouse. He slowed down even more, and gave her a quick tentative glance, seeing a bright-red face under straight-cut grey hair; she gestured at him feebly, though it was unclear whether it was a greeting or a plea for help.

George took another quick glance before and behind him to make sure there were no other cars, and then crammed his own as near to the road edge as he could, clambering out but not approaching the woman so she wouldn't feel threatened. There on her own ... Italy ... strange men, he thought disjointedly. Mustn't alarm her.

"I say!" he called across the few yards. "Are you feeling all right? Couldn't ... uh ... help noticing you look a bit peaky."

"Oh, thank heavens. An English voice," she managed to say. "I'm just a bit knocked out by the heat. My own fault – didn't think it was that far. And forgot my hat of course."

"Uh ... if you're going up to the village, I can give you a lift," he offered. "George Sutton...," and then heard himself add, "Engineer." Even as he said it he felt it was a very un-English way of introducing himself; it must have been the influence of Massimo and his "Engineer George".

The woman in fact laughed; her face was slowly returning to a more natural colour, losing the alarming crimson and puce of earlier. "Engineer, eh?" she said cheerfully. "Knight errant as well. Mind you," she went on, starting to push herself off the bank with one hand. "I haven't been a damsel for more years than I care to remember." Now George laughed, rather liking her humour and forthright manner. "Give us a hand, will you, Engineer?" she said, "I'm sure you've got experience in shifting awkward weights!"

George hurried forward, and with one hand under her elbow and the other round her ample waist, gently eased her into a standing position, and then relinquished his grip; she swayed slightly.

"Do you ... uh ... need a hand to get to the car?" asked George with some alarm, hand under her elbow again, and checking worriedly to make sure the road was still empty.

"Perhaps just a bit of steadying," she admitted, and they made their way slowly over to the car, George still glancing up and down the road.

"Didn't expect this kind of heat," she said, once they were both safely inside, and chugging up the hill again. "Never been this hot here before."

Which led naturally into her introducing herself ("Barbara Allberry," adding in her turn: "Stupid old woman, retired."), and explaining her annual visits to her old university friend, who lived in the nursing home down there over to left. From the hillside the clinic and grounds were clearly visible now: the main building, looking like a country mansion, the dark cypresses grouped over to one side of well-tended gardens, other tall trees dotting the sweep of lawn, and the curve of the stone parapet edging the grounds, with the discreet car park to the rear.

George himself volunteered the reason for his stay, the road-and-aqueduct tour, and here in Nemi his intention to visit Monte Cavo and the Sacred Way, though by now this last was beginning to sound more and more unreal to him. The few exchanges of small talk, which included the discovery that they were both staying at the *agriturismo*, took them up to the arch to the village, where George even managed to find a parking space not far from the arch.

"Well, all the best," said Barbara, heaving herself out of the small passenger seat, obviously intended for skinny dwarves in her book. She had completely recovered but was planning to sit down at a bar for coffee and a glass of water; she really had underestimated the distance up the hill.

"Yes ... uh ... you too," returned George, then hesitantly, "I say, do you need a lift back down? No problem, you know. Could meet back here in a couple of hours. No problem,"

"And very nice it is of you too, Engineer," said Barbara robustly. "About a quarter to one? But if I'm not here, you go on." And she strode off to look for a hospitable-looking bar and then a flannel.

George locked the car and wandered over to where a parapet separated a cobbled road running alongside the large palazzo from the sheer drop into the valley. With his back against the parapet, he could see the intersection of four different roads: directly to his left a narrow cobbled street abruptly veered off behind the palazzo; still left, but slightly at an angle, there was the road leading steeply down to the entrance arch where they had arrived, over to his right a third, more an alleyway or courtyard than an actual road, ended in a house and a flight of steps, and the last, Nemi's main street, a relatively wide thoroughfare with a large bar and tables in the foreground, the road itself, lined with shops, curving away towards the edge of the village.

As George looked around, he felt increasingly glum. He had not realized how very tiny Nemi actually was. He could see treetops immediately above the pink and cream buildings of the main street with their window boxes of massed red geraniums; the village was crammed onto a small ridge of the mountain, which then continued its upward sweep.

For a moment he considered having a coffee at the bar on the corner of the alleyway; it had small tables outside covered with cheerful sunflower-patterned cloths. Maybe later, he thought, after I've seen if there is a tourist office or something; he had given up on the idea of a bookshop. He too set off, only to retrace his steps because he had left his rucksack in the car. Must be going senile, he reflected gloomily. At his return from the car, rucksack now in hand, he saw a column surmounted by a bronze head on the corner of the alley and the main street. He ambled over to take a look and read the inscription: *Caligola*, it informed, *dono di Paola Maddaloia, A.D.MM* . Beneath the head was Nemi's coat-of-arms, three tall slender trees – cypresses? – on three mounds, and the inscription *Dianiae*. George looked at the expressionless Roman face under the short straight hair: Caligula, he thought, vague recollections of the old BBC series *I, Claudius* coming to mind. Creepy little bugger. Wonder what he's doing here. He set off again on what he already suspected would be a hopeless quest.

8 TUESDAY 4ᵀᴴ AUGUST

It is not often that two hands reach for the very same book in a bookshop. The two men had already gone through the manoeuvring that takes place when two people want to look at the same shelves, and now it was the very same book. Knuckles collided, apologies expressed but it was Gabriel's hand that was the first to swoop back to capture the volume. George, who had not had the benefit of living in Italy, where the law of the fittest – or at least the law of the most decisive – reigned, looked extremely crest-fallen. Gabriel relented, as far as he could, given his character, and said easily: "I'm so sorry but I do actually need this." George, bolstered by the certainty of *his* need for the book, straightened up, now looming over Gabriel.

Sensing a change in the atmosphere, the bookshop owner, a plump man sitting behind his till, looked up from his own book.

The bookshop in Trastevere had been open, advertising its presence with a box of yellowing paperbacks on a table outside. The box seemed to be a collection of what the owner considered to be holiday reading: old Agatha Christie novels, similar offerings in French and German, with a lone volume in Spanish on bee-keeping, all priced at one euro. The display in the window – the English books on Italy that had attracted George's attention – had been dusted and moved, the centrepiece now being a glossy coffee table book on famous fountains. George had arrived before Gabriel, and had been browsing methodically, while Gabriel, who knew the shop, spent a few minutes chatting to the owner before aiming immediately for the right section, where the conflict of interest arose.

"It's – uh – rather important for me as well, actually," insisted George, eyeing the book.

Gabriel considered the serious sun-reddened face of what was obviously an English holiday-maker, and glanced down at the book which he himself was now holding firmly in both hands. He was intrigued as to why this gangly sincere-looking man was apparently going against every ingrained instinct and rather than giving in gracefully, not making a fuss and politely withdrawing, was prepared to do the opposite of all three.

"Look, why don't you let me buy it?" he

suggested. Jane would have recognised the persuasive tone and disarming smile. The nice thing (the worst thing?) about Gabriel … "Then we can go for a drink and look at it together. Get it photocopied so we both have it. My name's Gabriel, by the way."

George, who had had no idea how the situation would be resolved – and had indeed been suffering the tortures of the damned – gratefully accepted, introducing himself in his turn, and, the book bought, the two went out into the sunshine. The bookshop owner relaxed and went back to his reading.

Gabriel chose a dim, run-down-looking café nearby; an overhead fan stirred the warm half-light inside, and the Formica-topped tables and woven plastic chairs were empty of customers. They collected their drinks from the counter, fruit juice for George, iced coffee for Gabriel, and settled in a corner. Gabriel took out the book, *Towns and Villages of the Alban Hills*, and placed it on the table; now that it was in his possession he could afford to be generous:

"Any particular part you wanted?" he asked, pushing the book towards George, and picking up his glass.

"Uh, Nemi, actually."

Gabriel's glass hesitated in mid-air before completing the journey. He took a sip before asking:

"Any particular reason?"

"I'm ... uh ... staying there. Interesting area ... uh ... very."

Gabriel was no fool and knew full well when he was being lied to. He sat back, and the disarming smile and persuasive voice came into play again.

"Sorry, I've been very rude, George. You're here on holiday, aren't you?"

George would have had to be a senseless clod to withstand Gabriel's charm, and that he was not. The complete attention of a listener who was never intrusive and who knew when a comment or question was called for, had him talking as he had never talked before. The "uh" disappeared, he described his road-and-aqueduct tour, employed a good fifteen minutes describing the museum in the former generating station, which – wonder of wonders – Gabriel was familiar with, and another twenty on the Claudian Aqueduct. Gabriel was not just an audience – he saw and re-lived everything that George had. For more than half an hour they walked through George's immediate past. Finally, Gabriel judged it was time to cut to the chase, but gently.

"You're staying in Rome, are you?" he asked casually.

George's light dimmed. He had avoided talking about Nemi, but now felt he had to be sincere with this interesting, understanding stranger. The "actually" and the "uh" returned:

"Uh ... actually ... I'm staying in Nemi – not the village, an *agriturismo* down by the lake." He paused. "For the Sacred Way ... you know ... then there's a minor road, the Via Virbia, from ...uh ... the Appian Way."

Gabriel had often found that sincerity – at the right point in a conversation – could move mountains.

"Hope you don't mind me saying so," he said slowly, "but you don't seem very happy about it. None of my business, I know, but ... you said the book was important for you."

"The thing is ..." said George hesitantly, all the tensions, uncertainties and worries of the last few days returning in full force.

"Yes?" That one word could not have been more persuasive, filled as it was with such understanding, concern and interest. And George, having encountered the right mixture of worldliness and empathy, told him everything.

Theo, the American, was working his way through college, and though he seemed young to George, he was older than his student contemporaries. He was not in any hurry to finish, believing that life was for living, and he wanted to see as much of the world as possible. To this end he had picked grapes in France, canned fish in Norway and once worked on a banana boat in the Caribbean, also simply travelling to places that interested him. His mother despaired, and being third-generation Greek-American, she reverted to her ancestry every time he embarked on another journey, spreading her hands in a gesture of reproof, incomprehension and entreaty. What she would really have liked was to see him become a success like his uncle Spiro, who had a chain of hardware stores, and settle down with a nice girl – she didn't even have to be Greek; Theo's mother could bend that far. Theo's father merely shrugged and winked at him; there were three older children who were all doing well, so let the youngest enjoy himself.

Theo loved and appreciated his parents, and happily went his own way. He had never managed to get to Italy before, though it was high on his places to check out, and he had been studying Italian off and on for the last two years. When the opportunity arose to go, it presented itself in the simplest of ways: a phone call from a college friend who could not take up a hotel job in Tuscany because of an illness in the family, and the ticket was already booked – the name could just be changed. And since the job was for six weeks Theo had the time to practise his Italian not only at work but on sight-seeing trips to Florence, Siena and Arezzo as well.

And then he read about Nemi in the German tourist's book and some kind of chord was struck. As he had recounted to George, he came there and found a job. And the job was not in Genzano or Nemi itself but in the valley that contained the sanctuary. When Theo subsequently reviewed the sequence of events, he believed there were too many coincidences; they must be links in a preordained chain, and one that had slowly but surely drawn him to this place and this time.

If George had shown more interest Theo would have talked more about the sanctuary and its roots in ancient legend, but the pleasant Englishman had seemed disinclined to pursue the subject. He did, however, advise Theo not to bother going to the museum to ask for the 'guide', explaining the way there and mentioning the large hole in the fence.

All of which turned out to be exactly as he described, and on Tuesday morning Theo was passing the tall arch-shaped recesses, walking left towards the partial excavation covered with rigid Perspex sheeting, and gazing at the plinth in the far corner. George had described the gifts left by neo-pagans, and Theo saw that there was a slender sheath of wild flowers, feathery grasses and corn stalks bound together with a strand of green wool. The strawberries, the tears of Diana, had gone, as had the misshapen biscuit. Theo had brought his own offering wrapped carefully in a plastic bag – bay leaves wet with spring water, and he laid them carefully beside the flowers and grasses, shaking the remaining water over them and carefully folding the bag to take away with him. He was sorry that the misshapen biscuit had been replaced; he would have liked to have seen it for he was sure it must be some kind of ceremonial cake.

It was cool and quiet beneath the Perspex, the corner being shielded from the rays of the rising sun by the cliff above, and the air still retained a hint of the moisture and freshness of night. Theo stood for a few moments, just enjoying the sensation of being there, though his concentration was broken by the low buzzing of a fly that had started somewhere behind him. He sighed. The spirituality he had talked about to George seemed entirely absent. Absent or dormant, he wondered; the site had not been neutralised or converted in some way by the early Christians, as had happened to so many pagan temples. There was no shrine to the Madonna that would have filled the void left by the disappearance of the goddess; everything had been abandoned and covered over. He sighed again; the buzzing of the fly seemed to fill the small area, and then stopped, intensifying the silence. What ...?

Voices sounded from outside, and they were coming nearer:

"Ma qua, non c'è niente," complained an adolescent voice.

"Attento alla cacca!" said – probably his mother, thought Theo smiling; he had seen the sheep droppings as he was walking along, and Italian mothers were always on the lookout for potential danger or dirt.

"Un po' di pazienza," came a man's voice (the father's?), and then the family came into sight at the top of the metal steps that bridged the few feet down into the excavation: father, mother and two teenage children: the boy who had complained,

and a girl, intent on sending a text message on her mobile phone. The father wore fawn trousers, a white shirt and a khaki fisherman's waistcoat with buckles and pockets, the wife was more elegant in cream trousers and a light jacket, while the children, both dark-haired, wore the summer uniform of the young: knee-length denims, T-shirts and trainers. Surprised, they stopped when they saw Theo, who smiled and said good morning. Striking up a conversation was easy, for they were all there for the same reason. "*Che carino!*" exclaimed the mother when she saw the altar and its offerings, while her daughter wanted to ask Theo about the States, the father took photographs, and the boy scuffed his trainers in the dirt and looked sceptical; Theo did not mention that he had placed the bay leaves on the plinth.

They walked back to the road together, the father practising his English, and the two teenagers joining in. The family were going to the *Museo delle navi romane*, said the father. Would Theo like a lift? They had the car down at the main road.

Theo accepted immediately. Despite – or because of – his expectations he had found the site of the sanctuary disappointing – there was really so little to see. It was frustrating too that it was almost impossible to imagine what the sacred complex had originally looked like; the small fields and ramshackle sheds were distracting. Still, he thought, the morning was not over yet, and he had the opportunity to visit the museum without having to walk there.

The museum was in the opposite direction, on the way to Genzano and on the same northern shore of the lake, the only shore with any real land mass behind it. It was here that the two Roman ships had been painstakingly raised to dry land in the 1920s, and a purpose-built museum constructed to hold their enormous hulls; the result was two interconnected exhibition halls – one for each ship – that from a distance could have been taken for two large warehouses. Outside the entrance, a dirt lay-by provided parking space, the plants edging it dusty and parched, while inside the grounds the museum was surrounded by lawns shaded by tall trees and the view showed the still waters of the lake. A ramp, ceremonial in size and effect, ascended to the entrance, also of monumental proportions and in the fascist style of architecture: massive blocks of plain stone in soaring vertical lines with IL MVSEO DELLE NAVI ROMANE carved into the high crossbeam. Theo and the family paused to look at the façade:

"Wow!" exclaimed Theo, making the two teenagers laugh; the girl had "Wow!" scrawled across the front of her T-shirt. "That is … really something."

The father said that well, you had to give Mussolini his due. Five years it had taken to recuperate the ships, not the first attempt to do so over the years, and an enormous undertaking, but ultimately successful; you know, they even drained the lake to do it?

"How did they manage that?" asked Theo, his interest engaged.

"Over there." The father gestured in the direction of the western shore and the dark smudge of Genzano, its roofs indistinct in the heat haze. "There was an emissary, an ancient gallery, dug out from here to the other side of the volcano, so that water ran away into the plain, then to the sea. They cleaned up the gallery, and used that."

Theo looked at the slopes to the west. "But that's incredible," he said. "How far is that?"

The father delved into one of the pockets of his fisherman's waistcoat, and found a small well-thumbed guidebook, which he consulted. "1,635 metres," he read, and then looked up, and catching his wife's eye, smiled sheepishly. "I know, I know," he said, "but I like …"

"… being informed!" chorused his family, laughing; it was obviously one of his favourite sayings.

"I can't wait to see the ships," said Theo, when the laughter had died away and they were walking into the building. "They must be wonderful."

"Ah, you don't know? They are gone," said the father sadly. "Destroyed by fire."

Theo looked at him stunned; the lake had been drained, a museum built to hold the ships, and they were burnt?

"It'll all be explained inside," said the father soberly.

Beyond the low-ceilinged entrance hall with statues flanking its walls and a large table showing a map of the area in the centre, the two exhibition halls lay to the left and to the right, huge spaces designed to showcase the hulls but now cool and empty, dwarfing the few exhibits the museum had since assembled. The family turned left and Theo followed, temporarily distracted from his original intention of concentrating on the history of the sanctuary, and stopped to gaze down the length of the hall. In structure it could have been a huge shallow swimming pool, for the floor was higher around the sides, and then had wide shallow steps leading down to the lower main area. On the walls were contemporary photographs of the salvage operations, one showing the sodden hull of one of the beached ships, surrounded by top-hatted men standing on rough planking, and another with the hull assembled inside the museum. It was this last that showed their enormous size: the hull completely filled the exhibition hall from side to side and end to end with very little room to spare; the shallow 'swimming pool' had contained the wooden cross-structures supporting the hull.

Other boards showed possible reconstructions of how the ships might have looked, with temples, baths, a colonnade and even fruit trees. Palaces, thought Theo wonderingly, floating palaces moored on the lake. And the sanctuary? Was there a connection between these amazing vessels and the sacred complex? He followed the displays down the wall to the far end of the hall, and then paused at some wall-mounted sections of lead pipes. The notice said that Roman pipes were usually engraved with the name of the person who they were made for, and these had been made for the Emperor Gaius Julius Caesar Augustus Germanicus, otherwise known as Caligula.

Caligula? thought Theo. Wasn't he the one who made his horse into a senator? He had completely forgotten to look for information about the fire that had destroyed the ships.

He had circled the main area without looking at the exhibits there, and now he began to retrace his steps to go to the other part of the museum, vaguely aware of a small group with a guide, who were gathered in the centre and appeared to be looking down at the floor, the guide saying, "… and this is the Via Virbia. You can see how perfect the flagstones are, with none of the ruts and grooves you see on the streets at Pompeii, for example. There was no heavy traffic of carts or chariots, for horses were forbidden to enter …" But Theo was already leaving the hall of the lost ships in search of the history of the sanctuary.

And there it was in the other exhibition hall. Theo made straight for the notice-board-size stands set among the statues and display cases, for they appeared to show long descriptions and explanations. Theo took out his pocket dictionary; this was the part he wanted to know more about.

The sanctuary of Diana, of such importance in

ancient times that a road was built from the Appian Way to accommodate the flow of worshippers, dated to pre-Roman times and was dedicated to Diana, but not in her traditional role of virgin and huntress. Here she presided over healing and childbirth, and apparently, fire played an important part in her ritual since at Nemi she also bore the name of Vesta, the Roman goddess of fire and the hearth. In its mixture of roles and responsibilities – confusing to a monotheistic culture – the story was little different from what Theo had read about other ancient myths, but there was a twist: the sanctuary was linked to a unique bloodthirsty custom. While in the valley reigned the cleanliness, order and piety of the sanctuary, above, hidden in the tangled undergrowth of the wooded slopes, reigned the Priest King of the Sacred Wood, the Rex Nemorensis.

By tradition this king was a runaway slave who had achieved his kingship by killing the previous king – the king is dead, long live the king, century after century, an unending line of challenge and battle, resulting in victory for one, death for the other. No parallel to it existed in the rest of the ancient world, and so strange and evocative was the custom that it had inspired the twelve-volume work by James Frazier, *The Golden Bough*.

Theo left the explanations for a moment to look at the display cabinets, thinking about how many contrasting realities had coexisted around the tiny lake: the northern shore with its greater land mass filled with the sanctuary itself, the woods the domain of the Rex Nemorensis, and then, moored over towards Genzano, the enormous sumptuous ships. Were they homage or challenge to the sanctuary? Or merely an emperor's whim for a summer retreat? He waved to the family who had now come into the second exhibition hall; they waved back cheerfully.

He strolled to look at a display cabinet which exhibited the smaller finds from past excavations: broken pots painstakingly reassembled, copper jugs with battered rims green with age, small Roman oil lamps, and votive offerings fashioned in the semblance of the afflicted part of the body. There were deceptively sturdy-looking feet with long straight toes, single hands frozen in a stop gesture, a lone thumb, looped intestines as stylised as a picture in a school biology book, and plump genitalia. Theo, being young and healthy, smiled at the collection of ills the clay objects represented, wondered if his mother would have been one of those seeking relief, for she suffered from arthritis in her right foot. Thinking of her, and her very real pain, the objects did not seem so amusing. Feeling a little ashamed, he averted his gaze from the cabinet.

Towards the back of the exhibition hall there was a long cordoned-off area. Theo crossed the short distance, and looked down into what appeared to be a long trench, rather like a water culvert. At the bottom of the culvert, about two

The Sacred Wood

metres below floor level, was an excavated tract of Roman road rising in gentle ascent; the flagstones were smoothed and rounded with time but as intact and unmarked as the day they were laid. The small placard on one of the metal poles supporting the cordon held the information that this was part of the Via Virbia, the road from the Appian Way that led to the sanctuary.

It was strange to look down on the road and see it emerge from the modern floor, run for some twenty metres and then traverse a huge glass wall to emerge again outside the museum. There, the stones were overgrown and stained brown with dead moss, following a straight course for about ten metres before disappearing again beneath the fence surrounding the museum grounds.

As Theo's eyes followed the course of the road from beneath the modern floor, along to the glass wall and then out into the sunlight a shadow passed across the sun. He heard the sound of faint singing, and as the shadow darkened and deepened (a storm cloud?), the sound came closer, a low musical chanting, with one clear sweet voice distinct in a counterpoint.

It became darker and darker; the air became hot and heavy and Theo smelt burning tar, then the scent of rosemary, thyme and mint. The singing was very close now, and the crowd (crowd?) leaned closer, Theo among them, as the first torches came into view. Above the bowl of the valley, the moon hung large and luminous, mirrored in the exact centre of the shimmering waters of the lake.

The heat of the night pressed down as dozens of torches now came into sight. Only women were in the procession, dressed in white, feet bare, most holding the flaming torches, others holding the leashes of large hunting dogs, whose collars were twined with ivy. The chant rose again, the single voice rising and falling in celebration and worship.

Sweating in the hot night, Theo looked to the left, up towards Genzano where the procession wound down from the rim of the volcano in a ribbon of flame, and then started with surprise when he saw the towering bulk of two enormous ships, immobile in the lee of the mountainside. They seemed like looming fortresses, the flaring light from lamps and torches showing the ripple of golden roof tiles, the sheen of marbled walls and the swaying canopies of slender trees; dim figures could be discerned moving on the deck. Homage or challenge? Involuntarily his gaze went to the sanctuary, now a blaze of lights, then to the darkness of the lake cupping the golden reflection of the full moon, to sweep up towards the gloomy slopes where the faint glimmer of a fire could just be made out under the trees.

The chanting swelled again, again the single clear voice broke free in celebration and worship, the fur of the dogs as they padded beside their keepers was sleek and glossy, sliding over the powerful muscles, the smell of …

"*Ma che fa laggiù? E' impazzito? Non è permesso*

oltrepassare ...!"

Theo came back to reality. He was standing on the Roman road, sunlight and the airy spaces of the museum about him, the angry face of a museum attendant above him.

"I'm sorry ...," started Theo. "*Mi scusi – non so* ..." He lifted his shoulders helplessly, started slowly towards the steps leading up to the floor of the museum. He was not aware that he held a sprig of rosemary in one hand, only heard, as once again he tried to apologize to the attendant, the shrill disgusted voice of the Italian family's teenage son: "She touched my face, the filthy old hag, she touched my face...!"

Down at the *agriturismo*, George was lying on his bed, hands behind his head, and contemplating his bare feet, the photocopies Gabriel had made beside him. He had intended to browse through them, but kept picking them up and then putting them down again. Grumpily – again! – he really must snap out of it – George wriggled his toes, and scratched the bump on his ear where a mosquito had bitten him. Rotten little buggers, he thought. He sat up and poked at the photocopies for the fourth time, abruptly deciding it was impossible to concentrate when it was so hot, he wasn't in the mood just then, and there was no rush anyway. He lay back again and regarded his toes; the nails would need cutting soon. And what about Monte Cavo?

Perhaps the next day? Got to get back on track … But it's just another stretch of lumpy stones, whispered some treacherous alien thought. Why even bother? You've done the Claudian Aqueduct, seen the Appian Way in Rome. Isn't that all enough? Restless and bothered, he closed his eyes, tried to put things into perspective and pin down just what was happening to him.

His original plan had been simple – relax in the country and visit the Sacred Way on Monte Cavo, but the plan had gone awry from the moment he had returned to the ruins for his guide book and was accosted by the mad woman. Since then he hadn't been able to 'settle', but why not? The visit to the old generating station had been pleasant (and the mosaic?), meeting Theo on Sunday evening had seemed normal enough, but then Theo had gone on about his 'spiritual quest' and the valley as a 'sacred place,' which was … loony. But he *is* young, thought George, trying for middle-aged detachment, and failing, since he was far off middle-age himself. There was the nice woman Barbara Allberry of the day before, English, normal, no nonsense about *her*. But didn't that seem a lot of people to come across in a small place in a few days?

And his second visit to Rome earlier that day, the result of being increasingly "bothered" and wanting more information about the area, had resulted in Gabriel. George looked down at the photocopies. Hadn't there been another two books tucked under Gabriel's arm? Probably other stuff, he thought. Otherwise Gabriel would have offered photocopies of those as well, wouldn't he?

The doubt had barely begun to worm into his consciousness when he suddenly sat bolt upright. Theo had been to the sanctuary that day. What would he have to say about it? A swift glance at his travelling clock and George almost leapt off the bed. Towel, and shower before dinner. No time to lose!

One hand stretched out to grab the towel, he suddenly stopped in his tracks feeling foolish. Theo would be working, he reminded himself, and would not be able to sit over dinner and talk. Now, with almost self-conscious slowness George picked up the towel, slung it over one shoulder and made for the bathroom, almost forgetting to duck his head to avoid the doorframe. They could talk after dinner, he thought. Another hour or so was nothing.

And the "hour or so" passed with maddening slowness, as George manfully ate his way through antipasti, pasta, and a steak with salad, washing it all down with mineral water; he had had enough of beer. Finally he spotted Theo, and waved, making sitting and drinking gestures, which sent the bread basket, luckily empty, flying. Theo waved back smiling and made "later" gestures. He looked tousled and heavy-eyed but when, some half an hour later, he sat, or rather slumped down opposite George, he summoned up a smile, and said, "Hi there. Have a good day? I can't remember what you were going to do – Monte Cavo, was it? The Sacred Way."

"I slept in," admitted George. "Ended up just going up to the village." Reflexively he looked round; he had not seen Barbara Allberry at dinner; she must be with her friend. "How about you? Did you ... uh ... go to the sanctuary?"

"Yes, I did," replied Theo; he too was drinking mineral water. "There's not much to see, is there? But I saw the altar with the offerings. The strawberries and biscuits had gone but there were other things; someone must be taking gifts there regularly."

George was nodding, but only out of politeness; he wasn't interested in the offerings. He fumbled at his water glass, and then "No ... uh ... problems?" he ventured.

"Problems?" Theo's young open face was questioning. "What kind of problems?"

George could feel himself going red, but persisted: "See anyone ... uh ... strange about? Uh ... anything ... strange going on?"

Theo looked at him with sudden attention, rested his folded arms on the table, paused for a moment, and then,

"Not there, no." he stopped, unfolded his arms and ran one hand through his hair.

Now George was alert. He watched puzzled as Theo half-rose, extracted his wallet from his hip pocket, and took out a folded piece of paper, which he laid on the table and began to unroll. It held a thin spiky twig. Theo pushed it towards George, who picked it up; it emitted a faint pungent perfume.

"Rosemary, isn't it?" he asked.

Theo nodded, again hesitated, again ran his hands through his hair, and began to recount his visit to the museum and what he had "imagined" (this was how he put it, but then, there was the withered sprig of rosemary). Initially he kept checking George's face for embarrassed disbelief or – worse – some kind of hearty interjection, such as "Yes ... uh ... these places can get you going", which would have effectively signalled the close of the conversation, but saw none of these signs, and told his story to the end.

" ... And that's it – one minute I was there and it was night and the next it was day and I was standing down on the road with no idea how I'd gotten there. The museum guy was furious but I was lucky – he got distracted by the Italian family who gave me a lift there. They were good and upset, I can tell you. It was weird, the teenage boy said that some old woman had come up to him and muttered at him and stroked his face. No sign of her but the museum guy ..."

He broke off. George had been listening with a mixture of sympathy and confusion but gave a slight start at the mention of the old woman.

"What?" asked Theo sharply, and George, now hesitating in his turn, admitted that he too had come across an "old woman" who had "muttered at him".

"But at least she's accounted for," he finished, giving a slightly forced laugh. "I met an awfully nice chap in Rome who knows the area. Apparently her son was drowned in the lake, and she went off her head. She's always frightening visitors. Very good at that disappearing act too."

That is what George said. However, even as he spoke, a doubt crept into his mind. What had seemed so believable when airily dismissed by Gabriel (and was it really plausible that a foreigner would know the area so intimately?) now reappeared in its original colours – unnatural and upsetting. (And Gabriel hadn't explained how he knew the area either.) He unwillingly remembered his own reaction to the encounter in the dim shade of the sunken track, and hoped rather incoherently that the teenage boy was safely away. (But why would Gabriel make up a story if it wasn't true?) He voiced none of these thoughts to Theo – it was all too tenuous. "I say, Theo," he said instead. "How about a beer?"

9 WEDNESDAY 5ᵀᴴ AUGUST

After the stupid squabble about computers on Sunday Jane and Gabriel had left it that they would phone each other. Jane undertook to keep calling Oxford, Gabriel, with his habitual secretiveness, had talked vaguely about "pursuing other avenues". He phoned her Tuesday evening and suggested she come round the next morning. She arrived about ten at the borrowed flat. Whoever lived there favoured minimalist modern – bare wooden floors, metal shelving and plain square furniture. It must have faced west since the living room was in shade, its one window giving a view of sunlit red-tiled roofs and clear blue sky. Jane flopped down on the pine couch with cream cushions set in one corner of the room. A few books lay on the low table (also pine) in front of the couch.

"What's this?" asked Jane, picking up *Towns and Villages of the Alban Hills* and looking at the contents page.

"You first. Any luck with Oxford?"

"They're still not answering." She said despondently, laying the book down, "but I did find out some bits about Nemi though."

"Anything useful?"

She took her notes out and read out the few details: strawberries, the wood sacred to Diana, and the ceremonial ship belonging to the Emperor Caligula, then recounted her own efforts to find some connection with the piece of paper, ending with, "So what would a professor have to do with the drug trade?"

Gabriel had listened carefully, nodding every so often but not commenting. "We need the Oxford info," he said at last. "I'll try someone I know there."

He used his mobile phone, muttering, "God, this will cost me a fortune at this time of day," and got through to someone apparently called Perce. While he and Perce exchanged pleasantries, involving some shared joke about the secret service, Jane started looking through the pile of books. Part of her was listening to Gabriel's half of the conversation and she registered "Oxhall Monographs", "Any idea who …?" And then, "I've got that. Great, thanks." A pause. "No, I'm still in

Rome, but you know where the key is." Another pause. "No problem – bring her as well. She looks OK in a bikini, does she?" Another pause, a laugh, and he ended the call, sitting back and looking triumphant but saying nothing.

"Well?" said Jane impatiently, part of her fuming, Bloody sexist pig! Bikini!

"I've got the number of one of the people who used to work at Oxhall. Retired now, but that's better – more likely to be at home." He re-dialled, muttering again, "A bloody fortune," then sat back to wait as the phone rang. At the tenth ring, just when he was about to hang up, someone answered it.

"Yes?" said a thin reedy voice. The line hummed and crackled as though connected to some deep underground bunker.

Gabriel, almost taken by surprise, introduced himself, and Jane smiled reluctantly as she recognised the charming intimate tone. Well, Gabriel does have a beautiful voice, she thought. She heard him mention Perce, which led to several minutes of reminiscences, during which Gabriel rolled his eyes but made sounds of interested agreement. She went back to the books again.

"Well," said Gabriel, finally ending the call. His face was expressionless. "That was a Mr Mitchel, and he remembers the professor very well, still in touch with her in fact. Christmas cards, that kind of thing."

"Her?" queried Jane in surprise.

Gabriel's face broke into an evil smile, "And you a feminist, Jane."

She reddened but didn't rise to the bait, "Go on."

"Professor Hannah Emelene Caseman. Ancient History and Classical Archaeology. Retired."

"Is she in Oxford? Did he give you her number?"

Gabriel smiled again. "She's here in Italy."

"What! Where?"

"Guess."

"Not Nemi?"

"Got it in one." He smiled into her astounded face.

Jane, who had stood up, abruptly sat down again. She still held one of the books, one finger marking the page.

"I can't believe this," she said limply. "I …" She waved the book at him. "Gabriel. What *is* all this, do you think?"

He didn't answer, had gone to stand and look out of the window.

"Gabriel …?" He turned back to face her. His face was partly in shadow and she could not decipher his expression. Thoughtful? Concerned? Calculating? She waited.

At last he sighed, sat down beside her, hands loosely clasped in front of him. "Professor Caseman is in a nursing home near Nemi," he said expressionlessly. *"La Clinica di Sant'Ippolito.* It seems to be rather exclusive, more like a hotel, communal public rooms but private suites, trained medical staff on hand, that sort of thing." He stopped. Jane waited again, and then said tentatively, "So ... we can phone or go there. Show her the photocopy, tell her what the ... man said to me." She had almost said "dead man", and now the scene of that night came back in all its shock and distress. The mellow lamps, the strolling couples in the cobbled streets, then the (dead) man, the slickness of sweat on his face, the agonised appeal in his eyes. And last ... the metallic smell of blood and their linked hands slowly parting. She shivered.

Gabriel sat there, hands still loosely clasped in front of him.

"Well?" she prompted, resolutely putting aside the memory.

When he did answer, it was very quietly:

"We should leave this now."

"But ... this is the connection we've been looking for," protested Jane. "You were the one who thought of phoning your friend in Oxford."

His expression changed again, now it was the charming smile she instinctively distrusted. He jumped up. "Have you had breakfast? No? Good. Let's go out. Coffee and one of those sticky pastries you like, perhaps with a side order of cognac. Come on."

Mrs Pleiades was content, no, more than content,

satisfied, triumphant, filled with a sense of power and – yes - with the certainty that success was within her grasp. The past seven years – autumn in London (opera), winter in New York (art and culture), spring in Paris (fashion), and summer in Greece (relaxation) – had been a search, though one that had been pursued well away from the public eye and the fashionable world.

Her hunting ground was the shadow-world that exists in all big cities – in those districts near a port or railway station, where steps lead down into a dim bar with small tables or private booths; there will be rows of gleaming bottles behind the counter, and a watchful and discreet barman who, if questioned, professes to know nothing about his clientele but – if he considers you suitable – may mention the inner sanctum where the real business of the night is conducted.

London, with a short flight to Hamburg, Paris, with a longer flight to Berlin, Athens, so near to Istanbul – these were her departure points for the other, more secret, aim of Mrs Pleiades' life – to find the right young man.

Six months to the day she had found him in Berlin, in the part of the city that was once behind the Iron Curtain but was now in a ferment of democracy and capitalism. There were many immigrants from the former eastern bloc countries in the city – they came from Bosnia and Transylvania, Estonia and the Baltic coast; some were known to the authorities, many were not.

Dev Yankovic (his mother's surname) was one of those who were not. The illegitimate son of an American serviceman stationed in Germany and a Serbian prostitute, he had inherited his father's height and blond Californian good looks, his mother's high cheekbones. He had grown up adored and petted by older women, most of them prostitutes, and soon learnt that money could be made easily and painlessly by flattering, wooing and bedding them. That night, in the smoky recesses of *Der Goldene Zuchthengst*, he noticed the smoothly sleek older woman accompanied by the pallid Englishman, and saw that the woman had noticed him. When the pallid Englishman glanced at his watch, murmured to the woman and left her alone, Dev was soon on the bar stool beside her, lighting her cigarette and offering her a drink, the only expense he expected to incur.

One drink led to another – all of them tactfully taken care of by the woman. "I have an account here," she explained in a low thrilling voice with the faintest of foreign accents.

"You have such magic ... such allure," he murmured, knowing that on no account must the words "for your age" be uttered in such circumstances. "I cannot believe in this fortune, this chance meeting when we could so easily have missed each other."

"You are right, my dear one," she said, briefly cupping the line of his jaw in a hand glittering with rings. Her eyes gleamed in the light from behind the bar. A momentary dizziness made her beautifully-preserved face swim before his eyes. "I may call you 'my dear one', may I?" He nodded speechlessly, suddenly aware that perhaps he had drunk too much. She went on, still in the same low caressing voice, "I too feel that this meeting – here and now – was meant to be, that we must seize the moment."

Again he nodded. Her eyes seemed to be the only thing he could see.

"So," she said, "I hope you will not think me too … impatient, if I tell you that I have a room upstairs," she stopped, took a sip of her drink. "We could …" Again she stopped but now he had enough presence of mind to catch her hand, press the papery softness of skin and the hardness of rings to his lips, the thought, "There must be millions here …" trailing like a comet across the darkness of his mind.

For those who knew, *Der Goldene Zuchthengst* had a few private rooms, and they were not squalid flea-infested holes for ten-minute assignations but spacious, beautifully-furnished mini-suites, all with bar and private bathroom. Leaving the bar, they went deeper into the building and through the concealed door that led to the upper storeys. "I've ordered champagne," she whispered. "It should already be waiting for us – I hope you don't mind."

He muttered something, aware only of her hand gripping – gripping? no, clasping – his arm and the deep pile of the carpet beneath his feet. Dark red with blue patterns, or was it blue with black patterns? Millions, the comet trailed. So easy, no coffee mornings, no cocktails, no helping her choose dresses or going to gallery openings.

The room was lit by one lamp, its light pooling in a dim glow beside the bed. On a side table beneath the window champagne was chilling on ice, two fluted glasses on the tray. A finger of brighter light came from the bathroom, the door of which was slightly ajar. He stumbled slightly as they entered and she steadied him, guiding him towards the bed. He began to fumble at his tie as she went to the side table, poured the champagne, which was already open but perhaps had only just been opened since it fizzed and sparkled in the glass. Her fingers flickered briefly above the bubbles before she brought the glass over to him, sitting beside him on the bed and raising her own glass in a silent toast. He raised the glass and drank as she smiled and started to ease the jacket from his shoulders, the prelude to the kind of sex that Dev Yankovic had never experienced before.

He was lucid, masterful, a king, and as a king she worshipped him, worshipped his body – the strong beautiful body – as was his right and his due. There was nothing she would not do, nothing she did not urge him to do and for the first time in his life he groaned aloud with the piercing pleasure of it.

Twice (or more?) he was ready to climax and twice (or more?), as though she guessed, she hurt him – how he was not quite sure – so that the moment passed. Then, finally, she beneath him now, her hands gripping his shoulders, her legs, long supple legs, about his waist, she whispered, "Now, my dear one. Give yourself to me. Come to me."

The pleasure swooped back, gripped him in curving talons and, soaring, ripped him from reality. Gladly and with relief, he surrendered himself to it, lucid, masterful, a king.

The orgasm went on and on and on, and then the pain began.

Only afterwards did David Levant – the perfect secretary – emerge from the bathroom. Mrs Pleiades was sitting on the side of the bed, a sheet wound around her, smoking a thin black Russian cigarette.

"And did you enjoy that, David?" she asked, noting with malicious amusement that the fine pale hair lay damp on his forehead.

"Yes, Mrs Pleiades. Two hours …?"

"Yes, as always," she said, "then we may see."

He gave an almost imperceptible bow and went out, closing the door noiselessly behind him. There was a click as the latch caught. Mrs Pleiades placed the cigarette in the ashtray on the bedside table, unwound the sheet, and rose and stretched, briefly admiring her reflection in the gilt-framed mirror above the bed. Smoke from the cigarette, drawn by the heat of the lamp, twirled upwards, casting tenuous convoluted shadows on the ceiling above.

She went to pour herself another glass of champagne, took it back to the bed, settled herself comfortably, sipped, smoked and watched the crumpled vaguely human-shaped thing lying on the floor. Two stages had been completed. Now she could only wait. Either it would happen or it would not. In either event, David Levant would see to the details.

But the 'creation' of Varian, as Mrs Pleiades termed it, was a success. The boy had been shallow enough to be consumed, but strong enough to survive the transformation. That February night in Berlin, in the dim room at *Der Goldene Zuchthengst*, time passed slowly but steadily. She watched the crumpled thing beside the bed, smoked her slim black cigarettes, drank champagne, and idly planned her next journey if this one should prove unsuccessful; there was – after all – still time.

It was a little after four in the morning when she finally saw a change in the slack skin of what had been Dev Yankovic, the merest hint of colour in the fish-belly pallor, the slightest lifting of the collapsed ribcage.

Now she hardly dared to breathe as the change spread and accelerated – from the shrunken trunk to the still-intact head, down the flaccid sacks of arms and legs to the fleshy scraps of fingers and toes. As dawn light filtered through a crack in the heavy curtains, the figure was complete. David Levant let himself soundlessly into the room, a brown suitcase in one hand, which he softly placed on the floor beside him; he remained near the door as she put her fingers to her lips. Both watched now as the naked figure on the floor stirred then breathed.

"It is done, David," she whispered, eyes flaring triumphantly, "You see how perfect he is."

"Yes, Mrs Pleiades," said David Levant, his gaze fixed on the figure. This scene had been played out many times. Twenty? Fifty? More than a hundred? The years since the death of Mrs Pleiades' husband had been dedicated to searching old Europe for The One. David Levant's role had been to dispose of the failures, the remains of those who had not survived. Now, at last, it was over, the suitcase would not be needed. Mrs Pleiades smiled and drank the last of the champagne.

"And now we begin ...," she said softly.

Six months later, in the rented villa near Genzano, everything was now prepared and in place. The temporary problem caused by Achille's treachery had been resolved, with the police conscientiously (no doubt) and uselessly (without any doubt at all) investigating the drug connection; it had been worth the expense of half a kilo of heroin. However, there was one small shadow darkening Mrs Pleiades' contentment. She hardly admitted it, even to herself, and when she did allow the thought to flicker briefly before her she quickly dismissed it in her peremptory way; it was the result of the tireless commitment and prolonged concentration.

The fact was that, every so often – not very often – though was it occurring more frequently? – but even so, very rarely – time passed that she could not account for. It might be minutes or it might be longer when she did not know what she had been doing or had done in the minutes (or longer) that had gone before. She would be in the same place, in the same room, but would suddenly come to herself and see that the hands of the gilt clock showed a later time.

It had happened again the day before, a little before lunch. It was at this time that the trained maid, an Argentinian called Dolorita, came to dress the shining helmet of chestnut hair, so that Mrs Pleiades could once again present a perfect image to the world.

Mrs Pleiades had been sitting before the mirror and contemplating her image with unalloyed approval, caressing one carefully-arranged lacquered curl, her one small concession to her inner passionate self. A bright spear of reflected sunlight lanced from the weathervane of the annex, and she narrowed her eyes against the sudden glare, looking down at the path below, where the foreshortened figure of the gardener was raking the gravel with circular looping strokes. Ignorant peasant! she thought in sudden fury. Straight lines I told you!

Which was when time stopped. An observer would merely have seen a woman sitting before her mirror, one hand raised to her hair, but the moment continued – the woman sat, her hand raised, and the picture did not change. She sat on, a character in a recorded film that has been put on hold, held immobile until the film is allowed to unreel to the next scene.

There was no clock nearby, and though afterwards, when she returned to herself, Mrs Pleiades could not be wholly certain that she had lost time, yet she knew that she had. Temporarily, complete control had not been hers to command.

At the clinic on the northern shoes of the lakes, if anyone had asked her, Lena would have said she felt "steady", a word from her childhood, when being 'steady' or showing 'steadiness' was her father's advice in the face of difficulty; not bad advice, since it was never accompanied by criticism or any kind of lecture. Barbara was there, and had agreed to do her part outside the nursing home, and though no word had yet come about the adversary's movements, Lena sensed the time was near and that her own allies could not be far off.

In the meantime, she had enjoyed their lunch out the day before. Barbara had been right – the air conditioning did indeed appear to be an open window, which made the two of them giggle, and then laugh when Alfredo the driver gallantly remarked that the two of them got younger every year. Lena smiled. Yes, laughter, she thought, that's what we need, more laughter. Still smiling, she folded her hands, sat straight and quiet, and let the stillness take possession of her mind.

Barbara herself was on her way down to dinner from her room on the first floor of the *agriturismo*'s main building. She had made her booking back in April, and when given the choice between a room or a chalet, had specified a room without a moment's hesitation: no chalet for her – too much like camping, and she wanted solid walls and reliable plumbing. She was happy with her choice; there was even a battered couch and a coffee table in the room, and though the room was under the roof, and hot in the day, in the evening its height meant that it caught any cooling breeze coming from the lake.

As she emerged onto the vine-covered patio, she was remembering what Lena had asked her to do. "So, could you just keep a look out, Barbara? A man, young or youngish. He could be any nationality. That's all, I'm afraid. I can't be more specific – but he will come here to Nemi, and to the valley."

The request was a severe test of Barbara's friendship for she was English to the core. To – somehow – engage a complete (young or youngish) male stranger in conversation, so that Lena could meet him seemed an impossible task. "Any nationality" meant that he could be Italian or German, French or Danish, or even from some other, much more obscure country; fortunately, Nemi was not the kind of place that attracted many tourists, otherwise the task would have been impossible.

Barbara knew that as far as just making conversation was concerned, her age was the perfect excuse; the cliché of garrulous old women rabbiting on to anyone and everyone was well-established. The problem was with the second part, the meeting-Lena part. She could perhaps start with George Sutton, the young man who had given her a lift to Nemi. And then? There was the other young man, of course, the American working at the *agriturismo*. So, there were two – fortunately English-speaking – possibilities and 'Engineer George' would be her first attempt. Now, when would she be able buttonhole him?

And there he was! Sitting at one of the far tables, a glass of beer in front of him, reading some sheets of paper and scratching one ear. No time like the present, she thought, but how …?

"*Signora* Allberry! *Buona sera!*" called Massimo, weaving his way between the tables. Hearing Barbara's name George glanced up from his reading, and smiled, detaching his hand from his ear to give a cross between a wave and a salute.

Massimo had seen the gesture: "Ah, you and Engineer George know yourselves. Good!" and Barbara was gently but firmly taken by the elbow and propelled towards George's table. "We have a little problem with many people this evening," explained Massimo. "Engineer George, would you mind if Signora Allberry shares your table?"

"Uh, not at all, not at all," said George, trying to rise but becoming entangled in the tablecloth. "Pleasure, Mrs Allberry."

"Miss Allberry," she corrected briskly, plumping herself down, as Massimo smiled and darted off; he did not think that people should eat alone, and considered he had arranged matters very skilfully.

"Uh, sorry," said George with an apologetic gesture that sent the photocopies to the ground.

Barbara gave her gruff laugh: "Not at all – never came up while you were being a knight errant. Thanks again, by the way."

"Pleasure," wheezed George; he was doubled over collecting his photocopies, and now straightened up, red in the face, clutching the disordered bundle. Barbara glimpsed the heading **Nemi** at the top of one.

"Ah, what's that you're reading?" she asked heartily. "Something interesting?"

10 THURSDAY 6ᵀᴴ AUGUST

The threads which Lena had waited for were drawing together. Jane and Gabriel would be coming to Nemi that morning. After Gabriel's apparent misgivings, Jane was relieved when, during the coffee and sticky pastries, he phoned the clinic, was put through to Professor Caseman and after a brief conversation, announced that the professor would see them at eleven the next morning.

The next day, Barbara, George and Theo would also be going to visit Professor Caseman, Barbara both surprised and triumphant at her success in finding not one but two "young or youngish" men, a seemingly impossible task. George's photocopies about Nemi had provided the opportunity for

Barbara to say at dinner: "Well, if you're interested in all that, my friend at the clinic is an expert." And then, breathing a silent apology to Lena, "Actually, you'd be doing her a favour. Cheers her up to have company – she's old and ill and hasn't got much to do. Why don't you come up with me tomorrow morning?" An expert, George had thought, and it was he who tentatively mentioned Theo, who managed to get the morning off.

In Rome, Jane was also pleasantly surprised, when Gabriel rang the bell of the apartment in the ghetto, and she found that he had hired a car, a nondescript grey Volvo; she had been so preoccupied with the meeting itself, she hadn't even considered how they would get to Nemi. I must have trusted him to sort it out, she thought. How strange ... but then, the nice thing about Gabriel ... She wondered what kind of driver he was. She had never been in a car with him before.

What Jane discovered was that Gabriel drove as he did most things – forcing though not clashing the gears, accelerating then stamping on the brake, muttering about the shortcomings of others, all with a kind of arrogant non-awareness. Jane, a 'good' passenger, found it more restful to look out of the side window than through the windscreen.

They followed the Via Appia out of Rome, crossed the *Gran Raccordo Anulare*, the city's only ring-road, passed the entrance to Ciampino Airport with its black-uniformed *carabinieri*, and took the turn-off to the Alban Hills. It was still fairly early and traffic was light.

The dusty city thoroughfares lined with furniture stores, supermarkets and indeterminate wholesale shops had now given way to narrow roads, woods and the large ornate gates of country villas. The road, Via dei Laghi, rose and widened with a sudden breath-taking panorama of Lago Albano, the other volcanic lake in the Alban Hills; Castel Gandolfo, now the temporary centre of the Catholic world as the Pope took his summer break, lay on the opposite rim, and the lake itself with its small tourist beach sparkled in the sunlight. The lake disappeared again, the road continued upwards through the woods until a sign pointed downhill to a steep side road. Hidden by thick woods, Nemi and its lake could not be seen; the road dipped and swooped via hairpin bends, with beech trees and oaks crowding on either side, until a dark unexpected tunnel and a sharp bend took them past a car park packed with vehicles on the right, then the village's first buildings, and after another bend, they had arrived.

The road had widened into a large intersection, a small delicate statue of the goddess Diana, holding her bow and accompanied by a hunting dog, at its centre. To the right lay the main street of the village, which was built on the lip of the crater, some buildings flush with the side of the sheer precipice. The first shops all seemed to be either restaurants or delicatessens with bunches of salamis hanging outside, and all of them had the sign *Fragole*. Gabriel stopped to ask the way down to the lake, and they found themselves venturing farther and farther into the village down the one main street, the tarmac of the road turning to cobblestones, then through an arch to a terrifyingly narrow road that wound down the hillside. So deeply set into the cone of the crater were the lake and valley below that the southern half was still in shade, the water appearing dark and fathomless.

As they descended (thank God Gabriel was finally driving slowly), Jane gazed down into the valley towards two warehouse-like structures, a patchwork of small allotment fields and what appeared to be a large tract of waste ground, the site of the sanctuary. Finally on the flat, at the bottom of the valley, they turned left for the *Clinica di Sant'Ippolito*, which was on the eastern side of the lake; their way took them past the sunken track to the sanctuary, then upwards again, where imposing wrought iron gates opened onto an immaculate gravel drive, and a discreet sign *Parcheggio* showed the way to the car park. The clinic itself was the shape of an unused staple – a long central part with two shorter wings – and had formal gardens to the front and right.

At the reception desk – Gabriel had been right in referring to it as "more like a hotel" – they were directed to the terraced gardens. Jane was nervous and clutched the strap of her bag more tightly (a sensible leather one; she had thrown the woven one away), suddenly discovering she had been holding her breath and gulping in air. Gabriel was himself, completely at ease and glancing about curiously.

Many of the clinic's guests, all elderly, seemed to be in the landscaped gardens, some in wheelchairs, some slowly strolling, others sitting on benches, and they could not see one woman on her own. Jane was about to ask a passing nurse for Professor Caseman when a hearty voice called, "Over here!" and they saw a group of four people in the shade of a tree by the balustrade: a small thin woman sitting with her legs up on a stool, a sturdy woman with a helmet of grey hair who had risen from the chair beside her and was waving at them, and two men sitting on the grass. Gabriel sighed.

The rest of Italy – with only nine days to go before the mid-August holiday – was on the move. Southerners were travelling to the cool of the north, while northerners sought the beaches of the south. Those with money were flying off to South America, the Caribbean, or London, while those without were simply returning to their home towns and villages. As for non-Italians, planes, trains, coaches and cars were constantly arriving and leaving as eager foreign tourists from Australia, Japan, the United States and everywhere in-between moved from hotel to hotel, from museum to museum and from art gallery to art gallery;

many of them found themselves in hospital with heat exhaustion and cultural overload as temperatures soared into the mid-thirties and stayed there.

And what of Mrs Pleiades in these days of holidays and travel? Nothing. She continued to be her perfectly-groomed lacquered self with her knife-shaped shoes and veiled eyes. While Lena would have described herself as "steady", Mrs Pleiades would not have given the matter a second thought. The time was drawing close, Varian was ready and eager for his part (his practice with the local help had amused him for a very long time). This time nothing had been left to chance, nothing had been overlooked; she was confident and well content.

If she had known of the meeting in Nemi, she would have laughed: two old women, a meddling girl, a callow American, a timid engineer, and a man who cared for nothing. Greater in number, yes, six to three, but when the three were Mrs Pleiades herself, Varian and David Levant – well, the others counted – at best – for one.

Among the 'one', in the gardens of the nursing home, the atmosphere was tense and hostile. After the introductions Jane had been the first to speak since it was the dead man's piece of paper that had started the search for Professor Caseman. She had made another photocopy for the professor, who studied it carefully but said nothing as Jane recounted the night in Trastevere. Gradually, as the story unfolded, supplemented and expanded by Theo and George, the explanations turned to recriminations. George had of course immediately recognised Gabriel, and in the light of what he now knew, felt that Gabriel had behaved badly. Where George was uncomprehending and hurt, Jane, whom Gabriel had not told about the meeting with George, was openly aggressive, while Theo and Barbara, in their different ways, were embarrassed. Gabriel justified himself by saying that he had seen George was worried and needed cheering up; it was not important. And as for Jane, he had not wanted to burden her with yet another odd coincidence. Lena sat and waited. 'Burden', she had thought. A strange formal word.

"And this is so absolutely typical of you, Gabriel!" spat out Jane, trembling with anger. "Not explaining our part, telling this poor man lies just for the sake of it, hoarding your secrets like a … like a … deranged squirrel!"

Unfortunately this made Gabriel smile, which incensed her even more, and she was just drawing breath to continue, when:

"Jane - may I call you Jane?" said Professor Caseman softly.

Jane, with a huge effort, managed to remember why they were there. "Please do, Professor Caseman. I'm so sorry but …"

The professor lifted a delicate blue-veined hand

The Sacred Wood

and smiled so affectionately that Jane felt herself relax and become calm.

"My dear," said the professor gently, "you have been so courageous and so great-hearted in what you have done, that I can only thank you." She paused. "The message you have brought me – it was a week ago, you said?" Jane nodded. "– means that our adversary is here and ready to act." She paused again. "Each of you has been chosen and each of you has experienced some part of the whole." She paused again to look round at them. What vivid eyes she has, thought Jane. "I will tell you what I know. Then, you must decide if you wish to continue." Her gaze rested thoughtfully on each of the three men in turn.

"Forgive me if I repeat some of the things you already know," she went on, settling her legs more comfortably, a shadow of pain passing across her lined face, "but it would take too long for you to tell me what you have already discovered for yourselves."

There were murmurs of agreement. Theo's face was rapt, George rubbed his right ear, Jane, who had been standing, now sat down on the grass and looked trustingly at the professor; Gabriel had been lounging with one shoulder against the tree but now straightened slightly and nodded.

"Diana is popularly associated with hunting and chastity," explained the professor, "but it is clear from the votive offerings found at the sanctuary that her role went back to a much more ancient time – an earth mother who granted offspring to men and women. Were not the very cycles of the moon – the waxing and waning – mysteriously reflected in each woman's body? Not chastity then, but procreation."

"Two lesser deities were also worshipped here – Egeria, who granted mothers easy delivery when they were giving birth – again the emphasis on procreation and renewal – and the last, a man, Virbius."

"Would that be where the Via Virbia came from?" asked George; now he was here he was listening carefully.

"Yes, Mr Sutton, the Via Virbia was indeed named after Virbius and, as you know, led to the Sanctuary; the name Virbius means "twice a man" – he was re-born, you see."

"I've never heard of him," said Jane.

Professor Caseman smiled. "Comparatively few have. He was killed as a man, and brought back to life through the intervention of the goddess Diana. She hid him here to protect him from further attempts, and it was here, in Nemi, that he was worshipped as a forest god in his second life."

"At the sanctuary?" asked Theo. He was thinking of the torchlight procession and the hymn to the goddess which had been filled with love and tenderness.

"Not within the sanctuary," corrected the professor. "That was sacred only to Diana. His province was outside the sanctuary, here above us

The Sacred Wood

in the woods."

Instinctively they all looked up. Above the site of the sanctuary and covering the slopes trees and vegetation rose to the top of the crater. It was a relatively small area but a wilderness for all its small size.

"Yes, there," said the professor softly, looking up as well. For a moment there was silence. The professor picked up the book that had been lying beside her. "I would just like to read you this." She put on the half-moon spectacles that hung from a chain around her neck and opened the book. "This is from *The Golden Bough* by James Frazier. 'On the northern shore of the lake, right under the precipitous cliffs on which the modern village of Nemi is perched, stood the sacred grove and sanctuary of Diana Nemorensis, or Diana of the Wood. ... In this sacred grove there grew a certain tree round which at any time of day, and probably far into the night, a grim figure could be seen to prowl. In his hand he carried a drawn sword, and he kept peering warily about him as if at every instant he expected to be set upon by an enemy. He was a priest and a murderer; and the man for whom he looked was sooner or later to murder him and hold the priesthood in his stead. Such was the rule of the sanctuary. A candidate for the priesthood could only succeed to office by slaying the priest, and having slain him, he retained office till he was himself slain by a stronger or craftier.'"

"May I see that?" asked Gabriel. She passed him

the book and he looked at the passage she had read, and then continued studying it. Jane half-opened her mouth to remonstrate, then closed it again.

"That is Frazier's description of the King of the Sacred Wood, the representative of the re-born Virbius, who was the first King, the first Rex Nemorensis."

"I read about him at the museum," commented Theo. "He was a runaway slave."

"Yes."

"But a man was killed ... now ... in the present," said Jane, "the messenger, you said." She opened her bag, brought out her own photocopy of the piece of paper. "'The artefact is ready. Where is the original?' then a date – the 13th August. What does it mean?"

"The 13th August was the annual festival to Diana, when a torchlight procession – the procession you apparently witnessed, Mr Manos – took the Via Virbia to the sanctuary. This is the important date, and we must be ready to act on that date."

"And the reference to the artefact and the original?" asked Theo.

"First, you must understand why Virbius was so important. Worshipped as a god of the forest, his successors, each of whom had challenged and killed the previous Rex Nemorensis, took and gave power to the natural world, thus maintaining its order and balance. The proximity of his kingdom to the sanctuary was in itself important. With his presence – outside the sanctuary but ever-present – no one could forget that renewal and growth is born of violence, sacrifice and blood."

The words seemed to hang in the warm air. The quiet scene about them, the sunlit lawns, colourful banks of flowers, even the nursing home behind them, suddenly appeared fragile and unreal. It was the thick woods above that held the power and mystery.

"That continuous renewal remained intact for thousands of years," went on the professor slowly, "until it was broken by the Emperor Caligula."

"The ships," said Theo wonderingly, remembering the ripple of golden roof tiles, the sheen of marbled walls and the swaying canopies of slender trees.

"Yes. The ships – one a floating palace, the other bearing a temple. They were moored there." Sitting more upright – again there was the shadow of pain – she pointed towards the museum. They all looked across to the slopes of the western shore, below the outline of the sunlit roofs of Genzano. "It was there Caligula had a summer residence, and perhaps he gazed across at the sanctuary and the woods. Perhaps the idea of another 'king' in the valley was distasteful to him, or perhaps it came about as a joke at a banquet. Whatever the reason, he declared that the Rex Nemorensis of the time had been there too long, so he *sent* a slave to challenge him. This of course broke the continuity because it destroyed the element of choice. It was laid down, you see - the slave himself had to take to decision to run away, the slave himself had to decide to come here and challenge the king. No outside influence should have entered into it."

Gabriel had apparently been absorbed in the book, but now commented, "But if I'm not mistaken, professor, the ritual continued after Caligula."

"You are correct, Mr Todd," the professor agreed with scholarly approval, "until the time of the Antonines. However, the damage had been done – the break meant that the following kings were not the true kings. The ritual continued but its meaning and power were lost."

"But why should it come alive now?" asked George. So much for cheering up an old, sick woman, he thought, glancing at Barbara, who caught the look and, rightly interpreting it, had the grace to look slightly shame-faced. He turned his attention back to the professor.

"Because we are approaching the next great upheaval in human history," she explained quietly, loosely clasping her hands in her lap. "There are still a few years left before it occurs, but before then the balance must be restored, ancient and modern forces must be reconciled."

Jane found she had been holding her breath again. She breathed deeply, almost missed the professor's next words.

"The artefact is the false reincarnation of Virbius

who will endeavour to take possession of the forces in the sacred grove. The original is the true heir to Virbius, who must re-establish the line and restore the balance." Again her gaze rested on Theo, then George, then Gabriel. "One of you three is that man." She finished softly.

Jane was incredulous, found her mouth open and closed it with an effort. Instinctively she looked at Gabriel, who appeared to have gone back to reading the professor's book. When she then looked at the other two, she saw her own amazement mirrored in both faces, but while George had gone bright red and was rubbing his ear, Theo's face held excitement and expectation. One of the three. But what would the one ultimately have to *do*, she wondered.

The meeting ended prosaically, with Barbara passing round a notepad and pen so that they could all write down their cell phone numbers, while Lena was weighing the behaviour of each person: Jane took the pad and wrote quickly but carefully, Theo had taken out his wallet to copy his temporary Italian number and he too wrote unhesitatingly, while George Sutton's pen wavered and he rubbed his ear before adding his own. Gabriel was the last, taking the pad with neither eagerness nor reluctance, his gaze scanning the list of names before he waved aside the proffered pen, took out his own and completed the list.

It was Jane who said, "Oh, we'd better take each other's as well. Could I have the list back?" and, with some confusion, the list made the rounds, numbers being keyed directly into phones, and goodbyes said.

Barbara was staying on to have lunch with Lena at the clinic, while Theo had to go back to the *agriturismo*; he was needed to help in the kitchen – a private party of twenty was coming for a celebration lunch after a christening.

"Why don't we give you a lift, Theo?" suggested Gabriel, as the four of them walked to the car park.

"Uh ... I can take you back," offered George; he had given Theo a lift in the first place, and was thinking he would like to get away from them all and think.

"Thanks," said Theo, and then to Jane and Gabriel. "I'll go with George – it'll save you a journey."

"I have a better idea, George," said Gabriel easily. Jane glanced at him; she knew that tone. "Why don't we follow you? You drop Theo off, and then I'll take you and Jane to lunch in the village."

"Actually, I think I'll ... uh ... just grab a sandwich or something at the *agriturismo*," said George feebly;

"Come on, George," said Gabriel with his most winning smile. "Don't tell me you don't want to talk over what the professor had to tell us."

"Yes, please come," said Jane, who thought George a very nice man.

Obstinacy was not one of George's faults, and it would have been discourteous to refuse. The two cars quickly arrived at the *agriturismo*, where Theo got out and disappeared into the kitchen; he was disappointed that he would be missing the chance to discuss the morning, but George would tell him later, he thought philosophically.

Jane climbed into the back of the Volvo so that George would have more leg-room in the front, and they drove up the terrifyingly narrow road again, through the arch and along the main street. "We'll park outside the village," commented Gabriel. He was looking from side to side as he drove. "Ah, that place there has air-conditioning," he went on, jerking his head towards a restaurant on the right, and then continuing along towards the car park outside the village.

Once there Gabriel told Jane and George to get out, and then crammed the Volvo into an impossibly small space under an overhanging brick wall, before somehow snaking his own way out. Jane watched, caught between annoyance and relief, the former caused by Gabriel's casual assumption that *his* organisation was the most effective, the latter because it really seemed it was, with no fussing or indecision.

Once back in the main street they made for the restaurant Gabriel had indicated, which not only had the promised air-conditioning, but also a fine view of the lake. The interior was dark-panelled, cool and dim, with signed photographs of Italian actors and other celebrities. Jane sank thankfully into a chair, and though she picked up her menu she did not open it for a moment, enjoying the feel of the cool leather against her hot palms.

"What do you think?" she asked Gabriel, who was pondering his own menu. She turned to George who had tentatively picked up his and was looking at the first page as if he had never seen a menu before. "George, what do *you* think?"

"I think we should decide what we're having," said Gabriel absently, still studying. "George? See anything you fancy?"

"Uh … perhaps a plate of pasta?" said George.

"No, come on. What about some antipasti to start off with? Then there's pasta with truffles – that looks OK – we're in the hills after all. And there's lamb as well, or a steak. Jane?"

Resistance was useless. Jane and George found themselves being relentlessly carried along, and a great deal of food was ordered.

"So?" said Jane expectantly when the waiter had brought bottles of wine and water.

George waited for Gabriel to speak but Gabriel leaned back and said, "Well, George?"

"… uh … it's all a bit … uh … strange," offered George. Gabriel laughed and Jane shot him a reproving look. George gave a sheepish smile and rubbed his ear. "But … uh … I was wondering … uh … where Professor Caseman got all this."

"You're right!" said Jane in a tone of discovery, "She never explained. How did she know about it all?"

"Probably some descendent of the goddess

Diana," drawled Gabriel. "Ah, food ..."

"And you're sure it's one of them?" Barbara asked when they were alone again. Lena had arranged a light lunch for them both in her room, and they were sitting at the table by the window.

"Yes."

"Any idea which one?" said Barbara abruptly.

"Yes. But I must not interfere past a certain point. The prophecy handed down is quite clear."

"Prophecy!" grumbled Barbara.

Lena smiled at her affectionately: "Barbara – you've listened to me all these years, you approached a young man and got him to come here – with *another* young man – and now you're rejecting the idea of a prophecy!" She returned to more serious matters:

"I've asked Mr Sutton and Mr Manos to come back tomorrow since they're close by. Mr Todd has said he will phone me." They exchanged a look.

"But then – when you've arranged it," Barbara went on, "your part is over," but her voice held a half-question. Her friend sipped at the half-glass of wine she allowed herself at lunch and smiled.

"Now, you're surely not thinking of racketing around in the woods yourself, Lena!" said Barbara shocked.

"I must." replied Lena firmly. "Without me they will never find the tree. It has been so long since I've been there, any directions I give would be useless."

"You might not recognise it." Barbara pointed out bluntly.

"I will feel it." Lena spoke with great conviction, then, with another impish smile." Anyway, I'll have three strong young men to carry me."

And now the day was finally over, and Lena was tired, her legs paining her quite badly. She looked longingly at the packet of pain-killers on the bedside table but decided to wait. She wanted to think and these particular tablets always made her a little drowsy. I must ask the doctor to change them, she thought. They are the best yet but they do cloud one's mind so.

She considered the day and the young people she had met. On the one hand she was glad that they had all been present, it saved repetition, on the other it meant that she had not been able to concentrate on individual personalities. She smiled as she thought of Barbara's summary: George was a "good chap", one of Barbara's highest accolades, Theo she labelled as "very young", Jane was "a nice girl", and Gabriel was "a difficult type". Lena understood what lay behind these sparse words and thought these initial descriptions very apt.

All in all, Lena was satisfied that the meeting had worked out as it had. In the recriminations following the explanations and sorting-out of events, George's meeting with the mad woman (recounted in the baldest and briefest of terms) had been lost in the confusion. But Lena had taken note, had her own thoughts about it and wanted to talk to him again.

She sighed. Perhaps she *would* take one of the pain-killers now, get a good night's rest. She sent them down with a sip of water, settled against the pillows, perched her spectacles on her nose and took up *The Golden Bough* again. Frazier had been right about so many things – it was a pity he had become distracted trying to find parallels in other countries. She re-read the passage about the King of the Sacred Wood that she had read aloud earlier, and then looked further down the page:

"To gentle and pious pilgrims at the shrine the sight of him might well seem to darken the fair landscape, as when a cloud suddenly blots the sun on a bright day. The dreamy blue of Italian skies, the dappled shade of summer woods, and the sparkle of waves in the sun, can have accorded but ill…" "Accorded but ill," she repeated to herself, relishing the nineteenth-century sonority of the phrase, "with that stern and sinister figure. Rather we picture to ourselves the scene as it may have been witnessed by a belated wayfarer on one of those wild autumn nights when the dead leaves are falling thick, and the winds seem to sing the dirge of the dying year." Yes, she thought. People forget that about Italy – the sun does not always shine. She went on reading: "It is a sombre picture, set to melancholy music – the background of forest showing black and jagged against a lowering and stormy sky, the sighing of the wind in the branches, the rustle of the withered leaves under foot, the lapping of cold water on the shore, and in the foreground, pacing to and fro, now in twilight and now in gloom, a dark figure with a glitter of steel at the shoulder whenever the pale moon, riding clear of the cloud-rack, peers down at him through the matted boughs."

Wonderfully over-written, she thought, smiling affectionately down at the page, but it does give one a very good idea. She put the book aside, switched out the lamp.

She was sleeping peacefully when something woke her, and as always she was immediately alert, with no intermediate stage of drowsy half-awareness. She had no idea how long she had been asleep. Perhaps not that long since the tablets were still working and the pain was a far-off ache, sealed away in a chemical cocoon. She could hear the few muffled sounds to be heard in any large building holding a large number of people, but there was something missing. She listened – the cicadas, which even at night rattled and droned, were silent.

Throwing back the light cover, she got out of bed, half-rolling then supporting herself on her elbow to get to her feet. It was still warm so she did not bother with her dressing-gown, and there was enough light for her to make her way to the window.

Her room looked out at a corner of the gardens to the left, and the sanctuary and village to the right. She stood, hidden behind the partially closed shutters, and looked down. Luckily there was nothing wrong with her distance sight.

For a few moments, as her eyes adjusted to the play of light and shadows, she saw nothing, then, a slight hissing and muttering from under a tree caught her attention and she could just make out a figure. It appeared to be swaying from side to side, hissing and muttering as it swayed. Lena's eyes narrowed.

"So, you *are* here," she whispered. She made her way back to bed, wondering whether she should have told the young people about the other forces gathering at the sanctuary. It was after all dangerous. Poor Achille, so faithful in all these years, had paid the price but by chance had found in Jane a way to deliver the vital message. Should she have warned the young people? No, she decided, it was better so – she had not lied, merely omitted a part of the whole.

11 FRIDAY 7TH AUGUST

When George arrived at the nursing home at 11 o'clock, exactly on time, he was skilfully fielded by one of the staff at the reception desk, and shown to the same chair where the professor had sat the day before, though now the stool was absent. The professor would be coming soon, the girl informed him. She sent her apologies.

"Uh …," started George but the girl was already going. "Coming *soon*," she repeated loudly, as if volume would make him understand. George stood rather helplessly, arms dangling, and then sat down in the chair. He had been going to ask for another one: sitting on the grass had been all very well with so many of them but … Oh, well, I can sit on the grass again, he thought.

He felt miserable and embarrassed. Having been carried forward by events, with the whole group seemingly quite prepared to go ahead with the (mad plan) strange idea, George had bitterly regretted having said he would come that day, and had seriously considered telephoning to make some excuse. He had even thought of the little speech he would make: Sorry, but not my thing, you know. All the best, anyway, with ... And then he hadn't been able to find the words to describe what he actually thought they were doing, and his innate courtesy, coupled with the residual idea of the professor that Barbara had planted (old ... sick ... frail ... glad of the company) had persuaded him that the least he could do was keep the appointment and gently explain why it all had nothing to do with him.

It was just then, as he was mentally setting his jaw, that the professor arrived – in a wheelchair pushed by the same girl as before. A wheelchair. George rose clumsily to his feet to greet her, now hopelessly entrapped and forced to listen to whatever she would say.

Lena smiled at "the nice chap" sympathetically; she knew exactly what he was thinking, and did not intend to keep him in suspense any longer than necessary.

"Mr Sutton," she began, after they had settled themselves. "I would like to reassure you that you will not be called upon to fight this battle. You are not the one."

George visibly relaxed. Apart from the general (looniness) strangeness of the whole thing, his mind had completely baulked at the idea that he, George Sutton, might be a key figure in some mythical re-enactment of an ancient rite. There had been no engineers of heroic proportions, with the possible exception of Isambard Kingdom Brunel, one of George's personal heroes, and George did not want to be the first. He rubbed his right ear and let out a long huffing sigh of relief, rather like a tired old horse being led into his horsebox at the bottom of a steep ascent; he would not have to plod up the hill after all. Professor Caseman nodded, leant forward and patted one of his hands, before continuing. "I know this must be difficult for you to believe," she went on gently, "but I would remind you that you yourself – from the little you said yesterday – seem to have had a ... visitation, if I may call it that. Can you tell me about that day? From the beginning?"

George rubbed his ear again and then, slowly and haltingly at first, gradually with greater speed and fluency, recounted the visit to the sanctuary with the museum man, the offerings left by the neo-pagans, the shriek of the bird and the leaving of the guidebook. He became tentative again when he told her of his decision to walk back to find the book that afternoon, and the meeting in the shadows of the sunken track.

"Do you remember her exact words?" asked the professor. George was looking at his hands, and

The Sacred Wood

did not see her sudden sharp look.

"Well, ... uh ... the thing is, professor," he said, now embarrassed again, but feeling he must come clean, "it wasn't ... uh ... words. I mean, she did speak but it was foreign." He looked even more embarrassed, and rubbed his ear. "I somehow ... uh ... understood the meaning." He looked away, did not see the slight nod the professor gave. "What did you understand?" she asked gently. He looked back at her.

"It was something like 'Where is he? I know he's here. It's useless to hide him'. I thought she was ... insane, some mad woman from the area. Then Gabriel told me ... well, I believed him until Theo showed me the rosemary and told me about the museum. All a bit much really," he finished lamely.

"Yes." Lena looked at the serious young man, who had found himself dragged from his natural element but was heroically continuing to do what he believed was right. *He's rather out of his time,* she thought, *he reminds me of those young idealistic empire-builders who are so unfashionable nowadays.*

"Who ... uh ... is she – that woman, I mean?" George asked.

The professor looked towards the lake: "A malign spirit, Mr Sutton, one that cannot rest. However, I do not think it has the power to do any actual harm. It can disturb and upset but it has no substance."

One of the nursing-home staff came up to see if

they would like a mid-morning coffee or cold drink. Lena asked for a fruit juice; George had a cappuccino. While they were waiting, and then sipping at their drinks, they chatted generally for a while, though – unlike with Gabriel – George spent little time describing his road-and-aqueduct tour; it had faded into the shadows of another life and another time.

Lena then returned to the present: "As I said," she continued, "I know you are not the one." George nodded vigorously. "And so, in effect, it has nothing to do with you." (George's very thought). "I understand that, sympathise with you, but what I *would* like to ask you, Mr Sutton," the professor paused, and George looked at her. With relief she saw there was no wariness on his face, only genuine curiosity and a desire to help. "... is whether you would be prepared to ... lend your assistance. No, don't answer for a moment." She marshalled her thoughts, not wanting to manipulate or coerce him in any way; the choice must be *free*.

"In a nutshell," she went on quietly and as though speaking her thoughts aloud, "on the evening of 13th August, the date of the annual festival to the goddess Diana," her gaze went to the sanctuary and woods, "the battle between the false Virbius and the true heir must take place. Whichever wins that battle will take possession of the forces in the sacred wood."

George's hand crept towards his ear, where the

mosquito bite had become quite inflamed in the last few days.

"What I did not say was that the battle cannot commence until one of the two has found a particular tree and broken off what Frazier called 'the golden bough'. The possession of the bough signals the right of the combatant to do battle for the title of King – conferring a moral advantage to the man who holds it. In a way, the real battle is the one to take possession of the bough. Is that clear, Mr Sutton?"

"… uh … yes," agreed George, thinking, … and now there's a branch in it.

"I am one of the people who know the location of the tree," said the professor. "So, I will have to go to the grove myself."

At this George stared at the frail figure in the wheelchair, the small elderly woman whose body was thin almost to the point of emaciation and whose bones were visibly deformed and twisted by her disease.

"Yes," she nodded, starting to smile. "I have to be present to locate the tree, but, as you see, I am somewhat … lame." The vivid green eyes, the glance of which had so impressed Jane, were alight with amusement. "I need strong muscles to carry me, Mr Sutton, and since mine are not, I would ask you to lend me yours." She laughed and the young George glimpsed the young Lena, strong and unafraid and infinitely amused by life and its vagaries.

He smiled as well, thinking, "What a game old girl!" And then George did attain heroic proportions: "It would be an honour and a pleasure," he said gravely.

When George had gone, Lena again turned her gaze to the lake below. Only six days were left, and she still had to talk to Theo and Gabriel. She thought about each of the young people in turn, cradling each image in her mind, and considering the little she knew of them. Jane was pure gold – her reaction to poor Achille and his message, and her single-mindedness in searching for Lena had amply demonstrated that. As Barbara had said, a nice girl, and the fact that she had added, "Reminded me of you, Lena, when you were young" awoke reassuring echoes.

George, the "good chap". Yes, practical, serious, but with a respect for the past and a glowing spark of hidden imagination, as witness his road-and-aqueduct tour, and his speed in suggesting that Theo too should come to meet her. In him Lena had recognised that rock-solid character that had reminded her of young Victorian idealists who believed in duty and commitment.

Theo. Barbara's label was "very young", but that very youth included an open mind, adaptability and also physical strength. She would have a better idea after she had talked with him. And then there was Gabriel Todd, a "difficult type". He had said little at the meeting (though he had – most politely – commented that the ritual had continued after

The Sacred Wood

Caligula), but he had protected Jane, talked to Robert Mitchel at Oxhall Monographs, and come down to Nemi. People are what they do, she reminded herself. Again, she would have a better idea when she had talked to him alone.

Her thin lined face took on a distant, detached quality as she reflected. The participants – with their differing qualities and skills – were now gathered together, of that she was sure. Barbara had been her link with the outside world – had persuaded George to come ("Said you were an expert on Nemi, and made out you were a poor old girl."), and George had suggested Theo. Of the four, two, Jane and George, had been … tested, there were two left. Theo that afternoon, and then … Gabriel Todd. Would he telephone, she wondered. Would he be 'difficult'?

She looked back at the nursing home. There was no sign of George Sutton, but the girl who had brought her out was coming back to take her inside. "No, thank you, my dear," said the professor, as the girl made to release the brake. "I think I can manage if you could just give me your hand." Lena rose from the wheelchair, steadied herself on the girl's arm, and then smiled and made her own way towards the communal dining-room.

George, driving slowly back along the road to the *agriturismo*, shifting uncomfortably in his seat since he had found that the car – though originally parked in shade – was now in full sun yet *again*, reflected that he had given his word, and in return had been given his instructions: carry the professor to wherever she wanted to go. That was that then; probably all a hare's nest anyway, but it would only be a few hours, he'd do his bit, humour the old girl. Though he was unaware of it he was secretly relieved at having received some explanation for the mad woman, however bizarre that explanation may be, and, with that load off his mind, was starting to feel he could 'get on with things'. He was whistling a little as he drew up in the dusty car park, and then abruptly stopped, lips still comically pursed. A small excited group of people were clustered around someone and apparently supporting him to the *agriturismo*'s station wagon. Stopping the car George strode over to see if he could give a hand, and saw that the person being supported – by his father and Theo – was Massimo, white beneath his tan and clasping his arm. Once he was gently helped into the front seat, his father climbed hurriedly into the driver's seat and took off, puffs of dust spurting up as he accelerated towards the main road. Massimo's mother, who rarely left the kitchen, looked after them, her face creased with worry, and then hurried back to the safety of her pots and pans.

"What happened?" asked George, bringing his gaze back from the road and looking at Theo, who was running his hands through his hair.

"He took a fall from his horse. But I think he'll be OK – the arm didn't seem to be broken."

"I didn't even know he had a horse,"

commented George, and then felt a little foolish; of course he knew that Massimo had a horse – they had met that day at the bottom of the leafy tunnel.

"A fantastic chestnut mare," explained Theo, "and usually as sweet and docile as they come, but he said something startled her, and the next thing he knew he was flat on his back, and the mare had taken off. I'm just going to check to make sure she's back. Want to come?"

"Yes ... uh ... do you know about horses, then?" asked George, following Theo towards the olive grove at the back of the *agriturismo*; they could already see the mare standing quietly in a patch of shade, idly swishing her tail to keep the flies away.

"I worked on a ranch once," replied Theo, "and you kind of get to know them when you're around them every day."

By this time they had reached the mare. Theo took the reins with one hand, and then smoothed the glossy neck with the other, continuing downwards so that he could check each of her front legs in turn, pausing at the joints to press them gently. She did not seem to be hurt in any way, and stood quietly, even nudged his head a little as though to reassure him. "*Principessa*," he murmured, "what's going on with you, uh?"

The mare gave a small whinny and tossed her head.

"Don't know? Come on, let's get you back to your stall. She's fine," he said to George. "I'll see to her, and then get you a cold beer before lunch. It'll be a bit late after Massimo's fall anyway." They started back, Theo leading the mare, George beside him, gazing around rather helplessly as he searched for the words for what he wanted to say. "Right ... uh ... Theo?"

"Yeah?"

George rubbed his ear, gazed up at the slopes: "Uh ... I'm coming along on the 13th. Promised the professor I'd ... uh ... help out."

"Good for you, George!" exclaimed Theo in delight, grinning at him. "I kind of took it for granted that you would anyway but ..."

George gave an apologetic smile: "Not my thing, you know, but when it's an elderly person and all that. Probably all ... nothing."

"Well, we'll see," said Theo, stroking the mare's neck. "The professor said it was one of us, and so whether you believe it or not, George, it might be you."

"Absolutely not," blurted out George vehemently. "The professor told me I'm ... uh ... not the one," He felt incredibly foolish saying this but ploughed on, "That ... uh ... means that it's you or that chap Gabriel."

Theo had stopped walking and was looking at George interrogatively. George had continued a few steps before he realised Theo was no longer at his side, and turned back. When he saw Theo's expression, he shrugged rather helplessly as an answer. Theo looked thoughtful, started leading the mare again. "Oh, right. Thanks for telling me,

George." He said no more, but his eyes were alight with excitement and he smoothed the mare's neck again. George was wondering if he should have mentioned it. The professor hadn't said *not* to tell Theo.

The day and the world in general continued on its drowsy summer course. Throughout the hills and ridges of the extinct volcano human beings went about their business – lunches were prepared, fans set on sideboards were switched on, families sat round tables, complained of the stifling heat, and irritably waved away flies. Televisions blared out news and sport, plates were washed, pots were scoured, until an after-lunch quiet descended. The lake shimmered in the heat, truly seeming the "Diana's Mirror" of ancient texts, the fields in the valley were deserted, the museum closed and the sanctuary baking in the afternoon heat.

Lunch was over too in the rented villa in Genzano. David Levant usually ate with Mrs Pleiades and Varian, who still showed a tendency to eat with his fingers and gulp at his milk, while bragging of his prowess and readiness to fight. He also enjoyed recounting how he had dealt with the local help, and had told the story numerous times, every time with the same words. "And then I woke him up by throwing water over him," he said gleefully. "So he could see me burning his cock off! And he screamed like a *girl*!" he said disdainfully, then, with sudden enthusiasm, "let's take one of those acetylene things to the fight! I'd be good! I know just the range, and everything."

Mrs Pleiades laughed fondly; David Levant smiled his burnt-out death's-head smile.

"It would burn the *trees*, dear one, and you *know* the weapons are going to be traditional." Varian looked sulky and began prodding at the table with his table knife. Mrs Pleiades patted his hand. "You will have your nice long fighting knife – and just think of the stabbing and slashing you will be able to do."

Varian cheered up, and then wrinkled his forehead: "No, not stabbing," he declared judiciously, a youthful Solomon weighing the alternatives. "Too quick, I'll slash, but slowly. Slash. Slash" he demonstrated with his table knife on the fruit in the centre of the table, but the knife was too blunt to have any effect on the slices of melon. He wrinkled his forehead again. "Well, maybe *one* stab to finish him off," and he plunged the knife into the melon, and beamed at them triumphantly.

"He will do well, Mrs Pleiades," said David Levant. "He has the will."

"Dear ones," breathed Mrs Pleiades, smiling fondly at both her familiars.

In the hot tobacco-smelling room in the servant's quarters, Byron Escobar and Dolorita Morales, the people behind Mrs Pleiades' 'gardener' and 'trained maid' lay together in his narrow bed, sharing a cigarette. She lay quietly while he smoothed her scarred belly with absorbed tenderness. She glanced down, drawing the smoke in deeply: "I almost died," she remarked. "Twenty, thirty hours in labour – what do I know? I only knew that I had to suffer for him. Whatever it took, I had to give him life." She passed the cigarette to her companion, who took it gently, lifted it to his lips, inhaled, and then again rested his hand on the scar, as if to recognise its specialness.

"And he was the first and the last," she went on. "After that, my body could bear no others – but that was not important. I had ... resisted." Suddenly she laughed: "My man – I could hear him outside – shouting, 'Don't let her die! Don't let her die', but I knew I would not."

"It was what it was," said Byron Escobar, looking down at the scar, a deep healed cleft that furrowed her belly.

"Yes," she agreed simply, taking back the cigarette, inhaling, and now resting her own hand on his. "So you see, when he disappeared, when there was no word from him – and he had always remembered, always – wherever he was – telephoned me on his birthday ... Well, of course I searched, went to Marseilles, the last place he was seen, searched and finally found a trace."

"A trace," he repeated, eyes still on the deep furrow of the scar.

"I went to bars, many bars, and then there was one in the alleyways near the port. I paid – I paid in every bar, even for nothing, but now I learnt that he had been there, drinking with a woman, a young-seeming woman who was not young. And then ... nothing."

Byron Escobar took the cigarette, inhaled, and then dropped it into the tin on the floor beside the bed. When he lay back, he smoothed her hair, repeated, "Nothing?"

"I bought the security tapes," and she smiled, rubbed her head against his hand. "All of them," she went on. "The bar, the stairs, the exits. And I found the link, found the faces."

"The Mask, the Pallid One," he supplied.

"Yes. She, at the bar, flattering him, offering herself, and then they left, together, first she and my son, then him, with a suitcase. A suitcase."

"A suitcase?"

"The police found nothing; no one would talk, but my son entered, and never left. What am I to think?"

They fell silent. A fly buzzed in one corner, but when Byron Escobar glanced over, it stopped and fell noiselessly to the floor; there were no sounds now. He cradled Dolorita's head, she clasped his arm, and so they remained as the day continued its lazy crawl through the hot still hours.

A stirring and an awakening – the first sounds of humanity leaving the refuge each had sought – began about four-thirty when Theo came to the nursing home. Lena was in her chair, feet on a stool, in her usual place under the tree, another canvas chair already ready for Theo; she saw him as a lesser challenge than George, and when she saw him emerge from the clinic and hurry eagerly towards her, she knew she had another ally.

She began, as she had with George, by asking him to recount his experience in detail. He repeated how he had been looking down at the Via Virbia when a cloud passed across the sun and he had had the vision of the torchlit procession. This time he went into more detail – the moon reflected in the centre of the lake, the looming bulk of Caligula's ships with their golden roofs, sumptuous marbles and delicate trees, the hunting dogs with sprays of ivy entwined in their massive collars.

"It was so *real*," he said, face alight with wonder. "I even smelt the burning tar of the torches, and the sweat of the people around me. It was amazing, professor, simply amazing!"

She smiled, charmed by his youth and enthusiasm. "Yes, indeed, Mr Manos."

"Theo, please, professor."

She smiled again, briefly touched his arm, a gentle butterfly touch. "Theo. And the sanctuary itself, Theo? Were you aware of a presence there, like Mr Sutton?"

"No," he said after a moment's thought; there had been that buzzing of the fly but that wouldn't count. "Nothing like George described. Perhaps because the Italian family were there."

"The Italian family?" she queried; he hadn't mentioned the family before.

"A couple with two kids – teenagers. The father was a Mussolini fan."

"Yes, many middle-class Italians are," said Lena abstractedly.

"We walked round together and left together as well. They gave me a lift to the museum, but we split up once we were inside."

"Were they still there when you came to yourself and found yourself down on the Via Virbia?"

"Yes. The teenage boy was upset – he said some old woman had stroked his face but there was no sign of her." He stopped, suddenly making the link. "That ... wouldn't be the woman that George met, would it?"

Lena considered, and then, "Very probably, yes." She repeated what she had said to George. "It is a malign spirit, one that cannot rest." She paused, and then, in explanation, "Every good arouses its twin evil, every light is menaced by its attendant darkness."

"And this old woman is the opposite of ... the goddess?"

"Yes. If you could just give me a moment to reflect, Theo." She rested her back against the cushions, settled her legs and gazed over towards the museum, where the long roofs of the warehouse-like structures were just visible.

George had seen the malign spirit, which had also appeared to the teenage boy, but Theo – through his proximity to the Via Virbia – had tapped into the past. From the details he had recounted – the barefoot women in the procession, the ivy twined in the hunting dogs' collars, the presence of the rosemary, thyme and mint – Lena knew that Theo had indeed witnessed part of the yearly ceremony. She chose her words carefully.

"Theo, you have seen … were privileged to see … what no one has witnessed for thousands of years. You were chosen." Her tone was grave, formal, that of an ancient queen to a young warrior who has sworn fealty to her. She paused before continuing. "The … encounter that is to happen, that *must* happen, will have its beginning with the possession of the golden bough. I will explain."

She repeated the explanation she had given George but where George had thought '… and now there's a branch in it', Theo nodded, accepting the power of the symbolic object.

"There is a prophecy," she went on. "'The true king will remember his kingdom'. I would ask you to be ready on the 13th, Theo. Do you understand?"

"Yes," said Theo fervently. "You can count on me, professor."

12 SATURDAY 8TH AUGUST

Already awake when dawn was only just breaking, Jane decided to take advantage of the cool of the early morning to water Silvia's plants. She had completely forgotten about them. After lunch with George in the village of Nemi, they had driven back to Rome, and Jane's intention to question Gabriel about what he thought was effectively nipped in the bud when she climbed into the car and promptly fell asleep. And I know that's what happens when I drink too much at lunchtime, she thought dismally.

By the time she woke up, hot, thirsty and uncomfortable, they were turning into a road near Silvia's flat, and Gabriel dropped her off, saying he had things to do, would be in touch. Jane, many glasses of water and a cool shower later, fell asleep.

Now, on Saturday (and it just doesn't feel like the weekend when you're on holiday, she mused) she was watering the plants. A couple of the poor things were brown and withered with only the merest trace of green visible. Guiltily, she spent time loosening the hard earth and carefully trickling in water (her own few plants would be long dead, she thought sadly, still ...). That done, she showered, dressed, lay on the couch to read and fell asleep again, waking to the sound of street-cleaners spraying water on the cobbled streets. She was surprised to find she felt rested and refreshed. She was on the point of going out to have breakfast when her mobile phone rang. Gabriel.

"I'm going down to see the professor," he said without further preamble. "Do you want to make the trip?"

"Yes, fine," she agreed, killing off several dozen questions that had sprung to mind. She knew Gabriel – he didn't go in for extraneous chatter. "What time?"

"I'll expect you in about twenty minutes. You remember where the flat is, don't you?"

"Yes, I ..." but he had already hung up. The trouble with Gabriel, she thought ...

It was still before nine, and the air smelled fresh and cool as she walked over to the borrowed flat, only stopping to buy hot *cornetti* from a bar on the way. Gabriel was waiting outside, leaning on a different hired car.

"What on earth is that?" exclaimed Jane looking at the black, chrome-trimmed monster.

"What's the matter with it?" said Gabriel shortly.

"It's ... you're not going to hunt lions, are you?" said Jane.

He muttered something that might have been "bloody women", and she changed the subject:

"I've brought breakfast," she said, holding up the bag, now become a peace offering.

"No, put it in the car. We'll go to a bar. Come on."

In the bar the smells of strong coffee and warm pastries and the attendant clatter were immensely cheering. It was obviously Gabriel's local while he was staying there, and he exchanged banter with the barman and the big woman behind the cash desk, who greeted him with. *"Gabriele, angelo mio! E chi è questa bella?"*, which was cheering as well until Gabriel replied that the *bella* was his mother, causing more hilarity all round.

Back at the car and strapped into the passenger seat, Jane looked round with a mixture of wonder and fear; the roomy interior made her feel child-sized, she had to sit bolt upright to see over the dashboard. Her thoughts flew to the terrifyingly narrow road from Nemi to the valley.

"Do you think it will get down to the valley OK?" she asked worriedly, pushing her hair back.

"No, I expect the wheels will slip off the edge and we'll roll to the bottom and burst into flames."

The Sacred Wood

"Oh, God! In that case ..." then she glanced at him, saw the evil smile, "You ... bugger!" she burst out feelingly. Gabriel laughed.

"You're so literal, Jane," he said, still smiling, "No, we'll go south through Genzano. There's a main road that goes straight to the valley. Have a look at the map."

Jane took the Touring Club map down from the dashboard to check, and was reassured. The road was a minor road, a white line rather than the yellow or red of main routes, but it looked fairly straight and twice the width of the road they had taken from the village. She spent a few minutes studying the area. How small the lake looked, she thought; you couldn't see the depth of the crater either, the coloured page flattened and diminished it.

Her thoughts flew back to the meeting on Thursday. The professor had said that one of the three men was the "reincarnated Virbius".

"Is it you?" she asked him abruptly, turning to look at his profile.

"Yes, I am definitely me," he said maddeningly, eyes on the road ahead as he swerved past a dusty truck with its number plate hanging half off.

"You know what I mean. It's supposed to be one of you three," went on Jane, opening her eyes again.

"Why should it be me? What about Theo? He's young and good-looking."

"Yes, but he seems very ..."

"Boring?" suggested Gabriel with another swerve, this time to avoid a car blaring rock music that had shot out of a side road.

She simultaneously flinched at the near miss and flushed at the accuracy with which he had read her thoughts. "I was going to say 'placid'," she said untruthfully, clutching at her seat belt. "I would have expected someone more …"

"Heroic?" suggested Gabriel with the evil smile, stamping on the accelerator. "Like Ulysses perhaps, or Beowulf, or King Arthur."

"You're not being serious!"

"Yes, I am. What about George?" He overtook another car but this time there was plenty of room. "Those shorts of his are heroic if you ask me."

That made her laugh and she gave up. Gabriel was obviously not going to give her any kind of answer she wanted. But at least there had been enough room to overtake that time.

Jane had assumed they would be going back to the nursing home together, and was looking forward to seeing Professor Caseman again. Who was she? How had she become involved in this remnant of an ancient religion defeated and superseded centuries before? Jane, in her instinctive and slightly dreamy way, believed in the professor implicitly. "There are more things in heaven and earth, Horatio …" was one of her favourite quotations; it included every possibility, and though she had never had even the smallest uncanny experience herself, she had always felt that magic and mystery lay close by, concealed from the everyday world by the thinnest of membranes.

But instead of continuing along the valley towards the eastern side where the nursing home was, some two hundred yards past the Museum of Roman Ships, Gabriel turned left, then right into a bramble-lined dirt road. A neat wooden sign with the words *Locanda Nemorensis* burnt into it in pokerwork hung from a pole at the corner. The whirring and clacking of cicadas could faintly be heard above the whisper of the car's air-conditioning.

"Why have we come to the *agriturismo*?" asked Jane, sitting up straight again to peer over the black expanse of dashboard. She had barely looked the first time when George had taken Theo back, but now took in the olive groves, the main building, the neat chalets and the vine-shaded patio, where a few people were sitting at tables.

"George will keep you company while I'm with the professor," said Gabriel, bringing the black monster to a halt in the unsurfaced car park to one side of the main building. "

"And does George know he's baby-sitting?" queried Jane acidly. She wanted to see the professor again, be part of it, and was ruffled and aggrieved that she was apparently being excluded. She grumpily started to undo her seatbelt.

"Jane."

She looked round. Gabriel was leaning against the car door; his clever, normally arrogant face, wore an expression she had never seen before. Affection? Protectiveness? Understanding?

"What?" she snapped.

"Don't ... take things so much to heart," he said (gently? but Gabriel was never gentle). He had said the same thing after the episode with the 'Greek scholar' and the 'archaeologist'. Jane was flustered, did not know how to reply but Gabriel was already opening the car door and getting out. Yes, she thought, when Gabriel has finished with one thing, he dismisses it completely and goes on with the next. Which was neither 'the trouble with Gabriel ...' nor 'the nice thing about Gabriel'. What an impossible person he is, she thought, uncomfortably aware that she was avoiding shades and nuances and taking refuge in black and white.

She got out of the monster vehicle, slithering rather than descending since it was so high off the ground. God, and isn't this just *Out of Africa*, she thought. This thing could take on a rhino and come out unscathed.

Gabriel had disappeared in the direction of the patio and she put on her sunglasses and followed, keeping to the shade cast by the main building. One of the doors was open and showed a large catering kitchen with white-tiled walls and stainless steel working surfaces. As she glanced in, a young man inside, apparently watching a coffeepot, turned his head, and called cheerfully, "*Buon giorno, signorina!*" He had a bandage round one sunburnt arm.

"*Buon giorno!*" called Jane back, smiling and stopping. "What happened to your arm?"

"My horse," said the man. "I fell down."

"Oh, painful," said Jane sympathetically. "Are you all right?"

He came over to the door, limping a little. "Yes, no problem. The doctor said a few days. Can I help you?"

"I was looking for George Sutton," explained Jane.

"Ah, Engineer George! The road and aqueduct man!"

"Yes," said Jane, laughing "The road and aqueduct man."

"The patio, round the corner."

"Thanks. *Buona guarigione!*" she added. "Get well soon!"

George and Gabriel were sitting at one of the tables on the patio. George was rubbing his ear.

"Hi there!" said Jane, much more cheerful after the brief exchange with Massimo. "How are you, George?"

"… uh … fine, thanks."

"Are you really?" asked Jane, inclined to be playful now her good spirits were restored.

George grinned, Gabriel laughed, and returned to the matter at hand. When one thing was finished, it was completely dismissed, next thing …

"So, how about we meet up for lunch?" said Gabriel. "OK? You two go out and about – why don't you show Jane the sanctuary, George? I'll see you back here about 12.30." He got up, strode off. George and Jane, having received their orders, looked after him. The sound of the car engine started, gradually faded away. Jane sighed, turned to George.

"I've found with him, it's easier just to do as he says," she remarked. "Sorry, George, do you mind baby-sitting?" This time she found the idea funny rather than insulting.

"No, ... uh ... fine," said George, looking faintly uncomfortable. Remembering his account at the meeting with the professor, Jane rightly surmised it was the idea of the sanctuary rather than her company that caused his hesitancy, and leaned forward.

"Do you mind going back there?" she asked sympathetically. "It's just ... well, I've never seen it, and it seems to have so much to do with ... all this."

George looked at Jane's pleasant face and understanding smile, and made a decision.

"No, ... uh ..." He started getting up. "Fine. Probably do me good – like getting up on a horse again after you've been thrown."

"That reminds me," said Jane. "There was such a nice young man in the kitchen ..."

The Sacred Wood

As she waited for Gabriel to arrive, Lena deliberated on how much she should tell him. She suspected he would not be convinced by the arguments she had used with George and Theo. She had been gentle with George and mythic with Theo, with Gabriel she would have to be much more specific and appear more open.

She received him in her room, away from the distractions of the valley, the sanctuary and the wooded slopes. She was also tired, drained by the heat, and was grateful for the cool of the air-conditioning that kept the room at a gentle 27 degrees. She rejected lying on the bed, even though her legs and hips were hurting badly, choosing instead to sit in the armchair by the window.

"Professor," he said, when he came in, eyes flicking to assess the room. High bed with a cord to call for assistance hanging to one side, bedside tables, one with a lamp and a small wooden tray holding bottles and boxes of tablets, the other with three or four books piled on it; table at the window, at one side a high armchair, where the professor was sitting, at the other a straight-backed visitor's chair; there was a door, probably to a bathroom, the cream doors of an built-in wardrobe and a beautiful antique chest of drawers. He crossed the room in his casual arrogant way, but bent over and took her hand very gently, the merest touch, as if he knew that the least pressure would be agony.

"Mr Todd. Thank you for coming."

He did not sit down but moved the other chair,

glanced out of the window and then leaned against the windowsill, still standing.

"Who is the adversary, professor?" he asked abruptly. And here we are, thought Lena but she could not help smiling. She did so enjoy a reaction other than patient deference to her age; it was so refreshing.

"Those who wish to establish the false Virbius," she replied crisply.

Now he smiled. "Yes, so we have established. But that's a little vague, professor. The messenger for example, the man who passed the slip of paper to Jane. Where did he come from? You were expecting him – or someone like him."

He had immediately identified the one element she had avoided during their first meeting. Yes, she thought, facts were what Gabriel Todd wanted, and she would give him facts.

"Achille," she said slowly, "a follower I suppose you would call him. He gained employment with … the potential adversary some years ago. He was perfect as an informant – half-Italian, half-Greek."

"Greek?"

"Yes."

"And his employer – the potential adversary?" His tone was neutral.

"A woman known as Mrs Pleiades, very rich, and as inaccessible as only the very rich can be," said Lena without hesitation. "She has an estate near Troezen, Achille's home town, and he became one of the security guards at the estate so that he could keep watch."

Gabriel had turned to look out of the window again. She could see only his shoulder and a part of his profile. "I see. Why?"

"She is the protector of the false Virbius. When she returned to the estate earlier this year she was accompanied by a young man. Achille wrote to tell me of their arrival, and also that the man was being trained in hand-to-hand combat and martial arts. Achille should have waited until they left to come to Italy, then come himself. But I do not know why he was in Rome or how they discovered him."

"Jane's flat was broken into, and two men were asking about her," said Gabriel flatly, turning to face her again. "On the Saturday evening." He appeared to be calculating, then." That was only two days after your messenger was killed, a week ago now."

"She did not tell me that," said Lena after a pause.

Gabriel smiled. "She wouldn't. I know Jane – she lives in the present. Once she decided on her course of action – going to stay at a friend's flat – she completely dismissed the *reason* for being at the friend's flat."

"Your friend Jane is exceptional – you know that, don't you, Mr Todd?"

Gabriel paused before answering. What a careful man he is, thought Lena, as if he has to consider the possible consequences of expressing any kind of opinion.

"Yes, I do, actually," said Gabriel. He had evidently decided he could admit that. "Now, what does the 'potential adversary', Mrs … Pleiades, stand to gain?" he asked, still in the same neutral tone. "Is this some … whim of a rich bitch?"

Lena was shocked, not by the word but the venom with which he had uttered it, though his face remained calm and emotionless.

"She covets the forces of the grove."

He made a sound of annoyance. Lena gathered her strength; she must make him understand.

"This woman is evil, Mr Todd," she said earnestly. "She has already killed – probably not for the first time – to achieve her aim. Her involvement – together with her money and resources – makes our endeavour all the more important. We must go to the grove on the 13th, join battle – and defeat this evil."

"Very well, professor." he said, his tone neutral again. "Is there anything else I need to know?"

"The golden bough," replied Lena. "Listen, Mr Todd …"

She repeated what she had said to George and Theo. Gabriel listened carefully, even nodding slightly as if she was telling him what he already knew.

"… so we will need to set out early to identify the tree," she finished. "Half an hour should be enough."

"An hour," amended Gabriel, "if not an hour and a half." Having left his place by the window, he carefully replaced the chair in its original position, and then once more took her hand. "I'll be in touch, professor."

When he had gone, Lena went slowly and painfully to lie on the bed and took some of her tablets. She did not close her eyes but gazed thoughtfully at the mellowed wood of the chest of drawers. It had belonged to her parents and was the only personal item she had brought with her to the clinic. As she regarded it, she dwelt on memories of the past; a technique she sometimes used to rest her mind. She thought with infinite affection of her father, a big bluff man who read Rudyard Kipling, Rider Haggard and Anthony Trollope, and her mother, a strong intelligent woman who possessed hundreds of books on mythology, archaeology and ancient history.

They lived in a large rambling house, a former rectory, every room containing books, and not one of them forbidden to Emeline Hannah, their precocious only child. What pleasure, thought Lena, when nothing was categorised. I really saw no difference between *Pride and Prejudice* and *Lord Edgeware Dies* – both just seemed a good read, and then there was *Hypatia*. Hi-pat-ti-ah I pronounced it, she remembered smiling. How impressed I was by the story: a woman philosopher *and* a respected mathematician, stripped naked and torn to pieces by fanatical early Christians. Yes, she mused, Christians as bullies and bigots, it came as quite a revelation. Perhaps that was the start, or perhaps it was that book of her mother's, *Women in Antiquity*, the first time she had heard about the Goddess Vesta and the Virgins who served her.

There were seven of them, living behind the round temple in the Roman Forum. Vowed to virginity – the penalty for breaking the vow was to be buried alive – their task was to keep the sacred fire perpetually burning. That was what she remembered from her childhood reading, and it was only at university that she had discovered how powerful and how sexually ambiguous they were.

Representing all women, they were legally recognised as men. As women, they wore the *flammeum*, the flame-coloured veil of the young bride; their hair was dressed in the six braids of the married woman, while their robe was the long *stola* of the matron. The three ages of women.

But they possessed male prerogatives: they were not subject to any man, save the *Pontifex Maximus* himself, and they had possession of their own money, the first requisite of freedom. They could give testimony at a trial and were entitled to a guard of lictors, a visible sign of power.

The Vestals – maidens, matrons and men. Through them Lena had discovered the existence of the sanctuary. At Nemi Diana also bore the title of Vesta, her worship celebrated in the flames of torches on the 13th August, while the Rex Nemorensis watched from his kingdom on the wooded slopes. And that was the beginning, thought Lena.

As 'suggested' by Gabriel, Jane and George went to the sanctuary. Before they left the *agriturismo* George had gone to get his photocopies of the Nemi part in *Towns and Villages of the Alban Hills*, which contained two maps, one of the lake and one of the sanctuary itself. He had studied them carefully and now had a clearer idea of the orientation of the sacred complex and its surrounding area.

He felt a little nervous as they left the main road to climb up the stony path, though it helped that it was morning, not the hot deserted hush of afternoon, and that Jane was with him. Even so, and quite unaware he was doing so, he kept one ear tuned to the whirring of the cicadas, monotonous but normal.

They reached the top of the stony track, and then took the path off to the left, past the small olive grove that still proclaimed its independence through its signs of *proprietà privata*. From there it was only a short walk to the high gate, where the large hole in the fence mocked the gate's massive padlock. Jane paused and raised her eyebrows.

"Neo-pagans," explained George and repeated what the man from the museum had said. Jane too was charmed by the idea of neo-pagans. They negotiated the hole and walked on.

"Do you think they have anything to do with the professor?" asked Jane.

"Who? Neo-pagans? She didn't mention them," said George doubtfully.

"Maybe they're New Agers," commented Jane idly. "You know, drapey skirts and amulets and sandals. Nuts and berries, that kind of thing. What are these anyway?" she went on.

The wide grass-covered track was flanked to the right by the crumbling walls of huge niches. It was in one of their corners that George had left the guidebook that first day. A cement pole held the remains of some explanatory notice, now faded and illegible from the effects of rain and sun.

George showed her the map, where B marked the position of the niches; they were in the eastern corner of the sanctuary. The guidebook hypothesised that the niches had probably contained statues and supported an upper level of the sanctuary. Now trees and tangled bushes sprouted from the top of them.

I'm the only one who hasn't been here, thought Jane, looking up, then corrected herself, no, Gabriel hasn't been here either. I wonder what he and the professor are saying to each other. There was some kind of … I don't know … hostility, no, that's too strong, some kind of … atmosphere between them. The professor was quite natural though formal, while he was … I don't know … guarded? Did he believe it all? And if he didn't, why is he here? Though he does act on whims – but he's always careful even with whims. Like the time we went to Pompeii. Now, that was strange. No, not strange.

Oh, do brace up, she told herself impatiently. George was studying the plan of the site, turning the page to align it with where they were standing; the niches (B) were a clear point of reference. R must be the room with the plinth and the offerings, he was thinking.

"Have you ever been to Pompeii, George?" Jane asked him.

He looked up. "Pompeii? Yes, years ago when I was a student. How about you?"

"Yes, a couple of times," said Jane. "But the first time was with Gabriel. He was teaching at one of the American universities in Rome and was taking a coachload of students." She was suddenly curious what George would have to say about one of her first experiences of Gabriel. "I'd only just met him," she said, aiming for a tone of light reminiscence. "He invited me, told me to phone the university secretary for the meeting-point, which *she* said was Piazza del Popolo. Then, the same evening *he* phoned to say it was near Via Veneto. Afterwards I wondered if he'd hedged his bets – you know – made arrangements in case he changed his mind. If he hadn't phoned, I would have gone to the wrong place, and it would have been the secretary's fault." She laughed but it did not sound entirely natural.

George looked faintly shocked. "That would have been ... uh ... rather devious, wouldn't it?"

"Yes," said Jane, "it would." Then she laughed more naturally. "I didn't hear you rushing to his defence, George! You didn't say, 'Oh, I'm sure he wouldn't'." George reddened, mumbled something, and Jane, contrite at having embarrassed him, said quickly, "It was still one of the best trips I ever made. He really was good as well – the students adored him."

"He's a professor then?" said George curiously.

"This time round – I mean, he seems to be at the moment," said Jane slowly. "Then sometimes he claims to have worked for the secret service. I don't know. If you ask him, he either lies or just doesn't answer. I asked him about his parents once, and he said, 'The usual – one of each sex.'"

"Uh … interesting chap," said George. It was half a question.

Jane sighed. "I can't make up my mind whether I like him or not," she confessed, looking toward the patchwork of fields. "Sometimes I think I go on seeing him because I just want to find out if I do or not, but he confounds me every time."

If Gabriel had been there, he would have thought, "confounds", that's a good one. George nodded. He too knew the feeling.

"What about the room with the altar?" said Jane to get away from the unresolved question of Gabriel; George had told her about it on the way there.

They left the huge niches and took the well-beaten path to the left. It really was difficult to imagine the original complex, most of which was still buried underground and hidden by vegetation.

The Sacred Wood

On the way they stopped again to consult the guidebook, which was detailed and informative. To the west of where they were standing there had been baths and living quarters, colonnades and the *celle* where votive offering and statues were placed. It went into more detail about the main temple (K), which had a large circular annex, explained by the guide as "probably a round temple of Diana in her character of Vesta, like the round temple of Vesta in the Roman Forum. Here the sacred fire would seem to have been tended by Vestal Virgins, for the head of a Vestal in terra-cotta was found on the spot."

To the north-west there had also been a small theatre, which the guidebook suggested was "the probable setting for the ritual duel for the succession of the Rex Nemorensis."

"The theatre? What about the wood?" asked Jane, looking in vain for anything which would give her some indication of what she was looking at. "Isn't that supposed to be the site of the battle?"

George, shading his eyes with one hand, was looking around. "That was probably in the early days of the cult, then things got more sophisticated. Like Morris dancers."

Jane started giggling. "Morris dancers!"

George laughed as well, then went a bit pink. "Well, the ... uh ... fertility symbols in Morris dancing were probably much more ... uh ... explicit at one time." Jane laughed even more. "You mean, instead of sausage-shaped bladders they whacked each other with huge phalluses ... or do I mean phalli?"

By this time they had reached the excavated room with its corner altar, but the room was not empty. Lying on a large blue blanket in front of the altar, a gurgling baby kicked and laughed, tiny pink hands waving joyfully in the air. Jane and George stopped dead, their faces a study in amazement. Then a young woman, with plaited fair hair and wearing a long leaf-green skirt, emerged from the shaded corner on their left. 'Neopagan,' thought Jane and George simultaneously.

"Are you seeking the goddess?" the woman asked softly.

Jane and George spoke together:

"Uh ...," said George.

"Yes," said Jane firmly, following the principle that "no" cannot be subsequently turned into "yes" while a "yes" may later become a "no".

"Come in," said the woman. They carefully descended the metal stairs that led down into the room. The young woman regarded them with a friendly smile while the baby continued to laugh and gurgle.

"Your baby looks happy," said Jane, smiling.

"She is always happy here," said the woman. She went over and sat on the blanket by the baby's side, caressing the child's cheek with her forefinger. The baby laughed again and grasped the finger as though shaking hands. George, who had had a moment of real fear, relaxed and smiled too.

Jane was wondering if she should ask about "the

goddess" but decided to wait.

"We come every so often to sit for a while," said the woman. "And at this time of year, this place is particularly sacred."

"Because of the 13th August," offered Jane.

"Ah, you know about the festival?" asked the woman eagerly. Jane wondered if she had been too impulsive but George held up the guidebook. "In here," he explained. "Sanctuary. Diana. Festival … uh … you know." The woman looked disappointed.

"I thought …"

"Sorry," said Jane, relieved that George had taken the lead.

"You are welcome regardless," said the woman but it sounded like a dismissal. Suddenly awkward, they turned to go.

"We wish you well," said Jane, wondering why such an antique expression had come to her.

"Wait." The woman rose gracefully from the blanket, the leaf-green skirt swirling about her, went to the altar and picked something up. She walked back across the room and offered it to Jane. "The goddess has told me that you are to have this," she said.

Jane took the small clay object. About three inches long and two wide, with a slight tapering at each end, it resembled a female figure, with exaggerated breasts and a groove where the groin would be. Traces of red in the groove showed that the figure had once been painted.

"Thank you," she said, looking at the figure with wonder. "Are you sure you want me to have this?" She could feel George beside her, tense and protective, as if the woman had offered Jane a bomb.

"Yes – the command was quite clear." The woman returned to sit beside the child, smiled and gave a small wave of farewell. Jane and George climbed the few metal steps and started back toward the gate. George began striding ahead and Jane had to hurry to keep up with him; she still held the figure in one hand, not wanting to put it in her bag where it would be banged and possibly chipped by her cigarette-lighter or mobile phone. George's eyes were fixed firmly on the ground and the photocopies were crumpled from the force of his grip.

"George, slow down! Are you OK?" she asked in concern.

He stopped, gave a sheepish smile. "Don't like it here," he muttered apologetically. "Too many strange women popping up."

That made Jane laugh even as she patted his arm consolingly. "Don't take it to heart, George. After all, this *is* a female sanctuary! Of course you feel put upon. Come on, let's get back to the real world. Oh, and now we can find out what the professor said to Gabriel."

Back at the *agriturismo* Gabriel was unusually punctual, but silent and withdrawn, uninterested to the point of rudeness in Jane's description of the sanctuary and the neo-pagan. In retaliation Jane did not show him the clay figure, which she had wrapped carefully in several paper handkerchiefs before laying it on top of the other things in her bag. George started murmuring "I'll be saying … uh … goodbye … uh … time for lunch …" but Gabriel suddenly became charming, wouldn't hear of George eating on his own, he must go with them to Genzano – yes, something sustaining and cheerful … beer and pizza, and whisked them off in the black monster. It was – as Jane had remarked – easier to do as he said.

"So, what did the professor say to you?" asked Jane when they sitting outside a take-away pizza place, which had thoughtfully provided some plastic tables in the shade of an awning. It was one of the businesses in a narrow side street and the only one staying open at that time of day; there was the rattle and clang as shopkeepers closing for lunch pulled down their heavy metal shutters and padlocked them in place. In a few minutes the only other place open was a tobacconist a short way down on the opposite side of the road.

"More of the same," said Gabriel; he had put sunglasses on.

"Oh, come *on*, Gabriel!" protested Jane. "Don't be so … niggardly."

Niggardly, thought Gabriel, that's a good one. He smiled.

"Did the professor tell you about the … uh … golden bough?" asked George. He felt rather inhibited with Gabriel and had looked for something relatively impersonal to say. He was enjoying the beer and pizza though.

"Yes," said Gabriel, taking a swallow of beer then holding the glass up and seeming to admire the effect of the light that turned the beer to clear golden liquid.

"What is it?" asked Jane.

"*Uno avulso non deficit alter,*" replied Gabriel unexpectedly, lowering the glass and giving the evil smile. Both Jane and George stared at him.

"What does *that* mean then?" said Jane in irritation, having waited in vain for a translation. George had buried his face in his glass.

Gabriel relented: "When one is torn away, another succeeds – Virgil."

"Succeeds?" asked Jane. "What succeeds?"

"Succeeds in the sense of one monarch succeeding another," said Gabriel. "It was what the sibyl at Cuma told Aeneas, when he went to ask her how to enter the Underworld. He first had to go to the forest and find a tree on which grew a golden branch. Then, he had to take the branch and carry it with him as a gift to Persephone, the queen of the Underworld, a sort of passport, if you like. If Fate was propitious, he would easily take the branch, if not, nothing could detach it. And then the sibyl added '*Uno avulso non deficit alter* – when one is torn away, another succeeds' – a new branch would grow where the previous one had been."

Jane was listening with a small frown of

concentration. George was thinking: so the professor explained it to him. I never even thought to ask. None of them noticed a pale man with thinning hair, eyes hidden behind the blackest of wire-framed sunglasses, who had apparently stopped to consult his newspaper in front of the tobacconist.

"Another one grew again," repeated Jane. "Another cycle. But what has that got to do with this?"

"You tell her, George," said Gabriel, apparently bored with the subject, and George recounted the part played by the golden bough in the ritual. The pale man with the newspaper must have finished reading whatever it was that had first caused him to halt. He folded the newspaper and moved away, not far since his car was parked on the corner. From there he could just see the three people sitting at the red plastic table.

13 SUNDAY 9TH AUGUST

"And you are certain it was she?" said Mrs Pleiades, tapping the photocopy of Jane's ID card with one crimson nail.

"Yes. She was with two men," confirmed David Levant; his pale bird-of-prey face seeming grey in the dim light of the brocaded sitting room.

"Two?"

"One of them was Gabriel."

The intake of Mrs Pleiades' breath was the hiss of a snake before striking, and then she smiled unpleasantly: "Well, well – Gabriel," her tone was musing, "so now we know where he got to. What about the other man?"

"He looked like an English tourist."

Mrs Pleiades laughed: "They do tend to be

The Sacred Wood

easily identifiable, don't they? Which man is she having sex with, do you think?"

"I couldn't tell, Mrs Pleiades. There was no touching or looks being exchanged."

"Not that that means anything," commented Mrs Pleiades. "Gabriel always was a cold fish."

"But they went back to Rome together, Jane Harrison and Gabriel."

"And?"

"They went for a meal in the centre, then sat drinking in a bar near Campo de' Fiori. And they went home together. I followed, waited for another two hours after the lights went out. By then Giorgio had arrived to take over – he reported back this morning. They're still there."

"So they did spend the night together ...," Mrs Pleiades said, showing her teeth. "Well, well ... I think we had better ... invite Miss Harrison to join us. Arrange it, David."

He went out noiselessly, limping slightly, the faintest of lurches, but Mrs Pleiades noticed, and thought without pity that it was a pity but unsurprising. Six years had it been? She sat for a moment admiring the crimson tips of her nails, and then rose languidly and crossed to the door to go to her room.

When she arrived, her trained maid was laying out the clothes Mrs Pleiades had chosen to wear at lunch, a dark blue-green dress and jacket; she was feeling mellow that day.

"And the amber necklace, I think," she

instructed the maid lazily. Dolorita Morales nodded, her thin dark face expressionless, and went to the large cabinet that held Mrs Pleiades' extensive collection of jewellery; her dead millionaire husband had been as generous if not more so than his predecessors, and there had been many predecessors. The maid laid the heavy necklace beside the clothes on the bedspread. "Do you require anything further, madam?"

Mrs Pleiades did not recognise the stilted cadence as being her own, but was always soothed and pleased when the maid spoke. "No, but come back in half an hour to dress my hair."

When the door had been gently closed, Mrs Pleiades slipped from her morning dress and then went herself to the cabinet; she had a sudden whim to view her collection. Opening the doors, she scanned the rows of drawers that filled the interior, and then began to open them at random to view their contents.

Ah, the Chanel brooch, a flower with curling gold leaves, its centre set with pearls and blue-green stones, and lying beside it the diamond comet necklace that clasped the neck but left the throat bare and inviting.

She opened another drawer: her *parure*, the suite of matching tiara, earrings, rings, brooch, and necklace, all in diamonds, a copy of the *parure* of the Empress Josephine herself, commissioned by Mrs Pleiades' besotted husband of the time, when Pleiades was not her name. It reminded her as well

The Sacred Wood

of the crippled English lord she had known; she had travelled with him to Nemi, and so impressed had he been with the view of the lake he had scribbled a few lines in the inn register, describing the lake as "calm as cherish'd hate". Not bad, she thought condescendingly. He did achieve some small fame if she remembered correctly.

Yes, she had returned at odd intervals over the years, just to see, just to make sure, and now, as she opened yet another drawer containing trinkets from the 1970s, a reminiscent smile curved her scarlet lips, closely followed by the slightest of frowns. It was in that decade she had almost succeeded – almost – in turning the Lake of Nemi into a cesspool. Having bought up a decaying monster of a hotel on the rim of the crater, she re-opened it as an old people's home, running the drains and sewers down into the lake itself. In the time that followed she had watched with satisfaction as the water clouded and thickened, took on a reddish hue as toxic algae proliferated and fish died, until the clear circle was reduced to putrid brown slime. But, after a surprisingly effective burst of indignation by local environmentalists, the clinic had been closed; the lake had returned.

She opened a fourth and last drawer, to the far right of the cabinet, where her most prized souvenirs lay, and contemplated the contents.

The jewellery that lay displayed on the white silk would have filled an historian with awed pleasure, closely followed by the incredulous question of why these precious items were not in a museum. The drawer held rings and bracelets, necklaces and earrings, all beautifully crafted in gold, and adorned with emeralds and sapphires, jasper and lapis lazuli, even a few pieces carved from the fossilized wood called jet from the barbarous Britannia.

There were the Etruscan filigree earrings, formed of fine gold wire, diminutive gold petals and blue gems. How well they had looked, shimmering and gleaming whenever she tossed her lustrous black hair; the five heavy-gold snake bracelets that she wore, three on her right arm, two on her left, the lack of symmetry subtly catching the eye; and the clasp earrings depicting the face of Eros with gold pendants of hearts and sapphire gems hanging beneath. She fondled them briefly, smiling. It was Gaius himself who had given them to her, as she helped him on his way to madness and excess. Lying beside him that summer evening in the sumptuous pavilion hung with drifts of rose-gold silk, she listened and encouraged as he drank and bragged and railed about his godhood; she had worn the snake bracelets, and the Eros earrings, lay watchful, feeling the shift of the massy ship as a mere hint, until the moment came. Hers was the voice which had whispered: "But do not you think he must be rather old now …? Is it not time for another to challenge and take his place?"

Still smiling, Mrs Pleiades took up the bracelets,

clasped them about her arms, three on the right, two on the left, then the Eros earrings, which she gently clipped to her earlobes, and turned to admire her reflection in the looking-glass.

Dolorita Morales, when her knock was not acknowledged, quietly opened the door, and looked into the room. When she saw the immobile figure decked in antique gold, half-turned towards the looking-glass, she nodded to herself and withdrew, smiling and feeling in her uniform pocket for her pack of cigarettes. Byron Escobar must be near, probably under the window, and they would smoke together when he had finished. He would tell her when it was time to return, and if lunch were a little late, well, lunch would be a little late.

Jane had drunk a lot the evening she and Gabriel returned to Rome and it hadn't helped that she'd eaten only one piece of pizza for lunch and was too tired and wound-up to have much appetite in the evening. They ended up in a bar somewhere near Campo de' Fiori, sitting at a corner table lit by a table lamp with an art deco shade depicting one of Klimt's dark ladies swathed in jewelled brocade; incongruously there was a row of cinema seats against the far wall, and the only other customers were two young men whispering together in another corner.

To Jane it had seemed an excellent idea to sip at

glass after glass of wine; it was a way to unwind, a pause in the onrush of events, and Gabriel was charming, interesting and funny. She teased him about his hatred for computers and he recounted that in fact a friend had once offered to set him up with an e-mail address so that he could write and receive messages.

"But he never wrote to me, you know," he finished, eyes on the row of cinema seats. He said it quite seriously, which made Jane laugh for he had so completely missed the point. How he hated the modern world and its instant disposable means of communication. Gabriel's idea of a letter was something on proper thick paper, possibly embossed, she thought, and ideally written with a quill pen.

Having now forgotten her earlier pique, she showed him the clay figure. He held it closer to the table lamp to study it, turning it gently between his fingers; he had nice hands, Jane decided, capable-looking, and she took another sip of wine.

"And why did she say she was giving it to you?" he finally asked, handing the figure back to her; she stowed it away again.

"The goddessh told her to," she said happily, wine-warmed and relaxed. "Isn't that nicesh, I mean nice, Gabriel? A goddess thinking of me and wanting to give me a present." She was proud she had said so many s-sounds without slurring.

"Yesh, very nicesh," said Gabriel with the evil smile. "Come on, let's go."

The Sacred Wood

They went back to the borrowed flat, drank yet more wine, at which point things became hazy though she did remember the warm furry feeling becoming a sad spiky feeling, ending with her recounting some long tearful story about her family.

When Gabriel put his arm round her she was too self-involved to notice and it was only when they were naked together in the borrowed bed, a low-built pine affair with huge pillows, that she had a moment's lucidity.

"I don't want this," she announced in a loud clear voice, and without a word Gabriel rose and disappeared into the living room. Jane immediately plummeted into velvety darkness, and did not hear Gabriel's quiet movements as he took the clay figure from her bag, held it under a table lamp to study it afresh, and then hid it behind some books. Then he too lay down, hands behind his head, feet propped on the arm of the couch, which was too short.

It was late when Jane woke up in the grip of the worst hangover she had ever known. Neither of them referred to the evening before, and Jane, dark glasses shielding her from the light and the day, said she was going back to Silvia's flat. Gabriel merely nodded, said he'd be in touch.

As she walked towards the old ghetto quarter and synagogue – the idea of which had so amused Gabriel – she did not know how she felt about the night before. At least he hadn't insisted, she thought. The nice thing about Gabriel ...

She came out into Via Arenula, and walked towards the river, intending to go past Isola Tiberina and then to Silvia's flat, but all at once, when she saw Ponte Garibaldi she wanted to go home; it was only five minutes away, and there must be post to collect. Surely it couldn't hurt ...

On the bridge, she stopped and, resting her arms on the rail, looked upstream to the small footbridge of Ponte Sisto, with its backdrop of the slopes of Gianicolo, and, further away, the dome of St Peter's. If I'd thought of it before, I could have gone home via Ponte Sisto, she thought. Much quicker. Still ...

She continued on her way, and was pausing before crossing Lungotevere, when there was a rumbling rattle and a large white van lurched to a halt beside her. Before she had time to realise what was happening the passenger door was pushed open with a metallic thud, a man jumped out and rough hands dragged her to the back to bundle her into the dark interior. Her bag sailed through the air as she flung her arm out, and one of two startled tourists who had been walking towards Trastevere shouted, "Hey!"

The van took off, veering left and accelerating, narrowly missing a family crossing the road, while the two tourists, Americans from Boston, suddenly noticed Jane's leather bag between the railings of the bridge; for a moment it lay perfectly balanced, but even as the husband started towards it – it would contain details of the owner's identity – there was a flap of wings, a screeching caw and a large ungainly bird landed on one end, taking off with another screech as its weight sent the bag falling into the river below. The two looked at each other. "You see that?" said the husband incredulously. His wife nodded, her face shocked; the warnings they had received about flagrantly inflated restaurant bills and bag-snatchers on mopeds, had now turned into visions of mafia-inspired kidnapping and possible murder. "Judy," he went on. "We have to report this to the police." She nodded again, pulled herself together, and gestured towards Trastevere. "You remember we passed a police station? There was that woman shouting outside."

"Oh, yeah, right. The Colosseum can wait till later. But did you see that bird?"

At the *comando di polizia* in Trastevere, Tommaso was explaining to the sister of the murdered man yet again that nothing further could be done. After the scene outside, he had persuaded her to come to his office, and sent out for coffee, which arrived on a battered tray with a heaped assortment of sachets of white sugar, brown sugar, sweeteners, and several plastic spoons. She added two sugars to her coffee, stirred it round and gulped it back in one swallow. "My brother had nothing to do with drugs," she repeated stubbornly, placing the plastic cup back on the tray. "He was a good man, he worked, supported our mother." She sat bolt upright as she spoke, a youngish woman, forty according to her passport, with dyed blonde hair caught into a knot at the nape of her neck, strong features and imperious black eyes.

Tommaso took a deep breath, reminded himself that she was bereaved, and sipped at his own coffee before replying.

"Signora Manousakis," he said gently, "I can assure you that we have carried out a thorough investigation, and this is what we know. Your brother rented a short-stay apartment on 27th July, but we have nothing else. The drug we found – half a kilo of heroin – is the only indication we have of his … affairs here." He paused but she regarded him silently, jaw set. "I am very sorry, signora," he went on, "but you must understand that having taken this as far as possible, we cannot now devote further resources to your brother's case."

Adelpha hesitated. She had the name and phone number in her bag, but apparently Achille had been quite specific in the letter he had left, had even underlined the words, her mother had told her on the phone. <u>Trust no one – not even the police</u>. She regarded the young policeman; he seemed in good faith but … No, she could not take the chance. She nodded, as though accepting his words, and began to rise. Tommaso walked round the desk to show her out, relieved that the matter was apparently at an end; families never believed that the son or the brother or the husband was capable of illegal activities – or so they said.

Adelpha walked towards the exit, passing two foreigners glancing about worriedly. She paid no attention; tourists getting robbed, it was the same in Athens. She would go back to her service flat and phone; she should have done so before, she reflected. Pointless to put any faith in the police, and if Achille had sent the letter as insurance, she must ensure she acted as he would have wanted. Decisively she quickened her pace, donned her heavy dark glasses, and left the *comando di polizia*; she made for Viale di Trastevere, where she had seen there was a taxi rank.

The back of the van was a hot dark box, with only one tiny jagged point of light coming from the cardboard covering the small window between the driver and the back. It was completely bare inside, with a floor of ridged metal and two rounded metal mouldings that housed the wheels. There was nothing to hold onto, and for a few minutes Jane rolled about helplessly in the rattling darkness until she managed to find the side of the van and sat bracing herself with her feet. At least I'm wearing trousers, she thought incoherently.

In the front of the van the driver glanced at his companion and grinned, and then applied himself to the task of driving, keeping just over the speed limit, eyes scanning the side roads.

While the white van sped southwards that

Sunday morning, George and Theo were following Massimo into the *agriturismo's* small office, having asked him if they could borrow his computer to do a search. Before he registered their expressions Massimo said jokingly, "Of course, but no porno sites, eh!" but then was unusually silenced by the seriousness of their faces. He logged on for them, pulled over another chair so that they could both sit down, and went off, still moving slowly after the fall from his horse.

"Good of you to come, George," remarked Theo as he sat at the computer. "I mean, since you're not really involved." George, trying to fit his long legs into some kind of comfortable position at the side of the desk, looked slightly surprised: "Best to … uh … find out what it's all about – or supposed to be about," he explained, leaning to squint at the first page of Wikipedia, where Theo was typing "Virbius" into the search box. "Yeah, right," agreed Theo abstractedly as the page came up.

They read its contents in silence:

"In Roman mythology, **Virbius** (or **Virbio**) was the name of the reborn Hippolytus. His cult believed that Artemis asked Asclepius to resurrect the young man since he had vowed chastity to the goddess. He was brought to Latium, Italy, where he reigned under the name of Virbio or Virbius."

"His name means "twice a man", in reference to the fact that he was mortally wounded, but brought back to life. He was worshipped as a god of the forest."

"The re-born Hippolytus," read George aloud. "Uh ... can we have a look at him?"

"Sure," agreed Theo, slightly annoyed he had not thought of it himself, and clicked on the link; the page changed:

"In Greek mythology, **Hippolytus** (Greek for "loose horse") was a son of Theseus and either Antiope or Hippolyte. He was identified with the Roman forest god Virbius."

"The most common legend regarding Hippolytus states that he was killed after rejecting the advances of Phaedra, the second wife of Theseus and Hippolytus's stepmother. Spurned, Phaedra told Theseus that Hippolytus had raped her. Infuriated, Theseus believed her and, using one of the three wishes he had received from Poseidon, cursed Hippolytus. Hippolytus' horses were frightened by a sea monster and dragged their rider to his death."

"This is it!" said Theo excitedly, the momentary annoyance completely forgotten. "This is all the stuff I read in the German guy's book up in Tuscany."

Now George remembered their conversation of the Sunday before, when he had first met Theo (and was it really only a week ago? it seemed that months had passed). Theo had read of the sanctuary to Diana and its connection with the Greek legend of a queen in love with her stepson, and had decided to come to Nemi. And George was also remembering how 'love', 'rejected', 'rape' and 'hidden' had suddenly come together in his mind, echoing the frantic whispers of the mad woman. "*Where is he? I know he is here. It is useless to hide him.*"

He sat back – the crouching was becoming too uncomfortable – and listened to the muted Sunday-morning sounds – a clatter of pans in the kitchen, a vacuum cleaner somewhere overhead, the twittering of sparrows from the trees outside – while Theo read and re-read the entry.

"Right, said Theo finally, looking up. "Hippolytus was falsely accused of rape by his step-mother and killed." He clicked back to "Virbius" again. "And then he was brought back to life by Artemis and hidden here at Nemi with a different name."

"Artemis not … uh … Diana?" asked George diffidently; the plethora of names was starting to overwhelm him.

"Artemis is the Greek name for Diana," said Theo absently, going back to the entry for 'Hippolytus'.

"And the … uh … Rex Nemorensis?"

"Greek Hippolytus became Roman Virbius, and the first Rex Nemorensis," said Theo with a hint of condescension, "that is, the first King of the Sacred Wood"

"Right-oh," said George. "Uh ... good."

Lena was spending her Sunday wondering about Gabriel Todd. She did not want to fuss but when she re-played their conversation in her mind, she realized that he had been courteous, concentrated and ... non-committal. Lena was skilled at reading people, was usually confident in her assessments and usually right, but this time she felt uncertain, was unsure whether she had gained the result she wanted.

When Barbara arrived with Alfredo in his battered Mercedes to go out to lunch, she found her friend uncharacteristically silent and withdrawn. Getting to her, thought Barbara. Wish she would give up the whole idea. But she knew that it would be useless to suggest it and would only add to Lena's preoccupation. So she said nothing as the car groaned its way up the hill to Nemi; they were going to a restaurant with air-conditioning and a fine view of the lake. The interior, dark-panelled, cool and dim was ideal, and the signed photographs of Italian actors, smiling or moody or caught in some moment of a film created a homely but celebratory background; Lena's favourite was of a radiant Anna Magnani receiving an Oscar, while Barbara favoured the jolly shot of Charleston Heston and Stephen Boyd clowning about with a moped on the set of *Ben Hur*.

They ordered pan-fried trout, "fresh this

morning", promised the waiter, with oven potatoes and salad, and Barbara added a half litre of house white wine to the order, thinking that Lena would probably have half a glass if it was there, and it might help to cheer her up. The wine and mineral water arrived immediately, and when both had a glass of each – Lena had indeed said she would enjoy some – Barbara took the bull by the horns and said gruffly:

"Come on, Lena, what's bothering you?"

Lena flashed her an affectionate smile: "Gabriel Todd," she said simply. "I am not entirely sure he can be relied upon."

"Like I said, a difficult bugger," commented Barbara robustly; she had actually said "difficult type" but she was feeling more belligerent that day.

That made Lena laugh, a sound of such joyful amusement that an Italian family, father mother and two teenage children, looked over at the two older women and smiled. Then, she became serious, leant back in her chair – they had thoughtfully provided a cane armchair with cushions – and gently pressed her swollen fingers together; Barbara's sharp eyes did not miss the gesture.

"So what happened yesterday?" she asked, partly to take Lena's mind off the pain, partly because she really wanted to know. "He came back, didn't he?"

"Yes," agreed Lena slowly, "he came back." Her eyes were considering as she gazed across to the hazy roofs of Genzano. Barbara took a sip of water, followed by another one of wine, and waited.

"I ... told him of the golden bough," explained Lena, now looking round the restaurant, "and said we would need to go early, perhaps half an hour. He disagreed, said an hour, if not an hour and a half. I suppose I took that as tacit agreement, and at the time believed that he would ... will come here on 13th."

Barbara nodded, and then the meal arrived, the trout already boned as they had requested, and it was only after they had finished arranging plates, cutlery and vegetables dishes and were eating and drinking that she went on: "Well, when you think of it from his point of view, it's all a bit ... strange." Like George, Barbara's own word would have been 'loony' but she was loyal to her friend. "I mean, Jane gets him down here to deliver the message from poor whatisname, which is fair enough, and then the next thing he knows he's being set up as ..." She stopped, unwilling to offend her friend but also unwilling to come out with something like 'champion of good', 'warrior', or anything else that might be sentimental or smacked of poetry.

Lena, adept at guessing the unsaid words, smiled affectionately again, picked up her fork, and went back to her own trout. Barbara took a sip of wine, wondering what could be done to help. All at once, she had it:

"Why don't you phone Jane?" she suggested. "Ask her if he's said anything to her. Get an idea

..."

Lena looked at her appreciatively: "Now, that is a very good idea," she said. "Thank you, Barbara. I'll do it now." And she took her mobile phone from her bag.

There would be no answer of course. The phone was zipped into the inside pocket of Jane's bag, and the bag itself was at the bottom of the Tiber. Having first sunk through the murky water, it had settled into the oozy sediment of the river bed, but was then slowly but relentlessly dragged forward by the current to tumble through the rush of the weir above Isola Tiberina, finally to snag in the twisted handlebars of an abandoned bicycle, where it again settled into the ooze.

All Lena heard was a recorded voice reporting that the number was "unavailable" and inviting her to "call back later." She looked at Barbara and shook her head. For a moment they regarded each other. "I'll try later," said Lena briskly, putting the phone away and picking up her wine glass. Barbara nodded. "What's your fish like?" she asked, skewering a potato. "Mine's still got some bones in it."

Jane herself, braced again the metal-ridged wall and floor of the van as it accelerated, braked, and accelerated again, was trying not to panic. One small consolation, she thought, was that she had not actually returned to her flat in Trastevere and been kidnapped there; Gabriel would have been impossibly scathing. And now?

You've read the books, you've seen the films, she told herself, this is the time to make some kind of plan, decide on some sort of strategy. I wish I didn't feel so ill though, she reflected dismally. That'll teach me – again – to drink so much. It's a miracle I haven't thrown up in here.

The van was going more slowly now. Jane was not to know, but it had arrived in Genzano, and now took the road leading upwards to the rim of the volcano; Mrs Pleiades' rented villa was on the outskirts of the town on the Via di Diana, the road that led down to the lake itself.

She did feel the van slow and turn, however, heard the clang of a gate and the muted crunch of gravel under the tyres, and then the van stopped; they had obviously arrived.

A muffled metallic thump as the passenger door was opened, more crunching on gravel as footsteps sounded from the side, and then the rear doors were swung open, and a black shape with rough hands hauled her from her precarious perch. Blinded by the sudden glare of light, she could see nothing as she was half-pushed, half-dragged towards house. It was only in the hall that she could see again, though her impressions were vague and fragmentary. A dim staircase, heavy dark furniture, a carved door, and then a spacious brocaded sitting-room, where there were three people: an immaculately-dressed woman, a tall handsome blond man, and a pale man with thinning hair. All three smiled when they saw her. Jane's skin, hot and sweaty after the close confines of the van, became damp and cool but she straightened and walked forward saying:

"Excuse me but what is all this? I have no idea …"

She got no further. The pale man, still smiling, walked up to her and quite calmly punched her in the side.

"Thank you, David," purred Mrs Pleiades. "Now, …"

But Jane – the nausea of the hangover now made unbearable by the vicious blow – doubled over and was at last loudly and comprehensively sick. Dimly she thought how nice it was that she had managed to throw up all over the pale man's shoes while completely avoiding her own.

Outside the rented villa, Dolorita Morales and Byron Escobar were conferring. They had been smoking an after-lunch cigarette in the sunken patio on the annex side of the building, but when they heard the sound of the van arriving, he swiftly darted to the side of the house and was in time to see the van doors being flung open and a slim young woman with ruffled light-coloured hair bundled through the villa's front door. He drew back when the van started up again, reversed and headed back towards the main gates.

Byron Escobar took a drag of his cigarette, eyes narrowed against the smoke, and was about to return to the sunken patio, when, for the second time, he stopped suddenly in his tracks, nostrils flaring, head cocked as though he had heard a far-off call. For a moment he stood, and then, again for the second time, gazed in the direction of Nemi. He now knew the source, had dreamed a dream and seen the Old One, who was also the key. He himself knew that the moment was approaching, he could sense it, but for all his efforts had not been able to discover the specific when and where. He breathed a few words in his native Tz'utujil tongue, and walked slowly back to Dolorita, who was smoking tranquilly and now looked at him trustingly.

"You want revenge?" he asked, sitting beside her again, his slanted black eyes holding her gaze.

A sudden flare of avid hope illuminated her dark eyes. "That is why I am here," she replied. "Tell me what I must do …"

14 MONDAY 10TH AUGUST

At six o'clock the sun was already flooding the dry countryside to the east, but the valley still lay in the cool protecting shadows of its north-western slopes. In the village of Nemi people were awake and about the business of the day, watering their geraniums, sweeping and washing floors, and even cooking sauce to go with the lunchtime pasta, since it would be too hot to do much after 9.00. The sky, now a delicate blue with a hint of rose, would become a blinding cloudless azure, the azure that looked so tempting in holiday brochures but that made shade and inactivity much more tempting in the real world.

The lake lay calm in the early morning, the reeds fringing its shores motionless in the still air. In the

Museum of Roman Ships, a cleaning lady – her days were Mondays, Wednesdays and Fridays – was carefully wiping down the glass of a display cabinet, one holding a collection of votive offerings, and as she wiped she glanced inside at the clay representation of a womb and sighed; her daughter was trying to get pregnant, so far with little success, which was a shame – she loved children so much, could not wait to have one of her own. It was the Pill, thought the cleaning lady, though she couldn't be entirely sure her daughter had taken it; no confidences had been exchanged. Useful when you didn't want children, thought the cleaning lady, but it probably upset the body, gave it bad habits. With a last critical look at the corners – that was where smears could go unnoticed – she walked over to the cordoned-off culvert of the Roman road, and saw that someone – probably a child, but the adults were just as bad – had thrown a sweet wrapper down there. Walking to the end, she unhooked the rope and went down the shallow steps, cleaning rag still in one hand. The wrapper had come to rest between two of the large stones edging the road, and she bent down to retrieve it, and then – since one stone looked so flat and comfortable, she sat down. She had swept the road the Friday before but now she ran her rag over the edging stones beside her, and then leaned forward to dust one or two of the massive flagstones of the road itself. Ah, my daughter ... she thought, looking along the road as it ran towards the huge glass window and emerged outside to continue on its way, she would be such a *good* mother too.

The empty spaces of the museum were cool and dim and quiet about her, and as she sat and mused, she felt more cheerful. It will be all right, she thought with complete certainty. Yes, everything will be well. She smiled, got up briskly, went back up the shallow steps and gently replaced the rope. It was time for her coffee with Alfredo; he would have finished in the gardens now.

After breakfast at the *agriturismo* George didn't know what to do with himself; he was just ... waiting, at a loose end. He thought of phoning Jane but did not really feel he could 'presume' (this was his word); they had only met twice, once at lunch in Nemi, and again on Saturday when they had gone to the sanctuary together. A very nice girl, he thought, but from the way she had looked at the professor absolutely convinced and absolutely loyal, and what George would have liked – though he wouldn't have couched it in the same terms – was to have some kind of reassuring man-to-man talk, involving much head-shaking and humming and haa-ing, which would have served to let off steam while not compromising his promise to the professor. Gabriel he did not trust, even though he was sure that the man would have worked his magic as he had when George first met him ("Knows how to talk to a chap," as George put it), and Theo ... Well, since George had passed on that he himself was not 'the one' and it was between

Theo or Gabriel, Theo had seemed different. The day before he had stayed glued to the computer after George, feeling uncomfortably hot and cramped in the stuffy office, went off to take a shower, and was now clearing the tables of their breakfast debris with a preoccupied expression ("moony look" were George's words). He gave Theo a half-wave as he got up from the table, and Theo gave a wave back but made no move to come over, disappearing into the kitchen with a tray of cups, and passing Massimo on the way.

"Engineer George!" Massimo called cheerfully as he walked over. "All OK? You have found what you wanted on the computer?"

George gave a half-guilty start and smiled sheepishly. "Yes ... uh ... thanks. Bits and pieces ... uh ... info, you know?" And then, with sudden inspiration: "The museum down the road there, thought I might go there today ... uh ... and Theo ... giving me a hand." He floundered to a halt while Massimo reflected that Engineer George was a very bad liar but it was none of his business anyway. (Curious, Massimo had in fact looked at the computer after Theo left, but the trail began and ended with Wikipedia). He grinned at George. "You are lucky – it is open all days."

"Thanks, Massimo. Uh ... See you later." And George escaped, thinking that actually it wasn't a bad idea, going to the museum; it would give him something to do. Massimo gazed after the tall lanky figure in the big khaki shorts, and then, as he picked up a coffee pot to take back to the kitchen, glanced down at his arm, where a dark bruise showed from his fall. He shook his head in wonder – he had been extremely lucky.

It was a mystery why Principessa had shied and stumbled for nothing had seemed out of the ordinary; one moment Massimo was in the saddle, the next flying over the mare's shoulder. When he sat up, shaken and with the breath knocked out of him, he saw he had only just missed falling across the jagged edge of a massive slab of stone protruding from the dry earth; another half-metre and he would have landed squarely on the lethal-looking ridge. "*Madonna! Che culo!*" he breathed, already aware that it was the kind of luck that he could never recount to his family; his mother would then worry herself into a state every time he saddled up.

Apart from his injured arm, which was not after all serious, the fall had had an unexpected consequence: it brought into focus the feeling that this year there was something different in the valley's summer atmosphere. The *agriturismo* was doing well, the visitors were the usual collection of Italians, both families and young couples, and a few foreigners. Now he thought of it, it was the foreigners who were different: the two who had come down from Rome, the nice girl who asked him about his arm, the man with her, the *signora* Allberry, Theo and Engineer George with their computer search. The foreigners – yes, the foreigners were different.

In George's case, Massimo felt – not guilty exactly but a little less than comfortable. He liked George, was charmed and amused at his road-and-aqueduct tour, another example of the endless eccentricity of the English, but had omitted to mention that there was a fine example of a Roman road, part of the Via Virbia in fact, on the land owned by the *agriturismo*.

The omission was not in any way a conscious decision. As a child, Massimo had been repeatedly warned away from the ruins and when the predictable desire to explore led to an unpleasant episode the warnings became real. Scrambling through the remains of some sort of circular structure, he suddenly found himself lost and alone. He could see the roof of the *agriturismo* in the distance but it seemed to belong to another world and one that was lost to him. The impression had been brief – he blinked and all was as before – but its effects were long-lasting. He did not even remember the incident now, but something remained: he avoided anything connected with the ruins, and that included the road.

George, blissfully unaware that he was such a bad liar, even congratulating himself on his quick thinking, went back to his chalet, collected his rucksack, and began filling his water bottle from the bottle of mineral water he kept in his room. The prosaic act of preparation for the morning ahead prompted him to start thinking of what preparations might be needed on the evening of the 13th. Sunset meant midges, and the wood meant brambles, and evening – what time did it get dark? About 9.00? 9.30? – meant torches. List, he thought. Check what stuff I need. Check what stuff *we* need, he corrected himself. I'll ask Theo what he thinks as well.

From the shadows of the *agriturismo*'s entrance hall Theo saw him go, and heaved a sigh of relief; for the moment he did not want to discuss the coming Thursday night with George, who would not be a main player in the battle; he wanted to get it straight in his own mind first. George was now driving out of the car park, and as Theo returned to his table-clearing outside, he wondered fleetingly why the malign spirit had appeared to him and not Theo himself, for of the two of them he reckoned he was more open to the mystic part of life. But then, his own vision – of the torchlit procession on the Via Virbia, the singing of white-robed women leading huge sleek hunting dogs – had been a manifestation of the sanctuary itself, with no alien presence contaminating the sacred moment. Theo shook his head, went on with his stacking and clearing. Anyway, he thought, George is certainly good back-up, and *reliable*. Theo was not aware that he was unconsciously comparing George with Gabriel Todd, whom Theo had not taken to at all.

After his three-minute drive George was just manoeuvring into a space in the dusty layby opposite the gates of the museum, where he locked the car, crossed the road, and was soon ducking his head to avoid the low lintel of the ticket office door. A stout Italian woman was just coming out, head turned to call back: "*Ciao, Alfredo! Ci vediamo mercoledì. Buona giornata.*" George sidestepped, but even so, she backed into him, then laughed like a young girl and – still laughing – apologised, patting him on the arm as if she knew him and was pleased to see him. Cheerful sort, he thought, obscurely cheered himself by the encounter. Now, let's see what's what here …

Lena, lying on her bed at the nursing home, was seriously concerned. She had phoned Jane's number at intervals on Sunday without success, and she was also remembering that Gabriel Todd had told her of Jane's flat being broken into and two men asking about her. I did not heed the implications of that, she thought; if Mrs Pleiades had discovered Jane's involvement – Achille's killers could not have been far behind him that night – she may have seen Jane as a threat to the triumph of the false Virbius in the enactment of the ritual. If that were the case, Jane had been in very real danger from the beginning, and Lena, intent on enlisting the aid of George, Theo and Gabriel Todd, had overlooked the fact. Lena closed her eyes, suddenly feeling weak and frail; Jane may already be dead, and it would be Lena's fault, Lena's lack of foresight. She raised a hand to her eyes, pressed her eyelids with finger and thumb, and felt the cool wetness of tears damping her skin.

The fact was that her years of experience had failed to prepare Lena for the painful reality that the battle would involve people who did not possess her belief and commitment. "Innocents", as she thought of them. It was different for her and the others, it was their life's work: the ten years of training, the ten years of service, the last ten of teaching, and, in their case, of holding the trust.

So it had been in the round temple in the Roman Forum, although other usages had changed over the centuries. With the final triumph of Christianity, the Vestals took refuge in the Alban Hills, returning to the original home of the first Latin tribes. The virgin Vesta and the huntress Diana fused into Diana Nemorensis, and those who swore to honour her were women not children, for knowledge and free will were fundamental to their power.

There were still seven of them, and Lena was the first to be called upon to act. The others, at Delphi, Cuma, Tibur, Lanuvium, Satricum and Lavinium – to give them their ancient names – had done as she had done, watching and waiting, since none of them knew where the cycle would begin. It was only known that it *would* begin at one of the seven sacred sites, and once begun would continue at two others, the mystical three that would bring past and present into harmony and protect humanity from what was to come.

Throughout the years the seven had been discreet, doing nothing to draw attention to themselves, safeguarding the ancient prophecies – which were often a mere sentence or fragment - and holding themselves ready.

Lena, as 'the first among equals' – it amused her to use Christian terminology – had done more. She suspected that Nemi would be the first, the bridge uniting Greece and Rome, the link between east and west. Her counterpart at Delphi already knew of the link and agreed when Lena suggested she herself should also keep close watch on the situation, hence the employment of Achille; poor Achille.

She sighed. Nemi as the first of the three was the most important. If they failed here the other two would be compromised, perhaps completely drained of their power. She opened her eyes, got off the bed with some difficulty and crossed to the window, where she looked across at the sanctuary and woods as if in challenge. Her vivid eyes grew hard and gemlike. No, she must not think of failure, and she must not think of Jane.

Slowly she crossed the room again, fumbled her mobile phone from the bedside table, and sat on the side of the high bed. Now, she dialled Gabriel Todd's number, and listened intently as a far-off ringing tone was replaced by a similar message to the one on Jane's phone. The number was "unreachable"; "invited to call back later". Her face thoughtful, Lena gently closed the phone and replaced it on the bedside table.

Jane was just waking up to find that both hangover and nausea had loosed their grip, though her side ached from being punched. Being so sick had proved a winning – if not deliberate – strategy. Varian giggled but Mrs Pleiades was almost comically astonished, and David Levant was a veritable death's head of revulsion and outrage. Faced with such a prosaic human occurrence, both felt at a disadvantage. Jane was bundled upstairs and locked in one of the spare guest-rooms, where she bathed her face, drank huge quantities of water and – despite everything – fell asleep on the bed.

Now it was Monday morning and the temporary respite was over. At least she no longer felt ill and could start to put her strategy, such as it was, into action. Years of greedy though shame-faced reading of popular novels, had given Jane – in theory at least – the means to deal with her present predicament. She remembered gems from Modesty Blaise like "starve the imagination", "take note of anything at all that may be useful" and "wait for an opportunity to act". I must add "be sick all over your kidnapper's shoes," she thought. Modesty Blaise never thought of *that* one.

It was an early John Le Carré spy story, however, that had given her the best idea. The truth must be hidden under layers of parts of truth; they did not know her and could not judge what the real person was or how much she knew, the less revealed the better. She must try and protect the others, especially Professor Caseman, who was elderly and vulnerable – no, more, she must forget she had ever met the professor.

So the Jane facing Mrs Pleiades in the brocaded drawing room was coarser and less intelligent than the real Jane. Protest and tears then falling over herself to answer their questions. The two men she had been with in Genzano were Gabriel Todd and George Sutton. Yeah, she and Gabriel had come down to see George, some old friend of Gabriel's who was OK but boring (Sorry, George, flickered the thought, immediately repressed). How did she know Gabriel? In Rome, you know, foreigners always meet up somehow, in a bar, a mutual friend, couldn't remember now. He was a weird guy, just an acquaintance really but he took her out for meals at nice places.

"When can I have her?" whined Varian, who was getting bored with all the talk. He had never had a woman to practise on and was becoming impatient.

"Hush, dear one, not long now." Mrs Pleiades said soothingly. Jane felt faint, wondered if they had believed her. She was sure they were involved with the story of the Sacred Wood, and sure that it was they who had killed the poor man in Trastevere. She was desperately frightened, the back of her neck tingling with the awareness of David Levant's eager presence behind her.

Mrs Pleiades turned her intention back towards Jane. "Gabriel Todd. 'A weird guy', you say. But I know you spent the night together." Her eyes were veiled, her tone non-committal but the atmosphere in the room became taut and watchful.

Memories of Gabriel crowded into Jane's mind. "I don't want this," she had said and he had got up and slept on the couch. Tears came into her eyes and spilled over. Mrs Pleiades sighed with pleasure.

"Ah ... and I wonder if he feels the same."

"I don't know," whispered Jane.

"Can I have her now? You said not long," complained Varian.

Mrs Pleiades thought, drummed her crimson nails and then decided. "No, dear one. There's still the nice dog you haven't started on. David, put our guest back in her room, will you?"

With the knowledge that Mrs Pleiades had decided not to let Varian "have her", Jane's legs almost folded under her with delayed horror. David Levant took her by the arm, a touch that made her flesh crawl with revulsion, and led her back upstairs to be locked in the guest room again. Once the door closed she did collapse, sitting on the bed and weeping until she managed to pull herself together and go to the en-suite bathroom to splash her face with cold water. She could see no glimmer of hope until she remembered her bag falling to the ground and the shout of the tourist. Some trace had been left of what happened. She prayed that the two tourists had done the right thing and gone to the police. Do the right thing and go to the police, she thought wryly. That was how it had all started.

Much later, a tray was pushed through the door holding an omelette with salad, some bread and a jug of water but she barely touched it. Sounds coming from somewhere behind the house, though deadened by the close-fitting windows, had made her head jerk up. When she opened the window, the terrible screaming howls, though faint and muffled, made her stomach churn with pity, revulsion, and anger. She took refuge in the shower, where the drumming water drowned out the sounds while she slumped against the shower wall sobbing. If I could kill them, she thought, squash them like the loathsome bugs they are, wipe them off the face of the earth. Just give me the chance, she prayed, just give me the chance.

15 TUESDAY 11ᵀᴴ AUGUST

The strange alliance of the gardener Byron Escobar, and the trained maid Dolorita Morales was born prosaically enough in their shared cigarettes in a sunken patio behind the rented villa. He sensed the grief and darkness in her, and like Maximón, the man in black sitting at a crossroads on the makeshift altar, had taken her to him. They were two strangers, two foreigners, who found comfort and solace first in the shared cigarettes smoked in silence, and then, when they were lovers, in the discovery that each had a task, each had a mission.

For Dolorita, nearly six years in Mrs Pleiades employ, her mission was simple – kill the woman responsible for her son's disappearance and probable death: Mrs Pleiades. Had not her son, her only son, entered a club in Marseilles and never emerged again? He had entered, Mrs Pleiades had entered, David Levant had entered, and only these last two left again.

Dolorita had watched the security tapes numerous times, especially the very last glimpse of her son. He drained his glass, strong throat gleaming as he swallowed, then turned, face alight with expectation and – yes – complacency, before he left the lighted circle of the bar, his tall figure melting away into the smoke and shadows, never to be glimpsed again.

And so Dolorita's quest – and then her mission – began, but had not proceeded as she imagined. To her linear mind, there were two parts to the task, the first – become Mrs Pleiades' maid, which would be difficult, the second – kill her, which would be simple once she had access to the woman's private life. One followed by two, difficult followed by simple.

But while the first had indeed been difficult, taking all of Dolorita's ingenuity, resilience, and remaining money, the second part, which she had taken for granted, turned out quite differently.

She added arsenic in ever-increasing amounts to Mrs Pleiades' strong morning coffee, but waited in vain for signs of headaches or confusion, the promised first symptoms, while of the later fatal final signs of vomiting and convulsions, nothing was to be seen; the only change seemed to be a heightening of Mrs Pleiades' fashionable pallor.

Arsenic was not enough then, concluded Dolorita darkly, and she turned to cyanide, which should have been immediate – coma with seizures, followed by cardiac arrest. Nothing, a result that now gave her serious pause. Reluctantly, though with no deep inner surprise, she concluded that Mrs Pleiades possessed inhuman characteristics and could not be killed.

Dolorita possessed her soul in patience, watching and waiting. Knowledge was power, and the more she knew, the more likelihood there was that some opportunity might arise, which finally did arise in the form of the Guatemalan gardener, Byron Escobar. "You want revenge?" he had asked, and she had replied, "That is why I am here. Tell me what I must do …"

His instructions were simple but involved very real practical problems. When could she leave the villa for a half-day? How should she get to Nemi, not even the village of Nemi but a clinic in the valley of the lake? Would she be able to gain entrance to speak to the old woman? And she had no name for the woman, only a detailed description of her physical appearance.

Dolorita had not come so far as to be deterred by lesser complications, and dealt with each in order. She had one day off every week, not a full day but one that ran from 10.00 in the morning until 6.00 in the evening, but she could decide on any day providing she gave 24 hours' notice. On Sunday evening she arranged to take the Tuesday, and was ready to murmur something about shopping in Genzano if asked; it was of course unnecessary since Mrs Pleiades was superbly uninterested – what did she care what banal plans the hired help had in mind?

For the journey Dolorita consulted the yellow pages for local taxi services, and booked a car, which would pick her up in the town of Genzano. As for the problems of gaining entrance and finding the old woman, she would have to trust to determination and luck; it was with the dark glow in her intense eyes that she looked out from the taxi as it carried her down the long slope into the waiting valley.

At the nursing home it was coffee time, and Lena and Barbara were sitting in the shade on the terrace, each with a cappuccino on the white metal table in front of them. Barbara was regarding her friend with an expression of blank dismay on her homely face:

"Neither of them, Lena?" she was asking. "Since when?"

"Sunday," admitted Lena. "I did not tell you yesterday for fear of worrying you but now, with only two days left, I am … seriously concerned."

Barbara leaned back, hands mindlessly smoothing the folds of her voluminous blue skirt; this was where Lena's feyness had led, no longer a harmless obsession with airy-fairy legends, but something that had put that nice girl Jane at risk. Barbara did not consider Gabriel at all, she was sure the 'difficult bugger' could look after himself, and he's probably buggered off, she thought grimly, also irritated by the realization she had spilt some of her breakfast tea on her skirt and hadn't even noticed.

She looked over at Lena again; she had never seen her look so frail and gaunt, though the vivid eyes gazing towards the sanctuary were as indomitable as ever. Barbara rallied and sat up straight again: "We should call the police, Lena," she said briskly. "I mean, an English girl goes missing in a foreign country – that's the point. Never mind all the rest of it."

Lena pressed her hands together; she should have guessed that Barbara would react as though she were in England, and in England you went to the police. Even as she was considering how to reply, she saw Barbara glance up and past her as a woman's soft foreign voice asked tentatively, "Professor Caseman?"

Lena turned, wincing a little, and looked up to see a thin dark young woman gazing down at her with intense eyes: "Yes? Can I help you?"

Dolorita Morales sighed with relief for the voice was low and encouraging; this then was the old woman. "I ... have a message for you, an important message."

Lena became all attention, and Barbara too, though for quite different reasons. In the light of

Jane's disappearance, Barbara was alert for anything that might threaten Lena, and now standing up, moved with a swiftness that belied her bulk to put her stout figure between her friend and the foreign woman. "And just who may you be to bother the professor?" she said belligerently. "Come on now! State your business!"

Dolorita was taken aback at being challenged by a fat old woman; if she had possessed a sense of humour, she would have laughed at the idea of a bodyguard in a voluminous tea-stained skirt, but she did not. She darted round Barbara and kneeled beside Lena. "Please listen. You are an Old One – the time is coming but he cannot know when. If I could just explain …"

Barbara looked as if she was going to shout for help, and Lena reached up to catch her hand, wincing as she closed her swollen fingers around Barbara's wrist. "Barbara, wait. This young woman could help us."

Barbara closed her mouth – she had indeed been going to start shouting, and reluctantly went to sit down again. Lena gestured at a chair. "Please sit down, and tell me your message," she said encouragingly.

In her service flat in Trastevere, Adelpha Manousakis was also pleading, speaking rapidly and vehemently into her mobile phone, fingers drumming on the Formica top of the kitchenette's work service, eyes gazing unseeingly at the mess of unwashed coffee cups and sandwich wrappers littering the surface; she would have preferred a face-to-face encounter but had only the scribbled phone number as a means of contact. When she had first phoned and found an answering machine, she quickly hung up, for she wanted to plan what she would say. Enough to arouse curiosity, enough to communicate the urgency. She had left the same message every day since Sunday, the last time that very morning.

This – finally – was the response, but the silence at the other end of the line after the first abrupt, "Tell me", had been disconcerting; she had expected either cold disbelief or immediate outrage. Initially she spoke in English and then, as she lost herself in explanations and repetitions, unconsciously switched to Greek. In her heart of hearts she disliked English, it muted and subtly ridiculed concepts that would be clear and strong in her own language, so that though the words "betrayal" and "murder" were the literal translation, they could not compare with προδοσία and δολοφονία containing as they did the echoes of ancient wrongs.

Finally her torrent of words faltered and stopped. She fell silent, now aware that there was nothing left to say." Σας ικετεύω," she said quietly. "Για τον αδελφό μου – για τον πατέρα σου πολύ."

By half past eleven the clinic clock was just striking the half hour, and Dolorita had delivered her message, prompted and encouraged by Lena, glowered at by Barbara, who was now sitting up, her face red and uncompromising to protest: "If you think the professor is going to ..."

"No, it's all right Barbara," said Lena; she thought for a moment; the gardens were almost empty now as people sought shelter from the impending midday heat. Dolorita waited in silence, the only sign of her tension showing in her tightly clasped hands. Barbara too waited, knowing that whatever Lena decided she would carry through, no matter what Barbara thought.

When Lena finally spoke it was as though she was speaking to herself. "I have been remiss," she said quietly, "even guilty of being overly ... parochial. Of course there are larger issues, more universal considerations." She paused, smiled reassuringly at Dolorita, who had understood neither 'remiss', nor 'parochial' nor 'issues', and was frowning in perplexity. "I will meet with Byron Escobar," Lena told her, and Dolorita's brow cleared; that was all she wanted to understand. "And if he cannot come here, we will find a place."

"He has a place," said Dolorita quickly. "It is near; he says you will know it too. Here ..." and she fumbled in the pocket of her skirt and brought out a crumpled slip of paper, which she handed to Lena.

Lena, carefully placing her spectacles on her nose, looked at the few words and smiled: "Yes," she said simply. "I know it. And at four o'clock tomorrow afternoon, he has written."

"Yes. Inside." And then, with a sudden burst of emotion, "I cannot come. I am the woman's maid and she must not suspect, but promise me ... I must be there when it is time. I must be there to see for myself. Do you understand, Professor Caseman?"

"Yes, Signora Morales," replied Lena gently. "I understand, and I promise you that you will not be excluded, that you will have justice."

Dolorita nodded, relieved, and then glanced at her small wristwatch. "I must go now. But you will tell Byron Escobar so that he may tell me?"

"Yes, I will," promised Lena, and leant back as Dolorita nodded, rose and walked off.

Barbara watched the thin figure disappear round the corner of the clinic towards the car park, and then squared her jaw. "Lena!" she said, returning to the attack. "What about Jane?"

Lena's gaze was serious: "Barbara, you remember I mentioned a woman called Mrs Pleiades as being involved in the murder of Achille?" Barbara nodded. "And she is probably also responsible for Jane's disappearance. Now, our visitor Signora Morales did not refer to her by name but she is Mrs Pleiades' maid."

"So why didn't you ask her about Jane?" exclaimed Barbara, who had the feeling she was the only one looking out for Jane's interests. And did George Sutton and Theo whatisname even *know* about the girl's disappearance?

"Because I do not know Signora Morales. For all I know it could be a trap. If I have knowledge of Mrs Pleiades, she may have knowledge of me. I could not take the risk."

Barbara was now looking at her old friend with dawning understanding, closely followed by respect. Lena might be fey, she was thinking, but she thought this one through all right.

"If, on the other hand, Signora Morales is who she says she is," Lena went on, "and Byron Escobar is what I think he is," – she gently stressed the 'what' – "then I will discover more tomorrow, including whether Jane is in the hands of Mrs Pleiades." And whether she is alive, Lena added to herself; she was not sure whether Barbara's concern had reached its logical conclusion, but if it had not … well, there are some things left better unsaid.

For a moment both fell silent. "So, anyway," said Barbara with an air of changing the subject; she had apparently accepted Lena's reasoning. "You're going to meet this …whatever he is?"

Now Lena smiled the impish smile, "Yes, my dear, I am, but I will book Alfredo and he will wait for me, and I would very much appreciate it if you could accompany me as well."

Barbara blew out her cheeks in a relieved 'whuff'; she had feared Lena was going to go haring off on her own. "Wild horses couldn't keep me away!" she retorted. "Someone has to remind you you're not twenty anymore!"

For the first time in two days Lena laughed outright; for all her inner strength and single-mindedness she was secretly relieved that she was not alone. "And now, my dear friend," she said gaily, "lunch is probably waiting, so shall we go?"

"And about time," said Barbara robustly. She came round the table to give Lena a hand in getting up. "In your room or with the oldies?"

"Now that is unkind," Lena chided, as she got stiffly to her feet, but she was smiling. "Since you and I are officially oldies too, but, as you ask, in my room. It is cooler there."

She had started walking slowly along the terrace towards the main entrance, Barbara keeping a sharp eye on her in case she lost her balance, when she stopped.

"Lena, do you feel all right? This heat is terrible …"

Lena turned to her. "No, sorry, Barbara, I am fine." She started walking again. "It just occurred to me that I should try Gabriel Todd's number again. Just to be sure …" She ignored Barbara's mutter.

For years Gabriel Todd had possessed two mobile phones, one 'public' and one 'private', sometimes adding a third for particular situations. It was the number of the public one he had written down for

Lena and the others, and the public one he had switched off as soon as he arrived in Rome after meeting with her; he had not switched it on again since, and had considered ditching it altogether now he was leaving.

The Wednesday morning saw him closing the door of the borrowed flat to go to the *Aeroporto Leonardo da Vinci*, better known as Fiumicino airport; he had a rucksack slung over one shoulder, and had tucked his passport into a side pocket. It was not the first time the rucksack and the passport had been gathered up as Gabriel left wherever he no longer wanted to be, or, in Barbara's words, "buggered off".

He was leaving much earlier than necessary since the flight to Athens would not leave until the evening, but he preferred to hang around the airport rather than in Rome. Normally he would have taken a taxi, but with so much time to spare he had decided to take public transport, walking to Largo Argentina for a bus to the main station.

Emerging from one of the side streets west of Campo de' Fiori, he walked across the piazza, past the van of the *Unità Mobile di Soccorso*, past the austere figure of Giordano Bruno, and past the fountain of water still flowing endlessly into the grill-covered drain. He did not look towards the bar where Jane and he had sat but crossed the piazza, skirting the stall hung about with flashing jewellery and trinkets, and made for the road that would take him to Largo Argentina, where nearly every bus that stopped was going to or past the station.

There was little traffic in Largo Argentina but quite a few tourists, many of whom were leaning on the rail to look down into the large sunken area in the middle of the square. The area, some 12 feet below street level, held the remains of four Roman temples that had been excavated and their broken columns reassembled; one of them was dedicated to the goddess Fortune, the huge head of which George had admired in the generating station. The bus stop was beyond Largo Argentina, and a bus arrived immediately, a 64, on its way back from Vatican City. Gabriel swung aboard, and sat at the back, rucksack wedged beside him, and watched as reference points flowed past: the dark wide canyon of Via delle Botteghe Oscure, the blinding glare of the white-marble monument in Piazza Venezia, the high brick walls of Trajan's Forum, and the fragment of Servian Wall set on a small grassed island. From here a sharp right took the bus into Via Nazionale that ran straight up towards the station, past the imposing façade of the Bank of Italy, past small fashion shops and a couple of abandoned-looking theatres, past the massy bulk of the Exhibition Centre, and at the top the sprays and waters of the Fountain of the Naiads in Piazza della Repubblica.

The bus reached the end of the line, and Gabriel collected his rucksack and walked into the station, which was dense with travellers – foreign tourists arriving to see Rome and Italians leaving for the holiday weekend; *Ferragosto* was only a few days away now.

Coffee, a ticket bought at a kiosk, a long walk down the platform for the shuttle train to Fiumicino, and Gabriel Todd was on his way.

16 WEDNESDAY 12TH AUGUST

Alfredo, the proud owner of the battered Mercedes that carried Barbara and Lena on their gentle trips around the area, was only too pleased to escort the two ladies that day. And when he discovered that their destination was The Museum of Roman Ships, where he also 'rounded out' his income by looking after the gardens, he was even more pleased; while his clients were inside he would be able to sit and have coffee and exchange news with the daytime staff, whom he knew but seldom saw.

"Long time you not visit there, eh, *professoressa*?" he commented jovially as he tucked Lena carefully into the back of the large car. Barbara was striding round to the other back door, determinedly clutching her sensible large bag, heavy with the weight of a brick; she hadn't been able to find anything else that could be classed as a weapon. "Big changes," Alfredo continued. "Now we have *congressi*, days of study, also music."

"How very nice," said Lena approvingly, genuinely pleased that the empty spaces were being given new life. "And you are right, Alfredo. It has been a very long time since I was at the museum. But today I am meeting a professor from South America, who is interested in the site. And I am happy to help."

"Ah," nodded Alfredo, obscurely relieved that there was an explanation for the unusual outing; he gently closed the car door, and went round to the driver's seat. "*Questi studiosi,*" he would say to the daytime staff. "*Veramente internazionali. Ecco cosa manca a noi italiani!*" And they would agree that they were not very international, that perhaps yes, it was a lack but that ... well, we are what we are.

And now Alfredo decided on an additional treat for his ladies – they would pay no entrance fee, and neither would the foreign professor! Foreign scholars must be treated with all the respect they merited. He was beaming as he started out on the short journey down the slope into the valley, along the lakeside road, and was still beaming as he parked as near to the entrance gate as possible so that Lena would not have to walk very far. The small man already standing by the ticket office must be the foreign professor, obviously a real professor since the jacket of his grey suit was crumpled and creased, and the trousers too long in the leg. As for the tie …!

"Enter! Enter!" he ordered boisterously. "No tickets! Not for *professori*."

Barbara, holding on tight to her heavy bag, felt she was there under false pretences. Her, a professor! And looking at the small stocky man with the swarthy face, (what was his name? Byron something. Ridiculous!), she wondered that anyone else would believe he was a professor either.

But Lena, vivid green eyes alight, smiled up the big beaming man, saying, "You are too good, Alfredo, too kind." And Byron Escobar, who had been eyeing the frail figure with critical and slightly suspicious attention, suddenly recognized that here too was power, a gentler power, a more … 'civilised' power, but in essence as strong as his own.

Lena turned to him now, and regarded him gravely, giving a small nod of greeting that could also have been a gesture of homage. "It is such a pleasure to meet you, professor," she said. "If you could give me your arm? Thank you so much." And she smiled the same luminous smile, which now held complicity and enjoyment. Byron Escobar found himself smiling back, revealing his sharp tobacco-stained teeth, but fortunately Alfredo had already turned away, and it was only Barbara who saw the transformation, thinking in horror, Lord, preserve us! A villain if not a head-hunter! But there was the villain and head-hunter holding out

The Sacred Wood

his arm for Lena, and then walking, as Barbara herself did, ever so slightly behind Lena, so that she could set her own pace. The three made their way slowly up the ramp into the cool airy interior of the museum.

Between the two exhibition halls there was a low-ceilinged area that was used for conferences and "days of study"; there was a large table for the speakers and a dozen or so chairs in front, which were usually set in rows but were now pushed haphazardly here and there. It was in this space that Lena and Byron Escobar sat down, while Barbara grudgingly moved away to walk around the museum; it had taken all of Lena's tact and diplomacy to persuade her friend to agree to this, but felt that Barbara might be overly protective and even jeopardise the meeting.

For a few minutes neither of the two spoke. Byron Escobar sat at his ease, still and upright, dark square-tipped fingers resting on his knees, and as he sat, he saw and heard the echoes of the past, and there were many: darkness, and then leaping flames, the terrified screams of women and children, the crash of burning wood, while men in uniform ran through the night, and there, just glimpsed, the woman he called 'The Mask' – for such she was – watching the destruction, watching the burning, and laughing with triumphant malice.

Lena sat quietly and waited. When she had said she had been 'remiss' and parochial' she meant that she had been guilty of considering the coming battle only in European terms. It was the first of three, "the mystical three that would bring past and present into harmony and protect humanity from what was to come", as she herself described it, but now the words sounded too glib to her; she had limited her understanding of "humanity." So now she waited for this man from another world and another reality to instruct her, for Lena, like all good teachers, was also willing to learn. She saw that for the moment Byron Escobar was absorbed in his thoughts, though she could not imagine the content of those thoughts. From where she was sitting she could look across at the exhibition on the Roman ships, and for an instant, just as Byron Escobar breathed deeply, and the focus returned to his eyes, she seemed to smell the acrid smell of smoke, and then it was gone, just as suddenly.

"The time is coming and the long cycle is ending," he said simply. "A crossroads. You know."

"Yes," agreed Lena, equally simply.

"In my land, my lake, Lake Atitlán is a centre of power in time and space. Here, in your land, this lake is also a centre."

"Yes." The museum was quiet about them, the few visitors walking and talking softly among the statues and display cases, the bright afternoon pressing at the window panes.

"But this lake has an evil spirit. It comes and goes, menaces the centre." He paused. "This is my work here: to watch, as you watch, and to make this spirit remain. But the destruction of this spirit is *your* work. I can only hold it here, make it remain so that it cannot go and then come again."

"I understand," Lena said. "What must be done?"

"When is the time?"

"Tomorrow evening."

"At sunset I will hold the spirit. I will not be there but I will hold the spirit."

Lena nodded. The two sat in silence, and then Lena said softly, "There is a young woman, a friend, who has disappeared, and I suspect ... your employer." Her tone was neutral, slightly questioning, and she gave no sign of her inner concern.

Byron Escobar regarded her, the flat planes of his face dark in the shadows of the low ceiling, and then said, "She is there. They hold her ... to barter. But she is well."

"Thank you. She is the one who has made this possible."

He began to rise, and Lena remembered her promise to Dolorita: "One thing," she said. He paused, turned back towards her. Barbara, who had been keeping watch from behind a large block sculpted into a ship with rowers, seeing him rise and taking a step towards Lena, began to hurry towards them. "Signora Morales," explained Lena. "I have promised that she shall be there. She must meet me here, outside the museum in the road at seven."

Byron Escobar again regarded her silently, finally said: "I will tell her," just as Barbara, one hand in her bag, arrived in the conference area, and was relieved to see that they were merely talking and that apparently the villain and head-hunter was about to go. He crossed to Lena, bent to take one of her hands, raised it to touch his forehead, and then turned to Barbara, giving her the sharp-toothed terrifying smile. "You are good friend," he said, still grinning, "but too old to carry stone!" And with that he was gone.

Lena looked at Barbara interrogatively. "Stone?" she asked. Barbara's homely face flushed red and she guiltily exhibited her brick. "Oh, my dear!" exclaimed Lena, laughing. "My gallant dear!"

George was sitting in his chalet making a list of necessities for the following day, not because he thought he would forget anything but because it gave him something to do. His visit to The Museum of Roman Ships had only served to increase his sense of unreality – half of it was dedicated to the ships and their salvage – historical, technical matters – but the other half dealt with the sanctuary and its legends: engineering on the one hand, myths and deities on the other. Unlike Theo, his Italian was only good enough for basic day-to-day communication, and since all the information was in Italian, he ended up looking at a collection of objects with no context, and could only hazard a guess about ways and means from the pictures. Demoted back to the nursery, he reflected gloomily.

It did not help when he unexpectedly came upon the tract of the excavated Roman road emerging from the modern floor as it ran towards the huge glass windowpane and then, grassy and weathered, continued on its way outside the building. He peered down at it, thinking disjointedly, Via Virbia, from Virbius, twice-born, Greek man, then Roman god or however it went. Not my thing at all. Very quietly he backed away from the edge as if it could hear him; he didn't want to find himself catapulted into the past, as Theo had been; his own encounter with the mad woman had been enough for him.

That did it. As quickly as he could without actually breaking into a trot, George left the museum and went back to the *agriturismo*, where he now was, and despite all his misgivings, all his sense of being in some strange dream-world, making a list of practical needs:

long trousers

anti-mosquito stuff

torch(es)?

water

He stopped. It didn't look much at all. Should he add sticking plasters? Should he add a *weapon* of some kind? But if he were thinking in terms of weapons, weren't sticking plasters a little ... too little? Bandages then, perhaps? Rope?

He decided he was in danger of disappearing up his own whatsit, and should keep it simple. Suitable clothes, yes, but he could put on the mosquito stuff when he was getting dressed – no need to carry it. A torch and a bottle of water, a couple of sticking plasters (brambles) that could be shoved in his pocket, and leave the idea of a weapon: he would be looking after the professor, and Theo and Gabriel would be there to look after the rest.

It was just then that his mobile phone rang. It was Professor Caseman.

"Mr Sutton, I was wondering if you and Theo could come to the clinic a little later. We need to talk about tomorrow."

"Fine ... uh ... yes. In fact I was just ... uh ... making a list."

"An extremely good idea," replied the professor warmly. "And when we meet, we can be sure that between us we have remembered everything. About six thirty?" she went on.

"Yes, but ... uh, I'm not sure Theo will be able to make it – work and all that."

"Actually," she admitted, "I have already spoken with him since he has time restrictions, but if you bring him in your car, he need – you both need – only be away for about half an hour."

Righty-o," agreed George, and as he hung up, was thinking that not only was the professor a game old girl, but she also had all her wits about her. He put his list in his pocket to take with him, suddenly cheered by the thought that the professor would know if there was anything else in particular.

As Lena hung up, she was thinking approvingly of George as well. Making a list. Of course. She was in her room, lying on the bed and marshalling her thoughts. Jane was safe – for now – and if Mrs Pleiades considered her of value to "barter" with, she would be safe until the battle was over. George Sutton and Theo: they would be there, and she would now have to tell them of Jane's kidnapping so that they would have time to assimilate the changed situation.

Barbara. Well, Barbara had made it quite plain she would not let her friend out of her sight, and at this point, Lena felt in need of as many allies as possible. Of Gabriel Todd there was no sign, and she reluctantly concluded that he had paid lip-service to her request, and rather than remonstrate or disagree, had taken the easy way out and simply disappeared – which was extremely revealing in itself.

Which left Dolorita Morales. Lena would have much preferred she had not insisted on accompanying them, but if she held her employer responsible for her son's death, she had the right to be present. Only ... Lena was not sure whether revenge could form part of the encounter, which was for and of itself and should not be used for personal ends. Could it even be affected – tainted – by the dark passion of Dolorita Morales?

Lena did not know, could only hope and trust that her provisions had been enough. Though she had told George he was "not the one", she now doubted her initial appraisal. The meeting with Byron Escobar had shown her that she did not possess knowledge of the whole; she had not known that the malign spirit was able to "come and go" nor that it had to be "held" if it was to be finally destroyed. She sighed. One thing at a time. The next thing was to see George Sutton and Theo.

Even at 6.30 the heat was too great to sit outside, and she did not want them to see her room with its high bed, bell-pull and bottles of pills; it was too much of an invalid's room and might give them pause. So she went downstairs, and left word at reception that she would be in the public lounge, which lay through an arch to the right of the reception area. The room was exactly like a large hotel lounge, with chairs and couches placed around small tables, and couches set in the recesses of bay windows. It was in one of the recesses that Lena sat down in a high chair, leaving the couch for George and Theo. As she expected they arrived punctually, coming through the arch from the reception area and looking around. She raised one hand and they hurried over.

She spent no time trying to soften the blow, but told them of Jane's kidnapping, using it quite dispassionately to stress the importance of the coming encounter. Both were shocked, but whereas George went white under his tan and was apparently struck speechless, Theo said buoyantly, "Don't worry, professor. We'll win, *and* get Jane back!"

Oh, dear, thought Lena, and could see that George was regarding the young American with British dismay as well.

"As I have said," she said, acknowledging Theo's optimism with a smile, "the only way to help Jane is to go to the grove tomorrow. And remember, the golden bough must be possessed before the encounter may begin. It ..."

George interrupted her, a more telling sign than anything else of the strength of his feelings. "But what about that chap Gabriel?" he asked bluntly; the "uh" had completely disappeared.

"He will not be coming," said the professor crisply. "He has not telephoned, and every time I have telephoned myself, there is only a recorded message that the number is unavailable."

They again looked at her dumbly. George was the first to speak:

"But does he know about Jane? They're supposed to be friends, aren't they?"

Lena's eyes were sad. "Since he is unavailable I have not been able to tell him, and I do not know how else he would know."

"Have you tried texting him?" asked Theo.

"Pardon?" Lena had leant forward.

"Sending him a text message," explained Theo. "If he's switched his phone off rather than it not working, he might switch it on to see if there are any messages."

"I see," said Lena, thinking wryly, And that's the problem with being old, you may think you are keeping up with things but it does not come naturally. "That is an excellent idea, Theo," she said.

"I can do it from my phone now, professor," and Theo took out his phone, quickly pressed several buttons, and then read aloud what he had written: "Jane taken by Pleiades. 13th now more important than ever. Please contact professor."

"Yes," agreed Lena, and Theo sent the message.

There was little else to be said or done. George's list, such as it was, remained in his pocket; he did not even think of it. The half hour was up, and Theo had to get back to help with dinner at the *agriturismo*. Subdued, they took their leave, and Lena, now exhausted by the long day, made her way to the lift to go to her room.

In the rented villa near Genzano Mrs Pleiades told David Levant to bring Jane down from her room to dine with them. Varian was bored and fretful and needed some distraction; he could tell Jane about what he had done to the hired help and the nice dog, and it would soothe him and prime him for the battle ahead.

When Jane arrived in the dining room, a long narrow room lit by an opulent chandelier suspended over the polished table, she saw that

Mrs Pleiades was already seated at the head of the table with Varian on her right. Mrs Pleiades was elegantly dressed in a long greenish-gold evening dress, her bare arms adorned with heavy gold snake bracelets, three on her right arm, two on her left; Varian's blond good looks were thrown into relief by the black shirt and black slacks he was wearing; even his tie was black, though with a dull satin sheen that glinted in the sparkle of the chandelier's pendants.

"Miss Harrison," said Mrs Pleiades in her metallic slightly-accented tones. "So good of you to join us." And she languidly gestured to the empty chair on her left. Reluctantly Jane took her place, reminding herself of her persona – the coarser, less intelligent version of herself – that she had established the first day; she contrived to look nervously admiring of the rich surroundings, and saw from Mrs Pleiades' small smug smile that she had succeeded. David Levant filled her glass with white wine, which Jane resolved not to touch, and took the seat next to her so that she was effectively surrounded on all sides, with her back against the brocaded back of the chair.

"Varian wanted your company so much," went on Mrs Pleiades, smiling fondly at him as she curled crimson-tipped fingers about the stem of her wine glass and raised it to her lips. "Didn't you, dear one?" Varian grinned and squirmed in his chair, looking at Jane with a kind of avid anticipation. Had Mrs Pleiades changed her mind and decided to let him "have her"? The terror she felt then was a huge aching emptiness beneath her ribs. Despite her resolve she picked up her glass and took a sip, smiling at Varian shyly and compliantly, again trying to infuse admiration into her glance. He grinned and preened, but the avid anticipation drained from his face. Not that then. But something horrible she was sure. She heard David Levant's murmur from beside her, and glanced at him, to be terrified anew – and nauseated – by the pasty fish-belly pallor of his profile; the skin looked like that of a corpse that had been immersed in polluted water, a sagging and slippage clearly visible. Jane took another sip of wine.

Mrs Pleiades had evidently understood the murmur, for she nodded, saying: "Yes, David, if you would," and he rose to cross to a where a small door in the wall opened onto the capacious shelf of a dumb waiter; the fitness fanatic who had constructed the annex with the gymnasium had been fearful of germs and did not want the staff standing over him when he was at table.

Jane, taking yet another sip of wine though she knew she shouldn't, discovered she was shivering, and realised that it was not from fear but that the room itself that was icy. Chill eddies from floor-level air-conditioning grills feathered her ankles, and she moved her legs, aware now that despite the uncomfortably low temperature there was a barely perceptible rotten smell to the air, the kind of smell that emanates from a refrigerator holding spoiled food. Jane glanced covertly about her. There appeared to be no windows to the room though peach-coloured drapes covered two of the walls from ceiling to floor; perhaps the windows were behind them.

In the meantime, David Levant had been ferrying numerous dishes from the dumb waiter to the table: rice salad, a whole salmon, a platter of cold meats, another of seafood, and a bowl of mixed salad.

Mrs Pleiades had begun speaking again, though Jane missed the beginning:

"So you see," she was saying with lazy contentment, "this is in the nature of a small celebration."

Jane berated herself for her lack of attention when she could perhaps have learned something. She reached for her wine glass, now consoling herself with the reflection that she was sure her alter ego would do the same.

"Sorry," she said humbly. "I don't understand."

Mrs Pleiades merely smirked as a response. Being convinced that Jane knew very little of the importance of the ritual, had in fact just tagged along with Gabriel – well, he always had to have some woman in tow – she didn't bother to repeat or clarify. Jane, all too aware that the next day was the 13th, guessed that the "celebration" was in anticipation of their winning the battle.

David Levant sat down, and for a few minutes

there was merely a prosaic filling of plates and wine glasses. Varian heaped rice salad onto his plate, hacked off a piece of the salmon and got up to lean across for the salad bowl, giving Jane another huge smile. Mrs Pleiades made a delicate arrangement on her plate, while David Levant merely took a thin slice of salmon and a piece of bread; it would still be on his plate at the end of the meal. Jane took some seafood and salad; she had no appetite but told herself that food meant strength and it was the only thing she could do at the moment.

Varian had been wolfing down his food as if there was some danger it would be taken away from him, though in reality Mrs Pleiades had told him he could tell Jane of his exploits when he had finished eating.

It was with a triumphant smile he wiped round his empty plate with a piece of bread, and crowed:

"Well, *now* can I tell her? You promised!"

Afterwards Jane would never know how she remained in her chair rather than trying to flee from the icy evil-smelling luxury of the dining room. Remain she did, eyes stricken and face blanching to pure white, as Varian recounted what he had done to the "two stupid men". He was particular in mentioning that it had been a good thing there were two of them, so that, for example, he blinded the first one – "I just scooped his eyes out" – but then of course the man couldn't see what Varian was doing to him, so for the second one he cut the man's eyelids off, so he wouldn't miss a thing. If he'd only had one, he wouldn't have had a second chance. He detailed his feats with the blow torch, but confided that he should have worked up to it a bit more – burned off the ears for instance, that would have been better. Smashing toes with a hammer had been fun though – they went all red and squashy. Oh, and fingers were good as well, he'd just snipped them off, not all at once of course but joint by joint. He'd really got the hang of it.

As Jane sat and listened – she was not expected to do more, it appeared – she slipped into a dim nightmare world where three ghouls grimaced and gloated, gradually shedding any semblance to the human shapes they had once had. The greenish-gold evening dress and snake bracelets adorned an empty shell containing death and decay, the man beside her, with his slack grey skin, increasingly resembled a human-shaped sack of decomposing flesh, which oozed and stank in the frigid air, while as for the handsome blond man, sitting and grinning and gesturing with triumph, he too seemed a mere vessel, a travesty of some young sportsman revelling in his triumphs.

And Varian also described the "nice dog", the agony of which Jane had heard, and it must have been at this point that Jane, still white-faced and immobile, felt her eyes filling with hot anguished tears, which spilled and trickled down her cheeks, the only warmth and humanity in the chill hushed room.

The empty shell in the greenish-gold evening dress and snake bracelets began to laugh with rich enjoyment, the rotting corpse chuckled, and the sportsman giggled, entirely sated and satisfied with the reaction of his captive audience.

"It had all its guts over the floor, and I stroked it, and, you know, it was so stupid, it licked my hand!" finished the sportsman jubilantly.

17 THURSDAY 13TH AUGUST

At the *agriturismo* Thursday was following its usual morning routine: guests were sitting on the vine-shaded patio having breakfast, chatting and planning the day ahead. George too was already up and about, sitting at his table and staring bemusedly at the mess of bread and jam on his plate; he had no memory of fetching it, let alone starting to eat it.

Even in the shade the bright morning light was making him squint and he shielded his eyes to look over the shimmering waters of the lake and then up at the cloudless sky. Going to be another scorcher, he thought, and then: Must check I've got water and go and buy some torches. Forgot to ask the professor what we need. He took a sip of orange juice and started on the mess of bread and jam, though he tasted nothing of what he was eating or drinking.

He was again struggling with a sense of unreality. Was a battle going to be fought? Would "the balance" be restored? And what about Jane? Was the only option to go to the wood and ... whatever? Or should the police be brought in? He felt completely at sea. Everything seemed both absurd and highly dangerous, and he was now at a complete loss as to how exactly he had become so involved. He was saved from further reflection by Theo, who came up with a pot of tea:

"OK, George?" he asked, setting the pot down, and turning George's cup, which had been upside down in the saucer, the right way up.

"Yes," replied George somewhat glumly. "Just ... uh ..."

"But you're still coming?" asked Theo, lowering his voice. "You're not having second thoughts?"

"No, I mean ... uh ... yes, I'll be there."

"We need you, George," said Theo earnestly, still in the same low voice. "You'll be looking after the professor, while I ..." He broke off, looking excited but somehow shy.

"Morning, you two!" came Barbara's hearty voice; she held a well-laden tray, and had apparently sampled everything from the buffet. "All set?"

"All set" could not begin to describe how they felt, but both greeted her, and she put her tray on the table and plumped herself down. Theo murmured something indistinguishable and went off to fetch another pot of tea.

"Now, young man, you're not going to let Professor Caseman down, are you?" Barbara went on in the same hearty tone. Having come to terms with the fact that Lena's feyness had led to this – including Jane's disappearance and the apparition of a head-hunter and villain – her behaviour was now dictated by past experience of village fetes and Women's Institute stalls when you had to jolly people along to get the job done.

George assured her that he would not let the professor down.

"She's not well," went on Barbara, her voice becoming more natural. "And with Jane going missing and …" she stopped, her kindly no-nonsense face suddenly so desolate that George had to say something.

"Miss Allberry – please … uh … don't worry. If what the professor says is true, the … uh … best way to help Jane is to go to the … uh … wood this evening, but I'll stay with her all the time and bring her back safe to you."

Barbara sat up straight; she had not yet begun on the well-laden tray. "You don't think I'm staying behind, I hope?" she said belligerently. "I'm with Lena – Professor Caseman – a hundred per cent even if I do think it's a load of codswallop. I'll be coming to keep an eye on her of course!"

George looked at her in dismay. It was bad

enough that there would be one frail old woman stumbling (no, being carried) around in the woods, but to have another one ...

Most of George believed that they would go to the wood, perhaps find the tree (or a tree) and then ... nothing would happen. There would be no false Virbius, no adversary and they would sit around, presumably with Theo holding the damn branch waiting for something that would not happen. It would be tiring, embarrassing and infinitely sad for the elderly woman who believed in it so implicitly. They would then trail back to the nursing home again, while Professor Caseman told them that a comet or something had upset the natural forces and nullified the encounter; they would all pretend to agree.

But – and this was the problem – Jane had disappeared, disappeared in the real world, and it had occurred while she was involved in the strange story of the twice-born Virbius, the first King of the Sacred Wood. The prosaic part of George wildly considered her vanishing in the context of a modern-day white slave trade or mad perverts but a part of him, that instinctive part containing a long-ago memory of the ancient world, believed it all and was afraid.

Jane awoke that morning filled with a sense of calm well-being; she stretched luxuriously and looked about the room. How was that even possible after the evening before, she wondered, after that dreadful recital of perversion, mutilation and pain, all recounted in gleeful boyish tones? It was too horrible to remember, too awful to contemplate, so why this sense of calm?

And then she remembered her dream, which came to her complete in every detail.

She had dreamt about the woman known to Barbara as Lena and to others as Professor Caseman, though in the dream she was neither. She was younger, her dark hair long and braided, sitting beside a circle of stones within which the flames of a fire wavered clear orange and then faintly blue, as fire appears when it burns in sunlight. She was quite simply sitting there, hands folded in her lap, and then she looked up – as though she had just become aware of Jane's presence – and said softly, in a voice as clear and pure as spring water, "You must be strong now, and brave. Remember, evil is not absolute – its every appearance arouses its twin good, just as every darkness is menaced by its attendant light." She gazed again at the fire that flamed and danced, glinting gold at its heart. "I promise you – the weak will be protected, the abused and the tormented will be healed and avenged … but you must be brave …"

Jane sat up. The dream had given her heart and courage but what could she do? And what were the others doing? Had the tourists taken her bag to a police station? Did Professor Caseman know? Did

Gabriel know?

And here she paused. Gabriel. The last time they had seen each other was four days ago – the Sunday morning after her hangover, which was after the Saturday night ... Jane tried to imagine what he would have done when she disappeared but could not. He was too ... Gabriel. But he helped find the professor, she reminded herself. Yes, but was he really involved, whispered a doubt. "Probably some descendent of the goddess Diana," he had said – no, drawled – about Professor Caseman. He had known about the golden bough and explained its origins but he had also smiled the evil smile. It was too complicated. All I can do is wait and watch for some opportunity, she thought, throwing back the sheet, and going towards the bathroom. There's the professor – she won't give up, I know – and George and Theo. I can only wait and watch for an opportunity, she repeated to herself. I must – those ... ghouls are never going to let me go now I know what they've done.

The morning had started for the other occupants of the rented villa as well. Attended to by the trained maid Dolorita Morales, Mrs Pleiades was engaged in her morning ritual and reassembling her perfect exterior, from the burnished backsweep of unnaturally chestnut hair to the hard crimson nails to her favourite shiny black shoes with their knife-shaped toes.

She was extremely satisfied with the way events were progressing. She had experienced none of the annoying gaps in time for three or four days, and in Jane now possessed a potential pawn in the encounter that was to come. She smiled at her mirrored self as she remembered dinner the night before. A frightened rabbit, the girl had been, but Mrs Pleiades had not missed her appreciation of the villa's wealth, nor her smile at Varian. Common little thing! As if she was worthy of the next Rex Nemorensis! No, everything was progressing in the most satisfactory manner, and there was only the small problem of David Levant, his physical presence, that is.

Jane's perception of the pallid Englishman as a rotting corpse was not far from the truth, for he was one of Mrs Pleiades' early failures during her search for 'The One'. Inexplicably, David Levant had undergone a partial transformation and somehow survived. Not a failure then but an incomplete success. Enough of the original David Levant remained to continue to live, and – fortunately – possessed enough memory to carry on so as not to arouse suspicion in those who had known him before. On the contrary, they complemented him on his wonderful new position as Mrs Pleiades' secretary, and she herself had found him invaluable.

Invaluable, yes, and with the ritual he would also be renewed, his decline reversed by the forces of the wood. An entirely satisfactory by-product of the main purpose.

In the grounds the gardener Byron Escobar was

watering the oleanders, keeping one eye on the sunken patio, where Dolorita would join him for a cigarette once she had finished upstairs. She would bring coffee as well, and he would tell her that the appointment was set for the evening, at seven, in the road outside the museum. He himself would be here at the villa, watching the westward journey of the sun, waiting for the moment when the spirit must be held, held and destroyed, so that it could never go and come again. And then it was the work of the Old One of the vivid green eyes. His work would be completed.

George's list of necessities was incomplete, and in his present state of mind he had forgotten its very existence. But Theo had had a similar idea and intercepted George just as he was going back to his chalet with no very clear idea of how he was going to spend the day.

"Was just thinking – we need to see if we're missing anything for tonight," Theo said, holding up a piece of paper. "Perhaps you could take a trip to the village for stuff?"

George brightened at the prospect of something concrete to do, and produced his own – by now crumpled – piece of paper, and they sat down to think over the practicalities: what to take and who would carry what. George had his battered rucksack and Theo said he had a small one as well, so between the two of them – each working from their different experience – George on his travels for work, Theo from his backpacking and various jobs – they came up with the essentials: long trousers, yes, insect repellent (and take some in case someone else had forgotten), and the water and torches that George had thought of, each could carry a bottle and a torch, and some light nylon rope (this from Theo), and what about a small axe and some pruning shears? added George with sudden inspiration. They couldn't be sure there would be a clear path. Heavy gloves! came from Theo, and what about weapons?

This stopped the flow, and they were looking at each other in silent interrogation when Barbara came up. She had gone to her room, and seen her half brick from the Museum of Roman Ships; it is true that her cheeks flushed red as she remembered the little man saying, "too old to carry a stone!" but, she reflected stalwartly, nothing wrong with the *idea*. At that, she had gone downstairs, where she saw George and Theo engaged in their list-making.

"A stick!" she announced as she came up. "I need a walking stick. Can you give me a lift to the village, Engineer?"

"Great timing! George was just going," said Theo, inwardly relieved that George would not be on his own; he had noticed George's preoccupied expression. As for George himself, he was not sure he would be capable of any kind of conversation, and Miss Allberry would surely expect it.

In this he was mistaken, however. Barbara herself was trying to think about other things she might need apart from the stick, and George was able to concentrate on the task of driving up the frighteningly narrow road to the arch that led to the village.

Their purchases in the local ironmonger's would cause some comment, though only after they had left the shop. No longer baulking at the thought of a weapon, George spotted a baseball bat and added that, buying some balls as well since the bat on its own might seem strange, even sinister. Barbara found a gnarled walking stick gathering dust in a corner and carried it triumphantly to the counter, where she insisted on paying half of the now-substantial bill. George, seeing the look in her eye, did not attempt to disagree, and the two of them carried their spoils back to George's car and loaded up. A clock was striking half past eleven as George manoeuvred the car through the arch and once more drove carefully down the hill.

A week had passed since they had all met for the first time in the gardens of the nursing home, but now there were still the remaining hours to be filled. Those hours would be like any before an event of great importance, with the same sense of expectation, the same concern that nothing had been forgotten, and the same treacherous elasticity of time, which was both unending and then impossibly short. And then – finally – it was time for the three of them, George, Theo and Barbara, to meet up in the *agriturismo's* dusty car park, pack the rucksacks, walking stick and the rest into the small boot, and collect Professor Caseman.

It was a little after seven when they arrived in the lay-by outside the Museum of Roman Ships, Lena having accepted Gabriel's estimate of how much time would be necessary, "an hour if not an hour and a half". She had also checked when the sun would set that night – just before 9.30 – for it was then that Byron Escobar would be engaged on his "work". She wanted to leave nothing to chance – nothing that was humanly possible that is.

To the Italians in a passing car the four in the dusty lay-by were obviously foreigners, and probably English, being dressed unfashionably and shabby-casually: Theo was wearing a dark T-shirt and trousers tucked into boots; George wore the only long trousers he had with him, faded khakis, and one of his well-washed shirts; Lena wore a long-sleeved blouse and slacks, both dark-blue, and Barbara had a roomy brown tracksuit, the top knotted around her ample waist, and a green blouse.

It was only when she stood up that they saw Dolorita Morales, who had been sitting waiting in the shade of a faded notice board that had once held tourist information; she too wore dark cotton trousers and top, and carried a plastic bag holding a small bottle of water and her cigarettes. Barbara already knew she would be there, and was not happy about it, and Lena had told George and

Theo in the car: The news that there would be a fifth member to the group produced little or no reaction – they were past reacting at that point – though George reflected it would be useful to have another pair of hands to carry the water.

The lay-by was bounded by a sprawling scrubby hedge, with a ramshackle wooden gate in the middle, and it was there that they had to start their ascent. Above them woods covered the slopes, dense and unbroken. While the small wilderness on the Nemi side had been constricted and cultivated, on this side there was nothing except the dark green of vegetation and the curve of the volcano above.

Initially the slope was gentle, and Lena could walk, though slowly; she had taken the precaution of asking the doctor to change her tablets, read the instructions carefully and taken the maximum number plus another half. Barbara and Dolorita stayed close by, Barbara behind, in case Lena swayed back, Dolorita, more agile, was beside Lena, who lightly held the younger woman's arm to keep her balance. Theo was leading, glancing back every so often for Lena's nod that they were going the right way, and George brought up the rear, keeping a sharp lookout. Even when the gradient became steeper the ground was still fairly free. There came a point however when any semblance of track ended and there were only trees and underbrush.

Lena called softly to Theo and paused to take

her bearings, happily breathing in the still warm air. It was still early, and though the sun had begun its earthward descent it would be light for some time to come. Midges danced in the sunlight that filtered through the trees and the scent of the dried leaves underfoot rose strong and – to Lena – heady; it had been so long. The others had stopped as well, Theo gazing expectantly forward, Barbara bending to rub some dry earth into her sweaty palm to get a better grip on the gnarled walking stick (Should have put some tape around it, she was thinking), and George offering the water round; one look at Dolorita's brooding gaze and he had decided not to ask her to carry the other bottles. Dolorita herself had sat down and sipped a little water, seemingly unaffected by the heat. Her expression was grave, her face calm, and in that moment she could well have been the model and inspiration for the crippled poet's scribbled words in the tavern register, "calm as cherish'd hate".

The short pause was over, for the professor was gesturing to the left. George went to lift her and was amazed at the lightness of the thin frame; in his imagination her weight had increased tenfold. Theo again led the way, while Barbara, whose long walks with her dogs now stood her in good stead, and Dolorita fell behind. The hardest part was yet to come.

For the next hour or more they toiled uphill, always tending to the left and entering further and further into the wood. All of them were tired, hot and uncomfortable with the effort of keeping their balance on the slope and the need to keep in the right direction; George was now feeling the weight of his burden and was placing each foot with extreme care. Not the time to slip, he was thinking. Might end up rolling all the way down. Under the trees the light was failing as well, and though the sky above the rim of the volcano had become a blaze of yellow, shades of peach were attenuating its brightness, heralding the setting of the sun.

The clearing in the woods and the narrow plateau came suddenly. One moment they were working their way up the hillside, brambles catching at their clothes and roots hooking at their feet, the next stepping around a fallen tree trunk onto flat ground. The mellow light threw long thin shadows across the withered grass, illuminating four figures beneath a twisted oak tree at the opposite end of the clearing.

The tableau froze. George put Lena gently down on the fallen tree trunk, and Barbara went to sit beside her; she knew better than to get in the way, and was only intending to act if Lena was in danger. George could feel his mouth hanging open and shut it with a snap, and then flexed his shoulders, where the straps of his rucksack were digging into him. Beside him Theo had tensed, and Dolorita had come to a halt slightly behind them.

The four figures by the twisted oak came forward from shade into light, one of them, a pale sick-looking man pulling Jane with him. One side of her face was bruised and smeared with blood, the result of what Mrs Pleiades had described as "a little something to take the heart out of them".

Jane, no longer aware of her hurt face or the bony fingers hooked into her flesh, was scanning the faces of the five opposite. Where was Gabriel? There was Professor Caseman, sitting and smiling at her in welcome and reassurance, Barbara beside her, looking serious but determined. There was George, red in the face and in long trousers rather than the 'heroic shorts', and Theo, young face tense but alight. But who was the thin dark woman with narrowed eyes? And where was Gabriel? "Some descendent of the goddess Diana," he had drawled, and so now she knew. Like all the casual lies ("But why did you tell them I worked in television?" "Oh, come *on*, Jane. No one listens or is interested anyway."), it had all been just ... a pastime, something to amuse his uncaring cynicism. Oh, Gabriel, she thought despairingly. What have you done?

Mrs Pleiades, wearing a purple designer tracksuit and incongruous pearl earrings, surveyed the small group opposite with growing disdain – two old women, two untrained men, and ... her crimson lips twisted into an unpleasant smile.

"Morales," she murmured malevolently. "Did you really believe I did not *know*?"

"*Puta inhumanos*," returned Dolorita flatly and deliberately. "*He venido a verte se muere.*"

Mrs Pleiades laughed. David Levant's pallid

features were slack, his eyes blank but filled with malice, while Varian stood stripped to the waist, the muscles of his chest glistening in the amber glow of the setting sun; he held a long curved knife in one hand, a strange fleshy branch in the other.

George looked at the twisted oak tree, and then at the branch the tall blond man was holding, thinking incoherently, Is that it? But it's not gold, it's yellowish.

It was then that Theo leapt forward, the baseball bat in one hand, and ran across the clearing. Ever since his vision in the museum and the explanations given by Professor Caseman, he had been sure that this was why he was there, why his journey to Italy had been so simple, and why he had come to Nemi. The professor had told him to be ready and the blond man with the brilliant but vacuous smile was the enemy, the false Virbius that must be defeated.

Varian preened and grinned, his day had arrived at last. In one fluid movement he laid the branch to one side and sprang forward to meet Theo, knife at the ready. Mrs Pleiades smiled. David Levant smirked. Jane gave a choked cry, while Barbara, sitting beside her friend, rubbed the palm of her hand against the dusty bark of the dead tree and gripped the gnarled walking-stick more securely. Beside her, Lena quietly checked the lengthening of the shadows and the dying of the light above the western rim of the volcano.

There was a swift flurry of movement, too fast to

be followed by those watching, a sudden splatter of blood and the baseball bat whirled across the clearing and disappeared into the underbrush. Theo had stumbled back, a ragged gash disfiguring one sunburned cheek, and losing his footing tripped and fell from the side of the clearing into the woods below. A crashing and thumping sound came back to them as he fell.

"Well, that's the dead wood cleared away," cooed Mrs Pleiades. "Bravo, dear one, perfect." Varian smirked again and postured his way through a series of complicated movements as though in a victory dance, waving the blood-stained knife in triumph.

With complete and utter dismay, George realised that it was up to him to protect the professor, her friend Barbara, Jane, and the thin dark woman. The adversary – the woman whose malign spirit he had encountered at the sanctuary – was real, the pretender to the title of Rex Nemorensis was real, the danger to them all was real.

He set his jaw, and began to shrug his shoulders free of the straps of his rucksack. If it was up to him, it was up to him …

He found himself suddenly freed of the rucksack by someone pulling down the straps from behind, and whirled to find – he could not believe his eyes – the man who was not coming, the man who had let them down, Gabriel Todd. Gabriel nodded, smiling slightly, handed George the rucksack, and stepped round him to confront the still-posturing Varian.

When Jane saw him, she was prey to so many conflicting emotions, she could not begin to identify them; her lips moved to say his name and though no sound emerged he appeared to hear for he glanced over at her, took in her bruised and swollen face, and then nodded as if to say "Only superficial. You'll be fine." Then his gaze went to Mrs Pleiades.

"Hello, stepmother," he said softly. "Tired of the fleshpots?"

Mrs Pleiades' crimson lips twisted into a snarling smile. "Gabriel," she exclaimed, and the metallic, slightly-accented tones were a travesty of pleased welcome. "So there you are. Such a shame about your dear father ..."

Gabriel said nothing, and Jane, eyes fixed on his face, saw no change in his expression. He walked into the centre of the clearing as he had always walked into a bar or restaurant, casual and arrogant. He held no weapon of any kind, merely walked forward, hands loosely clenched at his sides, while Varian, face alight with anticipation, crouched in readiness and began a weaving ballet-like advance.

When Gabriel did act however it was swift and sure – from one hand he threw something at Varian, catching him on the temple and interrupting the rhythm the other had established. Even as Varian stumbled Gabriel darted to where the branch lay and scooped it up. Mrs Pleiades hissed. Varian almost fell. In the seconds it took him to regain his balance, Gabriel had disappeared soundlessly into the woods.

"Find him!" screamed Mrs Pleiades, face now contorted into a mask of thwarted rage. "Find him! Kill him!"

Varian whirled, in his turn disappeared into the trees. Those watching were as still as statues as their ears strained to follow the sounds of his passage. A cry of pain reached them. Which of them was it? Mrs Pleiades for one seemed sure for she smiled and relaxed, came sauntering towards the stricken group. David Levant padded behind her, pulling Jane with him. The clearing was grey and dim in the dying light. Mrs Pleiades' gaze swept over the remaining four, coming to rest on Professor Caseman. And she nodded in recognition.

"You stupid old bitch," she whispered venomously, her mouth slipping to one side, "Did you really believe you could win? David, get rid of her, snap her scrawny neck." And she laughed, a horrid cawing sound that rasped and grated in the still air. David Levant, the perfect secretary, moved to carry out his employer's instructions, releasing his grasp of Jane. George lumbered forward to shield the professor, ungainly but determined. Barbara – exhausted from the climb but game for one last effort – heaved herself to her feet, walking-stick at the ready, only to have it snatched from her hand by Dolorita Morales, who sprang forward in her turn.

George, trying to remember the 'bit of boxing' he had learnt at school, raised his fists and made a clumsy feint. Swiftly and savagely David Levant punched him to one side, where he slipped and fell. At that point, Jane, maddened by her fear for Gabriel, terrified and infuriated by her days of captivity, launched herself at Levant and clung to his back. When she briefly touched the cool slack skin of his neck she almost loosed her hold. By this time George had got to his feet and now went in with arms windmilling. The weight of Jane and George's blows was weakening Levant who was trying to stagger away, when Jane remembered Barbara and the professor. With a last wrench at Levant's hair – she did not dare scratch his neck – she fell to the ground, managed to half crawl to her feet and then froze as another cry came from the woods, a despairing howl of pain and fury.

The stolen walking stick raised to strike, Dolorita too stopped in her headlong rush towards Mrs Pleiades, who flinched as though actually struck and whirled to scan the trees, lips still frozen in a snarling smile. Another cry came – this time in an unknown tongue but the meaning was clear – the cry rang out in a declaration of victory and possession.

Lena, holding onto Barbara's arm, pulled herself to her feet. Mrs Pleiades, the snarling smile now a grimacing mask, her fingers hooked into claws,

The Sacred Wood

sidled forward, though her movements were uncertain. Dolorita followed her, dark face set in deadly intent, but halted when the professor raised one hand.

"The true king has remembered his kingdom," said Lena slowly and clearly. "Now *you* must remember!"

And before his shrine, the small table with the lighted stubs of candles set in metal jar-tops, the charm flask and the picture of a man in black seated at a crossroads, Byron Escobar bowed his head. He had completed his own rituals, calling the spirit, and binding it to the moment when the sun left the rim of the volcano. It could no longer come and go.

The clearing became still. George and David Levant rolled apart. Mrs Pleiades hissed and her head jerked back; the pearl earrings gleamed in the half-light.

"*You ... meddler! You pious bitch ... you cannot stop me.*" But her voice was changing, becoming a whining mutter. "*I will have him, I will make sure this time!*"

"You CANNOT!" flashed back Lena, head held high and face imperious. "The true heir has triumphed and *you* must die for the last time."

Mrs Pleiades seemed to shrink and dwindle inside her clothes then slowly crumpled to the ground, her face slipping and sliding. Only the muttering continued. ""*Oida oti autòs entháde estí. Chrésimón esti autòn krúptein – chrésimón.*" "I know he *is here. It is useless to hide him – useless."* Dolorita walked forward, raised her weapon and smashed it down on the slipping melting features, once, twice, three times. "David, kill them," murmured the dwindling mess of blood and brains.

But David Levant was gone. When George glanced at what was left, he made a revolted sound, rolled yet further away and threw up. A smell of vomit and dissolution hung in the air, and then was dissipated by a sudden cool gust of wind.

Where Mrs Pleiades had been, there was nothing, not even clothes, only a faint depression in the dead leaves where she had fallen.

"Gabriel," whispered Jane.

But it was Theo they found, unconscious but alive, face bleeding, his arm bent and twisted out of shape. Jane poured some of the water onto paper handkerchiefs and bathed his face and lips, blotting at the blood, while George found a gauze pad and some tape to close the wound. Slowly Theo's eyelids fluttered open. "Is it over?" he breathed.

"Yes. Everything's ... uh ... OK," said George. "Come on, I'll give you a hand."

It took some time to half-carry, half-support him back to the clearing, where the others were waiting, and place him gently on the ground, back supported by the fallen tree. Looking up at Professor Caseman Theo said faintly: "I thought ..." There were tears in his eyes.

For a moment the vivid green eyes that had so impressed Jane were cool and detached. In the dying light her thin lined face had a pitiless hieratic quality. Then, her eyes became warm and human again. "I know," she said quietly. "But you fulfilled your part, your precious part."

It was now almost completely dark, for the sky had softly shaded from cobalt to indigo to luminous midnight blue; the lights of the village of Nemi were glowing on the opposite rim, the newly-risen moon just visible as it began its ascent through the star-filled evening. "We'd better come back in the morning," said George, rubbing his ear. "No point in …" He broke off.

They started back down the hillside. It was a long slow miserable journey. Dolorita went ahead, shining the light from one of the torches back to where George and Jane were carrying Professor Caseman. Barbara held the other torch in one hand, helping Theo with the other. Jane's eyes were filled with tears and the dark recesses of the wood wavered and sparkled before her vision. Their descent seemed more of a retreat than a victory, a struggle of refugees hopelessly searching for an end to their flight. When they finally – hours later – reached level ground, they stopped to rest.

From the village on the precipice came the sound of a church clock as it struck midnight, and across the valley, from the darkness of the sanctuary, came a gleam of light. The full moon now hung over the lake, luminous and golden.

"It is done," whispered Lena, and then repeated the fulfilled prophesy, "The true king has remembered his kingdom."

"But Gabriel …," said Jane, her voice choked with tears.

Before she received an answer the gleam from the sanctuary grew stronger, glowed and spread, lapping outwards towards where they stood or sat. Their faces were lit in the glow. Theo, face deathly pale, the gauze dressing stark against his skin, cradled his broken arm. George knuckled at his swollen eyes, unaware of the blood he was smearing across his face from the re-opened wound on his forehead. Barbara, sitting with Lena, put one arm about her friend. Lena herself smiled and raised one hand to touch her lips in homage.

The glow lapping from the sanctuary shimmered and danced, as though a million particles of gold were suspended within. At the heart of the dance stood a slim figure.

As they gazed on the figure each of them experienced something different. Theo was aware of stillness and the fiery throb of his wounds was cooled and then quenched; Barbara felt love and approval; George too; for Lena it was a recognition and home-coming. Only Jane, locked in her anguish at the disappearance of Gabriel, felt none of those things – but only she saw the man (man?) beside the goddess at the heart of the glow.

Between them, sitting straight on its powerful haunches, was a huge pale dog. Its muzzle was broad with black markings around the jaws, and its large eyes distant and dignified. The hand of the goddess rested briefly on its head, and the dog looked up at her, trust and adoration in its dark eyes. When it gazed back at the humans again, each of them remembered some special dog they had played with as children, and Barbara felt her eyes sting.

The goddess smiled with infinite tenderness and bent to caress the dog's broad head again. It lifted its head, opened the massive jaws and bayed. No other dog answered, and when the triumphant sound softened and died, the valley held only a deep hush.

Slowly Jane walked towards the trio. "Jane!" called Lena. "Come back!"

The million particles of gold danced in swathes and showers. For a moment Jane was bathed in their iridescence, her hair sparkling and flaring as though on fire, then she swayed and fell, and the darkness of the night closed in.

18 FRIDAY 14TH AUGUST

In the valley, in the dusty lay-by bounded by the sprawling hedge, Adelpha Manousakis checked her watch again – it was now more than three hours – and looked around at her surroundings: to the right the dark bulk of the museum, behind her, the road leading up to Genzano, ahead and above the lights from the village of Nemi, and to her left a sagging wooden gate and the darkness of the slopes. She was sitting in the black, chrome-trimmed monster that Gabriel had rented for the second time, the car that had so aroused Jane's incredulous amusement ("You're not going to hunt lions, are you?"). The windows were rolled down, and the cool of the evening was finally making itself felt.

The Sacred Wood

Having completed her survey, Adelpha lit another cigarette with her left hand while the fingers of the right continued their impatient drumming on her handbag on the seat beside her. She felt she had been brought here under false pretences. He had said her brother would be avenged and she had assumed she would be there, but one look at the place when they arrived – the steep wooded hillside and the clouds of gnats dancing in the heat, combined with the angry realisation that her sandals were completely unsuitable for such a trek – had forced her to agree to stay here and wait.

However, now she was here, she was going to stay, and besides, she wanted to get a look at Professor Caseman, who had drawn Achille into the whole mess and was thus responsible. Adelpha planned to give her a piece of her mind. Irritably she stubbed out the barely-smoked cigarette and glanced at her watch again, noting that the hands were standing at midnight. It was just then that she heard a clock strike the hour in the village of Nemi above, and she leant back against the headrest to ease the tension of taut muscles in her neck.

What happened next seemed immediate, but the glowing red numbers of the dashboard clock showed 00.30, and her neck was no longer paining her. Adelpha looked around disoriented to see a group of people slowly making their way towards the sagging gate, so slowly that she had time to make out the individuals in the group, six altogether, two men and four women. So many! She had never imagined …!

At the front of the straggling figures was a young man carrying a little old woman, close behind there were another two women, one old and plump, the other small and thin, and finally a second man supporting a young woman with light hair. Of the man Adelpha had come here with there was no sign, and with a sudden leap of intuition that dissipated her impatience and irritation, she knew that he would not be returning. Decisively she opened the car door and crossed the lay-by to drag open the gate. The group halted, seemed to draw closer together, and the man at the back strode forward; they obviously perceived her as a threat.

"Do not fear," Adelpha called softly. "I came with … Gabriel." She had been about to say his baptismal name but it would have meant nothing to them.

The group relaxed, resumed their slow progress, and filed through the gate, the man who had come forward first:

"George," he said by way of introduction, and then looked over at the huge black car. "We … uh … need a bit of help here. My car's not big enough."

"Adelpha," she returned. "Well, now we have two," and she scrutinised the little old woman, whose vivid glance belied the exhaustion of her face; that would be Professor Caseman, and

The Sacred Wood

Adelpha frowned. She would get to the professor later but this was not the time. Of the other women the old plump one looked exhausted as well, and was leaning on a misshapen stick, the dark one looked quietly serene but when she raised a hand to brush her hair from her face, Adelpha saw her forearm was speckled with dried blood. The face of the last, the young woman with light hair, was blood-stained and bruised, but she smiled at Adelpha, and said, "You came with Gabriel?" Adelpha nodded. "I ... am so sorry," said the other. "But he is not with us." There were tears in her eyes, and Adelpha, with another leap of intuition, sympathetically rested her hand on the woman's arm, before turning to the others. The little old woman was standing now, resting against the side of the car, the plump one beside her. "Professor Caseman?" queried Adelpha, and then, without waiting for an answer, "I am Adelpha, the sister of Achille."

Lena looked at the strong imperious features of the woman in front of her. "I am so sorry," she returned quietly. "We must talk but not now."

In the meantime George had been looking at the two cars, and working out the best way to use them; after all, he was thinking, when it comes down to it, you have to sort out the practical stuff, get people home. He crossed to Adelpha, asked her if she could take Dolorita back to Genzano in his small car, while he drove the large one and took the others home; they were all going in the same direction. "We can … uh … exchange the cars tomorrow. I'm at the *agriturismo* along the road there. Is that … uh … all right?" he finished; he had worked it all out. But Dolorita, who had been standing silently and listening, said, "But what about her? Where is she going?"

Adelpha did not know. She had not thought that far ahead, and if she had, she would probably have said that she would return to Rome with … Gabriel. But everything – every single thing – had been different from what she imagined. She managed to say, "Rome" but the word was tentative, even interrogative, and Dolorita, with no idea who Adelpha was, who only saw a woman in pain, said, "You stay with me. There is no problem." And Adelpha agreed, in her turn also seeing a woman who had suffered but was somehow cleansed. George fumbled his car keys from the pockets of his khaki trousers, now torn and smudged with leaves and dry earth, and handed them to Adelpha, who took them without a word.

"Tomorrow," said the professor to her. "Could you come to the nursing home in the afternoon? It is on the other side of the valley."

Adelpha nodded, still silent, and Dolorita saw she was now lost, had come so far and now did not know what to do, so she laid a hand on the other's arm to urge her toward the car. The sound of its tinny engine starting up and then driving towards Genzano held the rest of them motionless, and then there was a sudden flurry of activity as Lena was lifted into the front, and the other three climbed into the back.

At the *agriturismo* Barbara took Jane upstairs, the battered settee in her room was going to come in handy, and Theo, with a quiet "goodnight" walked off to his own room, where he did not expect he would get much sleep.

George drove up to the nursing home, and saw the professor in, where she was greeted with small cries of remonstrance about the late hour.

"I am so sorry," she said, and then, with an impish smile at George, "but it is not often my favourite nephew comes to visit." George laughed and went off, still engaged in his practicalities, which blessedly lasted until he too went to bed.

In Genzano the rented villa stood silent and untenanted. Byron Escobar was gone. When they returned, Dolorita had looked after Adelpha, making sure she had everything she needed, and then sped softly to the narrow tobacco-smelling room. The bed covers were neatly folded on the bare mattress, along with the red curtain that had covered the alcove, and the small altar was empty of candles and the photo of the man at the crossroads. Only the charm vial remained, now bearing a label with her name, and Dolorita smiled and cradled it in her hand.

She stood for a moment and then, with a sudden

thought, put the vial down again and raised her cotton top to look at the terrible cleft of the her scar. It was still there, and protectively she ran her hand across its ridged contours, sighing with relief. When the Golden Goddess had appeared in the shimmering swathes of celestial light Dolorita had felt her belly bathed and soothed and healed, and she had thought ... No, it was still there, though beneath her fingertips the skin felt softer and more elastic. It was only later, some years later, she would know that she had indeed been healed. She fell pregnant and gave birth to twins, one boy and one girl, children who were cherished for the miracle they were, but she would always lovingly carry her lost son in the scar that had given him life.

The next morning was no different from any other summer morning: the same bright sun shining on the slopes and patchwork of fields, the same shimmer on the placid waters of the lake, the same lazy holiday atmosphere as people coped with the heat and made their preparations for *Ferragosto* the following day. And yet, for those who had gone to the wood to join battle, there was something wonderful and infinitely special in their return to the everyday world. It had never seemed so beautiful or so precious.

The practicalities went on however. Theo and George went back to the wood after breakfast to look for Gabriel, though both suspected it would be pointless. Jane would have insisted on going with

The Sacred Wood

them if she had known, but she was still in a deep exhausted sleep on Barbara's settee, bruised face deep in a soft pillow, and Barbara tiptoed out and went to sit on the vine-shaded patio to read; she hadn't started her new paperback, what with everything else.

She was still there, dozing rather than reading, when George and Theo came back just before lunch, and joined her at the table.

"Anything?" she asked simply, waking up.

Theo shook his head: "We couldn't find the clearing," he said.

"Not surprised," said Barbara heartily, secretly relieved they were back safe. "Everything looks different in the dark. All those woods, one tree looking like another."

"No, that wasn't it," said George. Theo was shaking his head and glancing down at his healed arm, where a slight bump in the bone was the only sign it had ever been broken; his face too was unmarked save for the thinnest of white scar. "We found the baseball bat all right. Just ... uh ... there was no clearing."

"Nonsense!" retorted Barbara; she had completely recovered. "No missing it if you found the bat – long flat sort of area, with that oak tree at the end. The bat fell over the side."

"It wasn't there," said Theo, looking up from his arm. "There was just a slope, right, George?"

"That's it," said George. "We found the bat, climbed further up and then across to look down but ... uh ... as Theo said, it was just a slope."

"Well, I'll be damned," exclaimed Barbara. "If you'll excuse my language ..."

"The thing is," said George tentatively. "Should we report ... uh ... that Gabriel's gone missing?"

Barbara opened her mouth to rap out "Of course!" and then closed it again. What she said instead was: "Better wait for Jane to wake up. She was his friend, wasn't she?"

In the rented villa outside Genzano two women were having coffee and quietly talking in the kitchen.

"I saw her die," Dolorita was saying, "her and her ... creatures of darkness. Your brother is avenged, as my son is avenged."

Adelpha sat back, sipped at her coffee. And a father too has been avenged, she thought, but said nothing to her companion. Instead she picked up her pack of cigarettes, took one out and then offered the pack to Dolorita; they both lit a cigarette and relaxed, watching the blue smoke curling in a shaft of sunlight.

"And now," asked Adelpha. "What will you do?"

"I will go home," said Dolorita. "Now. Today. Here, there is nothing now. No one will know, no one will come. The other staff – only a cook and a girl and they did not live here – I have telephoned. I said the people were called away urgently, a

The Sacred Wood

death in family," her smile was dark and ironic as she said this. "No one will know," she repeated. "And you?" she went on. "You return to speak with the professor?"

"No," said Adelpha simply. "Last night I wanted to confront her, shout, scream, make her know what she had done but now ... Enough. My brother was foolish and full of crazy ideas but he was also a man. He chose. Now I choose." Dolorita nodded, took a sip of coffee, and looked questioningly at the other: "That man," she said. "The man you came with. There in the wood he called her stepmother."

Adelpha regarded the glowing tip of her cigarette, and then, "I only know what Achille and our mother believed," she said slowly. "She was crazy too," she added with a shrug. "Full of old tales. According to them, my brother and our mother, that woman was from the past, she had always existed, and always with the same story. The father, the son she desired, and when he refused her, she told the father of rape and abuse. But this time it was different – the father had doubts, was thinking to see his son, and was murdered for his doubts. I don't know. They were both crazy, my mother and brother," she finished with another shrug and a resigned smile. "Now, when we are ready, we will take the car, and then we can go."

Dolorita kept her own council. She believed the story; maybe she was crazy too, but her own attempts – repeated attempts – to kill the woman had all been to no avail. No matter. If Adelpha wanted it to be "crazy", it was better so. Here too it was "enough".

George had left the car keys to the black monster at the *agriturismo* when he and Theo went to look for Gabriel, and when they returned he saw that Adelpha had been and gone. His hired car was again baking in the dusty car park, by coincidence in the same spot he usually parked it so that it was as if it had never been used.

The rented villa stood empty in its spacious grounds, its front door left ajar. As Dolorita had predicted, no one knew. It was mid-August and the rent had been paid in advance until the end of the month. The villa could have remained so until the agency came to take re-possession, only … the girl who worked in the kitchens told her boyfriend of the tenants' desertion, and he, a smart boy already known to the local police, rounded up a couple of companions, and went to "have a look".

It was a rich haul, and could have been richer, they suspected, for they found an empty cabinet with numerous small drawers that must surely have held many precious things. Still, there was enough to make the foray well worth the trouble, and the agency would have to call their insurance company to cover the cost of missing furniture, curtains, and even light fittings. A very rich haul.

At the nursing home late that afternoon Barbara was sitting in Lena's room; she had pulled over the

The Sacred Wood

high armchair, and was sitting comfortably, thinking of all the similar occasions over the years, when the two of them had talked endlessly and unreservedly in one of their bedrooms. Lena had spent the day in bed and was still there – the night before had taken all her reserves despite the painkillers and George's excellent care. To Barbara's concerned eyes, her friend looked thinner and frailer than ever, but her face showed an inner glow of quiet happiness.

"But they couldn't find the clearing," Barbara was saying; she had recounted George and Theo's return to the wood. "So what do you know about that, Lena? You could have saved them a hike." Her tone had wavered between interrogation and criticism.

"Well, I didn't actually *know*," replied Lena, inwardly amused that Barbara, having reluctantly accepted and then acted upon what she had termed "feyness", was now taking it all in her stride and passing judgement. "Now you have told me, it makes perfect sense. But before, well, the only thing I did know was that I would find the place. I did not think of what would be necessary afterwards."

"That's all right then," Barbara commented, and Lena, rightly translating the few words into an apology for having doubted her good faith, looked out of the window and then at the clock, remarking:

"I do not think she is coming. She would have

been here by now."

"Who? That Greek woman?"

"Yes. And I am sorry, for I would have liked to …" she broke off, and Barbara said bluntly: "What? Apologise for getting her brother killed?" It was too close to the truth for Lena to smile her friend's forthrightness. She merely nodded and looked sad.

"Least said, soonest mended," commented Barbara, brisk but consoling. "Over now."

Jane had slept for most of the day, and now, slowly taking a shower in Barbara's en-suite bathroom, felt limp and washed-out. Her clothes were a mess too – she only had the same trousers and top, and wondered if she could summon the energy to go to Genzano to buy some things – George would probably give her a lift, and she would only buy the minimum anyway; back in Rome she would have not only all her own clothes at home but also the ones at Silvia's that she had bought at MAS.

She had seen Barbara for a few minutes before Barbara went out to the nursing home, but it had been long enough to talk about what, if anything, they should do about Gabriel's disappearance. "Just have a think about it," Barbara said. "You're the only person who knows anything about the man."

And Jane had thought about it, finally coming to the decision – was it the right one? – that it would be better to say nothing.

It was not only that it made things easier not to be involved in official investigations (that night in Trastevere had shown how time-consuming it could be, and on that occasion there was Tommaso as well), it was also a matter of how much, or rather how little, she actually knew about Gabriel. His reluctance to talk about anything personal, combined with the off-hand lies and arrogant detachment, meant that she really no idea who he was. All she could really tell the police was his name, Gabriel Todd – if that really was his name. She sighed. No, there was nothing she could tell the police that would be of any use.

She also wondered if the police were looking for her after her own disappearance. When she got back to Rome she would find out, she thought, picking up her top and trousers with distaste; Loretta her neighbour would know. And now, George and shopping. Everything would be closed the next day.

19 SATURDAY 15TH AUGUST - FERRAGOSTO

Ferragosto, the oldest public holiday in Italy, is what remains of the *Feriae Augustae,* month-long holidays proclaimed in 18 BC by Octavian after being proclaimed the Emperor Augustus by the Roman Senate. In modern times it is traditionally a time for picnics in the countryside with family and friends and – also traditionally – the weather changes after that date and the end of the summer is at hand.

That morning George was walking across the dusty car park to move his car into the shade; he thought he had finally identified a spot that would actually stay in the shade all morning, and this was important today. Later he would be collecting the professor from the nursing home to have lunch at the *agriturismo*, and a boiling-hot car, even for a short journey, would have been too uncomfortable; Alfredo had offered to come in his battered Mercedes – a huge compliment since no one works at *Ferragosto* – but had been reassured that the professor's friends would look after her.

He was just turning the key in the lock when he heard the sound of footsteps and turned. It was Massimo, who was now no longer limping. "Engineer George!" he called in his cheerful way. "How are you?"

"Fine, how about you?" asked George. "Everything OK?"

"*OK-issimo!*" said Massimo with a sudden huge smile. "Never so well! And now, *Ingegnere Giorgio*, I have something to show you. Come, come with me!" And he walked away from the *agriturismo* towards the fields. Mystified, George relocked the car and followed him, past the large vegetable garden with its neat rows of lettuce and glowing clusters of tomatoes, through the orchard and over a rough uncultivated field towards a line of scrubby bushes. Massimo's mare Principessa appeared to be grazing on the other side.

Massimo hurried ahead, slipped through a gap in the bushes, and then turned back to George.

"Come! Look!" he called joyfully. "Here is another road for you, George!" And George, infected by Massimo's enthusiasm and haste, burst through the bushes and saw a perfect stretch of

Roman road. Still glistening with the morning dew, its rounded flagstones worn and trodden by countless pilgrims, it led from west to east, from the direction of Rome and the Appian Way towards its end in the great sanctuary of Diana Nemorensis.

"The Via Virbia," said Massimo, gesturing along its length. The mare, which had been cropping the short grass at the side of the road, ambled over, gave George's shoulder a friendly push, before nuzzling at Massimo's neck and blowing lovingly into his hair. "Fine, isn't it?" he went on, throwing one arm about the mare's neck and rubbing his face against the glossy coat. "Danish archaeologists – two, three years ago – they came to excavate."

George's gaze travelled from west to east, from the warehouse-like structure of the Museum of Roman Ships, upwards to the wooded slopes that had contained the ritual of the golden bough, and lastly towards the sanctuary, where the neo-pagans had left cakes and strawberries, and he himself had left his guidebook. His gaze returned to the smooth stones of the road. It held no menace now, no feeling of onward-rushing pressure. It rested, a gentle invitation, a promise of places to go and life to be lived.

"This is wonderful, Massimo," said George, grinning. He knelt down, gazed along the length of gleaming flagstones, and ran his hand over one of the raised edging stones. "Fine engineering, built to last." He stood up and took a few steps down the road, looking round at the sun-filled bowl of the valley.

Massimo too was grinning, pleased by the success of his surprise and with his conscience finally at peace; everything was, as he had said to George *"OK-issimo!"*.

They started back towards the *agriturismo*, the mare following and nudging Massimo every so often as if to remind him that she was there.

"And my horse, you know," said Massimo. "I found her there this morning. Before she never went near – no, never. Animals, eh?"

Some hours later Lena, Barbara, Jane and George were celebrating the holiday with lunch on the vine-shaded patio. A set lunch was laid on and all the tables were full. Theo was working, but he would join them later for coffee, saying little but quietly listening, his young open face serious and somehow more mature.

The light was golden and hazy as they sat looking towards the lake, where a small evening breeze crinkled the still waters. Theo came to sit down.

"Your friend Gabriel was very cunning, very wily," the professor was saying to Jane. "From what I saw of the other, he was over-confident and that was his undoing. He expected to fight in the clearing and had not considered the wood. Gabriel knew of course. He took the battle to ground he knew."

"But ..." Jane still looked pale and exhausted, the bruises on her face standing out dark and painful-looking, but her expression was quiet and tranquil. "I still can't believe that he ..." She stopped.

The professor smiled at her, said, "I almost forgot – I have something for you." She fumbled in her bag, which had been hanging from the back of the chair, extracted a small clay figure and gave it to Jane. "It is what he threw at the other – with exceptional aim, I must say – and that gave him time to seize the golden bough, take the battle to the wood."

Jane held it up to show George and laughed shakily, "It's the figure the neo-pagan girl gave me. But what on earth was Gabriel doing with it? How did you come to have it, professor?"

"Barbara – Miss Allberry – found it in the clearing."

"Thought it was just a stone, but that you might like to have it," said Barbara gruffly. "But the professor recognised it."

"That was so kind of you, Miss Allberry," said Jane quietly. "Thank you so much." Barbara, spiritual kin to George, looked embarrassed and picked up her empty coffee cup.

"He probably recognised it for what it was and took it," said the professor in answer to Jane's question.

"But why? What is it?"

The Sacred Wood

"May I?" The professor took the figure back and turned it gently between her fingers. "This is a Venus figurine if I'm not mistaken, immensely old and immensely valuable. The statuette of a prehistoric fertility goddess. It contains enormous power, you know, enormous *female* power," she added with one of her impish smiles.

They all fell silent. The valley with its shining lake and wooded slopes cradled the day and seemed to breathe a sense of well-being and peace. Barbara sighed and relaxed. Soon she would be going home, home to her friends and the village, where her beloved setters would surely be pining for her; Theo, gazing at his arm, was remembering with wonder his vision of the torchlit procession and felt again the peace that had enveloped him in the glow from the sanctuary; George was thinking: it is not often that two hands reach for the very same book in a bookshop. It would take him a long time before he could weave the events of the past days into the fabric of his life but at that moment he was content. When all was said and done, he had followed a route that no road or aqueduct had ever taken, and it was Gabriel who had set him on his way.

Jane was still holding the figurine – it was warm and comforting to the touch and seemed to nestle in her fingers. Immensely old and immensely valuable. She could not encompass this along with everything else. Gabriel had recognised it. Had he known of its power and that he would need it?

And the professor too …

"Professor," she said abruptly, her pleasant face perplexed but determined. "Who are you?"

Lena smiled, gazed towards the sanctuary. "No one in particular," she murmured. "Just a passer-by."

ABOUT THE AUTHOR

Joanna Leyland was born in South Wales but grew up in England. Leaving the UK in 1984, intending to work temporarily in Rome and then go on to Tokyo, she has lived in Italy ever since. She has made her home in the Monti Lepini, south of Rome and the Alban Hills, where she has set the first novel of her Goddess Trilogy, *The Sacred Wood*. The second in the series, *The White Sibyl*, will be available in late 2013.

Printed in Great Britain
by Amazon